MW00904891

JASON *and the*
WONDER HORN

IN THE SAME BOAT

JASON *and the* WONDER HORN

LINDA HUTSELL-MANNING

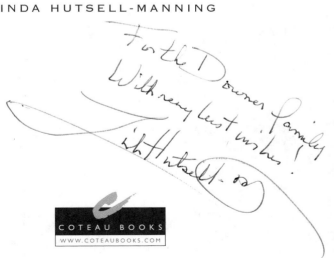

COTEAU BOOKS
WWW.COTEAUBOOKS.COM

© Linda Hutsell-Manning, 2002. First US edition, 2003.

All rights reserved. No part of this book covered by the copyrights hereon may be reproduced or used in any form or by any means—graphic, electronic, or mechanical—without the prior written permission of the publisher. Any request for photocopying, recording, taping, or storage in information storage and retrieval systems of any part of this book shall be directed in writing to CanCopy, 1 Yonge St, Suite 1900, Toronto, Ontario, M5E 1E5.

This novel is a work of fiction. Names, characters, places, and incidents either are the product of the author's imagination or are used fictitiously. Any resemblance to actual persons, living or dead, is coincidental.

Editor for the Series, Barbara Sapergia.
Edited by Barbara Sapergia.
Cover painting and interior illustrations by Susan Gardos.
Cover and book design by Duncan Campbell.
"In The Same Boat" logo designed by Tania Wolk, Magpie Design.
Printed and bound in Canada by Houghton Boston, Saskatoon.

National Library of Canada Cataloguing in Publication Data

Manning, Linda
Jason and the wonder horn

(In the same boat)
ISBN 1-55050-214-X

1. Coburg (Germany)–History–Juvenile fiction. 2.
Germany–History–To 1517–Juvenile fiction. I. Title. II. Series.
PS8576.A563J37 2002   JC813'.54   C2002-910913-2
PZ7.M3156JA 2002

10 9 8 7 6 5 4 3 2 1

COTEAU BOOKS
401-2206 Dewdney Ave
Regina, Saskatchewan
Canada   S4R 1H3

available in the US from:
Fitzhenry and Whiteside
195 Allstate Parkway
Markham, Ontario
Canada   L3R 4T8

The publisher gratefully acknowledges the financial assistance of the Saskatchewan Arts Board, the Canada Council for the Arts, including the Millennium Arts Fund, the Government of Canada through the Book Publishing Industry Development Program (BPIDP), and the City of Regina Arts Commission, for its publishing program.

For my children
Bruce, David, and Laura
and my grandchildren
Chad, Byron, Aaron, and Dylan.

CHAPTER ONE

JASON STARED OUT HIS BEDROOM WINDOW PAST THE sprawling weeping willow to the fields beyond. And beyond those fields to more fields, as far as he could see. Why would his parents move away out here, near some dumb little town called Cobourg? No arcades, no friends, no place to go for the whole summer. This rented house was older and more run-down than any he could remember, and he could remember quite a few. He kicked at one of the many boxes still piled in his room and wished desperately he was back in Toronto.

Now, with every room in the house still full of unpacked boxes, his mom was taking off for a week to teach a music course in the city. In the fall, she'd be back playing clarinet in the Toronto Symphony Orchestra. And his dad wrote mystery thrillers – he could live anywhere. So why had they moved?

He listened to his mom in the other bedroom, opening and closing boxes and packing crates, trying to find the stuff she needed to take with her. It was kind of funny, except she could leave her room in a mess and get away with it. Jason would be expected to clean his up. "Okay," she was always saying, "let's get organized."

His dad never had to pitch in because he was always on a writing deadline. When his mom left, Jason would be on his own, stuck out here in the middle of nowhere.

"Look," his mom said, bursting into his room, "what I found packed away with my clothes. Your corduroy shirt."

"I won't be needing it in the summer, Mom."

"I know, but let's hang it up in that closet of yours anyway."

"I've already tried the closet light," Jason said, jumping onto his unmade bed and grinning at her. "And it works."

So far, his closet was the only good thing in the whole house. It was huge for a closet and had floor-to-ceiling shelves on one side. Last week when they'd moved in, his mom had said he could pick his room. When he'd seen this closet – that had been it. He could stuff everything he owned in there. It would make cleaning up a piece of cake.

"I know you're less than thrilled about being here," his mom said, pulling the chain to turn off the closet light. "But try to give the place a chance." She sat beside Jason on the bed. "This was a grand house once, especially when your great-grandparents lived here."

"Uh-huh."

"I remember coming here in the summer to visit Grandma," his mom went on. "She was in a wheelchair by then and your great-uncle Joseph used to wheel her into the sun-porch downstairs."

"Where Dad has his office now?" Jason tried to sound interested.

"Yes," she went on, jumping up and going to the window, "and your Aunt Kate pushed me in the swing right out there on that willow tree. I must have been about four."

"You can remember that?" Jason asked. "Cool."

"That's exactly why I wanted us to move back here," she said, sitting beside him again. "It will give you a sense of your own family. Kate was named after your great-grandma Käthe."

"Uh-huh."

"Before I was born, your grandparents and Kate came here every summer," she went on, staring toward the window. "And before that, both your grandad and great-uncle had gone off to war. Grandma used to say, when her sons left, their farming days were over."

Jason had heard most of this before. How the house ended up belonging to his great-uncle, who didn't take care of it. How, after he died, it went up for auction and his aunt Kate, who was in real estate, bought it back.

"You should look around," his mom said, getting up. "Your great-uncle was in both wars. He even performed in a circus for a while. Who knows what might be stashed away?"

"What?" Jason asked. "A clown suit or something?"

"Family history. Boring stuff, I know," his mom said, tousling his shoulder-length blonde hair. "Look, we'll get your computer hooked up as soon as I get back, okay?"

"Sure, Mom."

"Gotta dash." She stopped at the doorway. "It won't be

that bad," she said, "you and your dad here alone. Maybe you can do some guy stuff."

"Like what?"

"Go exploring. Climb the hill behind the house. Your aunt Kate piggybacked me up there once. Sat me on a fence post and I still remember being able to see the lake."

"Why couldn't I come to Toronto with you?" Jason asked suddenly. "I could hang out somewhere. Dad wouldn't miss me. He's glued to his computer."

"Hey, now," his mom said, throwing him a kiss. "It's your job to look after your dad – get him out of the house once in a while."

"So the answer is no?"

"Not this time."

A half-hour later, Jason listened to his mom's ramshackle car backfire out of the driveway. Their old station wagon wasn't much better. His dad talked as though this new book would be a best seller, and Jason sure hoped so. Maybe they could fix up this place so it wasn't such a dump. Get a decent car.

Jason pushed a couple more boxes into the closet and turned on the light. Pulling the door closed, he sat on one of the boxes and thought about his mom saying there might be something hidden in the house. It was a "mom" thing to say. The house was boring. The rest of the closets were small, the rooms ordinary. His dad called the basement "gothic," which probably meant it would show up in his next novel. Jason supposed the basement might have a secret cupboard or door, but it also had a dirt floor and leaky stone walls. Jason had no interest in checking it out.

Maybe, he thought, looking at the still empty closet shelves, I could tear these out and have my computer in here. Cool. He pushed the few clothes on hangers to one side. I'd have awesome sound, he thought, especially if I hung speakers from the ceiling, one on each side. He looked up and that was when he noticed the outline of a trap door.

This door was less than a metre across, its square wood frame painted the same pale blue as the ceiling. An attic, he thought, my closet opens into a secret attic. The difficult part was figuring out how to get up there.

Jason tried piling up boxes of books, but they didn't reach high enough and one box split open, books scattering everywhere. He knew they had a stepladder, but where was it? Before she left, his mom had been putting up curtains. He tiptoed across the hall to his parents' bedroom. Behind a bunch of opened boxes, there it was, leaning against the wall beside the window. "I'll put it back, Mom," he whispered as he hauled the ladder back to his room. Before he closed his bedroom door, he listened to his dad's computer keys clicking at double-fast speed. Good, he thought, no interference. My closet. My secret.

The trap door pushed up easily when he shouldered it, a shower of dust and dead flies falling onto his clothes and books. He was too excited to care. Anything might be up here. A square of light bounced onto the slanting rafters above him, highlighting rough boards and cobwebs.

Once his head and shoulders were through the opening and his eyes were adjusted to the dark interior, he thought he saw floorboards stretching out on all sides. He might actually find something hidden up here in the darkness – old picture albums, sports equipment, antique guns, maybe even a secret compartment.

Pushing down with his palms on either side of the opening, he lifted himself to a sitting position on its edge, pulling his legs through onto the floorboards. It was then he realized the flooring only covered half the attic. Long wooden beams spanned the other half, and between these beams was some kind of greyish fluff insulation. He sat cross-legged on the floor, following the slanted rafters to their peak, searching back along the floor and beams. It appeared the attic was empty.

When he turned to climb out, convinced there was no hidden treasure, no secret door, he saw the outline of a large box up against the eaves where the roof slant met the floor. Heart pounding, he crawled on his hands and knees, carefully putting weight on one creaking floorboard after the other. He had lost perspective as to where he was, what room was below him. What if he suddenly crashed down into his parents' bedroom or, even worse, his mom's studio?

The box seemed even larger up close, at least a metre long, and seemed too heavy to move. What if it contained family jewels or a gun from one of the wars? What if his great-grandparents had hidden their money up here instead of putting it in a bank? As he yanked at what looked like its fasteners, something clunked back and forth inside, metal against metal.

It's an old gun, he thought, or another smaller box. He needed a light and remembered the flashlight his dad kept in the station wagon.

The doorbell rang. Jason couldn't believe it. No one had wound that doorbell since they'd moved in two weeks ago. When it rang a second time, he wriggled back down through the opening onto the stepladder and ran from his room.

Clang ring clang ring. The old bell handle was going non-stop, now, and his dad would be furious if he was interrupted. Jason catapulted down the stairs, ignoring his mom's advice to be careful of the loose stair rails and the holes in the scruffy carpet. Grabbing the end of the banister, he skidded into the front hall and was momentarily dazzled by bright sunlight.

"See, told you there was someone here."

CHAPTER TWO

J ASON SQUINTED AT TWO FIGURES SILHOUETTED ON THE other side of the sunlit screen door, one taller than he was, and a smaller one who was kicking the bottom frame of the door, winding the bell handle again even though Jason was right there.

"Hey, cut it out," Jason hissed between his teeth. "Keep it down, will you?"

"Why?" the door kicker hissed back, mimicking him. "Somebody asleep?"

"Squid, smarten up."

Jason's eyes adjusted, and he found himself staring at a girl whose wavy dark hair was pulled back in some kind of braid. She looked about his age even if she was taller. The younger kid, with the same dark hair, had switched from door-kicking to air-punching.

"Gran said someone had moved into the old Elmhurst farmhouse," the girl said, staring at him. "Squid and I thought we'd check it out."

Jason slipped out through the screen door and beckoned them down the steps onto the front lawn. "Have to be quiet," he mumbled. "Dad's got a deadline."

Squid charged ahead of them and attempted to run straight up a tree trunk down near the fence. He fell, hard, on his butt and howled, seemingly enraged that he couldn't accomplish the impossible.

"Be careful," the girl called, but there was no conviction in her voice.

Squid paused a millisecond and then jumped for the lowest branch, wrestling his way up.

"Is he always like this?" Jason asked. How could she stay so calm and unconcerned?

"He's my brother," she replied with a grin, "and he's been totally hyper since he was born. I'm used to it." She turned back toward the house. "Is your dad a writer?"

"How did you know that?"

"Gran said she'd heard..."

Jason had no idea what to do with these two. He felt he should be polite, but the sooner they left, the sooner he could get the flashlight and check out the box.

The girl was staring at him, expecting something to happen. He couldn't invite them in, not today. He didn't even know her name. She seemed perfectly at ease here, as if striding through fields and knocking on strange doors were no big deal.

Squid was three-quarters of the way up the tree now, rapid-firing at some unseen enemy.

"My name's Charlotte Cannington," the girl said,

smiling. "We're here for a couple of weeks while our parents are in Europe."

Jason knew this game and he hated it. It was one of those "getting to know you" statements, and he never knew what he should say. He could say that his dad was on the final edit of his third espionage thriller and that a New York agent was waiting to see it. He could say that his mom was a professional musician and was in Toronto teaching clarinet at the Conservatory. He could say that he'd just found a beat-up-looking metal box in his newly-discovered attic, a box containing something heavy, metal-sounding. Instead, he shrugged his shoulders and felt embarrassed. "I'm Jason Carter," he said, shuffling his sneakers in the grass. "Sorry I can't invite you in."

Squid charged between them and flung himself against Charlotte. "Lottie's got a boyfriend, Lottie's got a boyfriend..."

Jason jumped aside as Charlotte grabbed her brother and swung him flailing in a circle until they both fell onto the ground.

"Doesn't," she yelled, pinning him with her body.

"Does," Squid roared back. "Does, does, does..."

Jason had no experience with little kids. He expected blood any minute.

"Time to go," Charlotte said, jumping up and striding toward the gate. "Gran says come on over. She's dying to meet you."

Squid raced ahead of her and climbed the wire fence, yelling a war cry on the way up and over. He ran full out across the driveway and disappeared into the cedars on the far side.

"You have any brothers or sisters?" Charlotte asked as she closed the gate.

Jason shook his head.

"Lucky you," Charlotte said. "Better than lucky. Five-year-old brothers are the plague. See you." She paused at the edge of the cedars. "It's easy to find our place," she called. "We're right next to you, through the field."

"Yeah, see you around," Jason said, not wanting to promise anything. Right now, he had more important things to do.

He retrieved the flashlight from under the front seat of the station wagon and tiptoed back inside, glad his dad hadn't heard anything. In the kitchen he managed to find the peanut butter and make himself a sandwich. He leaned against the door frame and looked at all the unpacked boxes in the living room. His mom had cleared a space around the piano, though, and found his piano books. Lucky for him she'd forgotten to mention practising.

Past the piano, through the open door, he could just see his dad's back – hear the incredibly fast clicking of his keyboard. He would stay like that for another couple of hours at least. Best to stay upstairs until he heard his dad's chair push back, a signal he was taking a break. The man turned into a Jurassic Park monster if he was interrupted while writing.

Once in his room, Jason stuffed the flashlight into his jeans pocket and pulled himself up through the dark opening. The flashlight changed everything and, when he zeroed in on the old box, its rusted edges disappeared beyond the ring of light. It was not something he could move.

He traced a finger over the rusty lid where parts of letters

or numbers or both had faded into what looked like strange hieroglyphics. The two metal clasps on the lid wouldn't budge. Laying the flashlight on the flooring beside him, Jason struggled with both hands, holding the box down and against the wall with his knees, pulling at the spring end of the rusted clasp until sweat ran down his forehead and his knees burned against the rough metal.

When the first clasp finally gave way, he took a break and scanned the light over the box's exterior again. Under layers of dirt and rust, it was dull green. Military green. He rattled the box again. Another box? An old pistol? He tried the second clasp, but it proved more stubborn than the first, giving way only after he hooked the edge of the flashlight under it and shoved hard. The flashlight promptly died, and no amount of shaking revived it.

Jason opened the creaking lid and put his hand gingerly inside. What he pulled out was definitely not a gun.

In the dim light shining up through the trapdoor opening, he could see it was a musical instrument of some kind. As he ran his hand along its smooth curved surface and funnel-like opening, a tingling sensation ran from his fingertips to his elbow. He barely noticed as reality kicked him with disappointment. It was only a dumb instrument. A trumpet maybe. No, it was too small and had no valves. He remembered an old war movie he'd watched with his dad where a soldier blew a horn to lead the infantry charge. It was a bugle, somebody's beat-up old bugle.

As he pushed it back inside the box, his fingers brushed against paper. He pulled it out to discover an envelope and moved close to the trapdoor to have a look. Inside, on a water-streaked piece of paper, he made out the letters – *W u n d e r* ___ and beneath it – *19*__, the second half of each line blurred by water stains. *Wonder?* He thought. Some bad speller. He shoved the envelope back in the box and closed the lid.

So much for finding something interesting, he thought, as he climbed back down into his closet. But then, if I get really bored, I guess I could try to play it.

CHAPTER THREE

W HEN JASON CAME BACK DOWNSTAIRS, HIS DAD WAS IN the kitchen eating cold pizza. "How's the writing going?" Jason asked.

"Not bad," his dad replied, "but I'm beat. You want some pizza?"

"No thanks, I made a sandwich a while ago." Jason went to the fridge for milk. "Dad," he said, sitting down, "Mom says there's a great view from the top of the hill."

His dad smiled. "And she said you should get me out of the house, right?"

"Well, sort of, I guess."

"Look," his dad said, standing up, "why don't you go and check it out? Be good for you, hiking up there on your own."

"What do you mean?"

"Better air out here," his dad said and then, in a western drawl, "lots of wide open spaces, son. Get out there on the rough and tumble land."

"Why? 'Cause I'm a city kid?"

His dad threw him a mock punch. "Rain check until this chapter's finished," he replied, "then you're on." Two seconds later he was back at the computer.

"ROUGH AND TUMBLE LAND," Jason muttered to himself as he strode through long, scratchy grass, batting at giant nose-diving grasshoppers. The slope was steeper than it looked and he was sweating by the time he reached the top. His mom was right about the view, though. He could see right across to Lake Ontario, a huge blue paint splotch against the skyline.

A bird trilled somewhere, and when he looked around, he found it nearby, on the branch of a small poplar tree. Jason whistled, trying to imitate the call. To his surprise, the bird fluffed its feathers and trilled back. Jason whistled again, and again the bird answered. Cool, he thought. The bird turned its head sideways to look at him, then flew off.

He looked around at the long grass, at a pile of big rocks nearby. It was weird to think of his mom being up here, years and years ago when she was a little kid. And she remembered it all, even being pushed on the swing. Jason guessed that was why she was so excited about living here. Maybe he could get to like this place.

Trudging further along the fence line, he spotted a rooftop below. Figuring it was the house where Charlotte and her brother were staying, he climbed over the rusty wire fence and started down the hill. After pushing his way through more shoulder-high grass and coarse smelly weeds, he found himself looking down into an amazing back yard – perfect-looking flower beds and lawn – almost like a park. The old stone house was much bigger than his, with shiny dark green window frames and trim. It was the kind of house his mom would point out in a magazine.

Charlotte burst out of the house carrying something that looked like a drum. She disappeared around the corner just as Squid came out shouting, "I'll get you Lottie. I'll get you."

Jason watched as she reappeared on the other side. She looked both ways before racing up the hill toward him.

"I'll tell Gran," Squid yelled, coming into view a moment later. "I'll…"

"Jason," Charlotte called, stopping suddenly. "Come on down."

Even though he wasn't sure he wanted to, Jason waved back and ran the rest of the way down to meet them.

"Lottie's got my drum," Squid called as Jason approached. "Make her give it back." It was an elaborately painted tin drum with a yellow braided cord. Jason noticed a dinosaur bandaid on Squid's forehead and two more on his knee. He wondered what the kid had hurled himself in or out of this time.

"Here, take your old drum," Charlotte said, handing it to him.

"It's not old," Squid said, grabbing it. "Daddy gave it to me on my birthday." He looked at Jason. "I'm five," he said, holding up five fingers. How many are you?"

"Too many for my fingers," Jason said, smiling. "Ten plus two."

"How many's that?"

"Twelve."

"Octavius?" a voice called from the open back door. "Gran needs you to help her."

"Perfect arrival time," Charlotte said after Squid was out of earshot. "He was driving me crazy with that drum."

For the next little while, Jason followed Charlotte around what she called *the grounds* of her grandmother's house.

After looking at all the flower beds, they crossed the driveway and through a row of huge old cedar trees to a pond. "It's too muddy for swimming," she said, casually, "but there is a rowboat on the far side." Jason noticed a larger-than-life grey stone toad sitting at the end of a short dock anchoring the boat.

"Cool toad," he said.

"Gran calls it Chaucer," Charlotte said, rolling her eyes. "She tells Squid it rides off on boat adventures at night when he's asleep."

Jason nodded and stared at the toad. He had no idea who Chaucer was.

Charlotte pointed at the stone garage nearby. "And I'll show you the fort we made in the garage after we do the tea thing with Gran."

The whole place was awesome, and Jason momentarily considered leaving before he even met Charlotte's gran. He'd always lived in rundown rented places and, most of the time, it didn't bother him. Right now he felt like the pauper about to enter the palace. "I found an attic in my house," he blurted out as they passed a little fountain in the middle of another perfect flower bed.

Charlotte turned and stared. "An attic," she repeated. "Gran always said that house was full of secrets."

"The opening to it is in my bedroom closet."

"You've been up there?"

"Today before you and Squid came."

"And...?" She stared at him directly.

"It was empty, mostly."

"But you found something."

Jason shrugged.

"Gran says the Elmhursts had that place for over a hundred years," Charlotte said, standing a bit too close to him for his liking. He could feel the curiosity in her, the questions.

Jason realized he was staring at the flowers. "Nice fountain," he muttered.

"Gran only knew Mr. Elmhurst after he 'got respectable,'" Charlotte continued, "after he came back to live where you are now."

Jason nodded and walked slowly toward the house.

"He was in a circus or something," Charlotte was rattling on behind him, "I don't know. Mr Elmhurst had money and then he didn't have money. Ask Gran." She pushed him aside when they reached the back door, planting herself firmly in the doorway. "So what did you find in the attic?"

Jason breathed in the smell of freshly-baked cookies and took a split second assessment of his choices. Tell and enter the palace, or exit and probably lose someone who might be his only friend for the summer. "A bugle," he said after a few moments silence.

JASON SAT UNCOMFORTABLY on the scratchy couch, a *settee*, Charlotte called it, and sipped his lemonade. The room was like the inside of one of the country antique stores his parents visited on weekends. Charlotte sat opposite him and Squid, unusually subdued, was cross-legged on the floor. Grandma Cannington was in the kitchen.

"Your father's a writer," she said, returning with a plate of homemade chocolate-chip cookies. "Thrillers, and so they tell me, quite violent." She stood holding the plate out to him, her silk dress smelling vaguely like dried flowers.

Jason wasn't sure what to say. Was she implying that he, Jason, was responsible for his dad's writing? Ridiculous. Did she think that because his dad wrote *thrillers,* he, Jason, was, by association, potentially dangerous, a wild card? Like father, like son? He had dealt with that one before.

"Dad's got a vivid imagination," he said, helping himself to a cookie. He took a large bite and smiled at her. "Delicious cookies," he continued, watching her lower herself carefully into an elaborately carved armchair. She poured tea from a shiny silver teapot, her long, tapered fingers old but graceful. He had already noticed the grand piano beside the curtained French doors. He wondered if she or Charlotte played.

"And your mother?" she continued, squeezing a wedge of lemon over her teacup.

"Mom plays clarinet with the Toronto Symphony."

"Such a talented family."

Jason waited for her to go on: *And what do you play?* Or, *With such parents, you must be incredibly talented.* But she didn't. Instead, she turned to watch Squid, who had inched himself, cross-legged, around the settee and was about to zero in for another cookie. He paused and turned the snatch into a wave.

"Go ahead, Octavius," Grandma Cannington said in a matter-of-fact tone, "and when you're finished, I want you to get a *nice* bouquet of flowers for Jason to take home to his family."

Octavius, Jason thought. No wonder the kid was wild. Jason imagined him pulling flowers out by the roots, tramping blossoms as he went.

"Remember to hold the scissor points away from you," Grandma Cannington called as Squid disappeared toward the kitchen.

Jason glanced at Charlotte and grimaced. Squid loose with scissors? Jason could only imagine what kind of bouquet he would get. He watched Grandma Cannington pour a second cup of tea. No one drank afternoon tea in his family, and any flowers they'd ever had were from a florist. "Octavius?" he said, not intending to say it aloud.

Grandma Cannington smiled and ran her finger delicately around the rim of the empty teacup. "He was born when my son, Richard, was teaching ancient history. The Roman Empire, I think it was."

Jason nodded, feeling totally out of his depth again.

"We tried *Octopus,*" Charlotte added, "but he went ballistic over it."

Grandma Cannington nodded. "So we switched to Squid."

It didn't seem like a very good explanation, but when it was obvious that was all, Jason asked if he could have another cookie.

Charlotte passed the plate to him. "So tell Gran about the bugle," she said, as if its discovery were as commonplace as cookies.

Jason was horrified. Dumb, dumb, dumb, he thought to himself. Never tell someone you've just met *anything.* Never tell anything. He didn't, usually: the ideas his Toronto friends thought were too weird, things he saw that other people didn't, the way he felt about almost everything. The bugle itself was ordinary enough, but it had *implications* and *consequences* he wanted to keep to himself.

To begin with, it was his find, and if he told his parents, they would take over. His mom was big on organizing his life, his stuff. And his dad? He would probably do a bunch of research on it; put it on the cover of his next book. No way. They both meant well, but this was his secret – he would make the choices.

"I was wondering if it might have been my great-grandpa Elmhurst's," Jason said, watching Mrs. Cannington and carefully choosing his words. He was going to see if he could figure out how to play it. It had to be easier than piano. All those wretched scales and boring little pieces. He would surprise his mom, who despaired over his reluctance to practice – impress his dad, who said maybe the kid's talents lay elsewhere, i.e., that maybe with his obvious imagination Jason would turn out to be a *writer.*

"Most likely his brother's," Mrs. Cannington said, more than a little wistfully. "That would be your great-uncle Joseph. He always said there was a bugle, but I was never sure." She reached for the cloth napkin on her lap, dabbing her lips with a quick little flick at the corner of one eye. Then she smiled at Jason. "Your secret is safe with me. Do you play piano?"

Jason rolled his eyes. "I was taking lessons before we moved."

"But even with those long fingers, you're not interested. Right?"

Jason nodded, wondering how she could possibly know.

"Bring the bugle over sometime," she continued. "I could show you how to play." She paused and stared out the window. "Besides, I'd love to have a look at it."

"WHY IS YOUR GRAN so interested in the bugle?" Jason asked. They were seated on two old cushions in the garage attic – on Charlotte's side.

From the opening at the top of the stairs to the window at the far end, old packing boxes, trunks, and two dressers formed a barricade down the middle. On the other side of this barricade, Squid was crashing about, roaring out commands to the enemy, occasionally misfiring some object that crashed over to their side. Each time something landed, often close to them but never a direct hit, Jason winced.

"He *knows* where we're sitting," Charlotte said calmly. "He wouldn't dare hit us."

"The bugle," Jason asked again. "Why did your gran say 'he always said there was a bugle but I was never sure'? What about my great-uncle Joseph and the bugle?"

"I don't know very much," Charlotte replied. "She and Mr. Elmhurst used to do a lot of stuff together after my grandpa died."

"So?" Jason replied. She seemed a bit defensive about the whole thing.

"It's one of those adult things," Charlotte began, after

staring at him until he felt uncomfortable. "She and Mr. Elmhurst were more than just friends. When they were both old, they wanted to get married."

"Married?"

Charlotte gave him a look. "Gran had been a widow for a long time. I don't know about Mr. Elmhurst. Anyway, my mom and his nieces had a big argument about it. They thought Mr. Elmhurst wanted to marry Gran for her money, so they refused to allow it."

Jason almost wished he hadn't asked. It was none of his business, really.

"Mr. Elmhurst used to do odd jobs for Gran after Grandpa died," Charlotte continued after an uncomfortable silence, and then added almost as an afterthought, "Mom says that in the evenings he would come over with his trumpet and she'd accompany him on the piano."

"So he played trumpet too?"

"I guess so. You'd have to ask Gran."

ON THE WAY HOME, Jason remembered Grandma Cannington saying "Bring the bugle over some time. I could show you how to play." He started to run as soon as he saw the station wagon gone. His dad was probably in town getting groceries. Jason wanted to try the bugle alone. Maybe he didn't need anyone to help him. Three years of piano lessons should be good for something.

No flashlight and he had to grope his way to the metal box in order to find the cold metal bugle. Once back down from the closet, he took a look out the front bedroom window before giving the bugle a try – no station wagon yet. As soon as he picked it up, a tingling ran through his fingers again. He was probably squeezing too hard, hoping he could get even one sound out of the thing.

He knew it would play notes if he pressed his lips together the right way – *embouchure* his mom called it. Pulling his lips as tight as he could, he puckered them up and blew into the mouthpiece, but all he heard was the sound of his own breath, and after a few tries he felt dumb. Grandma Cannington had offered – so why not?

That evening when his mom called home, he asked her about his great-uncle Joseph. She said that Joseph had been ten years older than Jason's grandpa and played trumpet in a military band in the Second World War. She could only remember him being mentioned as *the wild uncle* who faked his age to get into the First World War and then afterward joined a circus.

"Your great-grandma Käthe Elmhurst was a serious, no-nonsense German," Jason's mom said. "She thought circuses were the devil's playground." She laughed and continued. "Uncle Joseph did come home, though, to look after her before she died."

Jason didn't say he already knew this. "So I'm part German?" he asked.

"A tiny part," his mom added. "And you look a whole lot like a picture I have of your great-uncle Joseph in his World War I uniform. I'll try to find it when I get home."

Jason stared at himself in the bathroom mirror that night

and tried to imagine a military jacket and beret. He stood at attention and saluted himself. "Private Elmhurst," he said. "Ready for service."

CHAPTER FOUR

J ASON WOULD NEVER FORGET THAT FIRST DAY HE CAME TO Charlotte's with the bugle. Charlotte's Gran served tea again, which meant lemonade for himself and Charlotte and the notorious Squid. Today, shortly after Jason arrived, Mrs. Cannington found something important for Squid to do, upstairs.

Charlotte's Gran was *proper,* that's what his dad would call her. She carried herself a certain way, spoke slowly, and never seemed rattled or ticked off, even with Squid. When she saw the bugle, though, her eyes sparkled and her face changed, seemed younger. She took the bugle as if it were something of great value, something that might disappear or break if she didn't hold it carefully. She lifted it toward the sunlight pouring in through the French doors and waltzed around in a circle, saying what sounded to Jason like *Vunderhorn,* over and over again.

"Jason wants to know more about the bugle," Charlotte said, obviously surprised by her grandmother's behaviour.

Grandma Cannington stopped then and, almost as if she had been acting a part, came back to being herself. She sat in her chair and, placing the bugle carefully in her lap, pulled a stray wisp of hair back into place.

"I don't think I ever really believed him," she began, her voice sounding far away. "How he found it, yes, but the rest..." She stared past them on the settee as if they weren't really there anymore. Charlotte cleared her throat and Grandma Cannington nodded. "Memory is a strange thing," she began again. "You're never quite sure if what you remember is correct."

The clock in the front hall chimed the quarter-hour and ticked the seconds as they waited.

"Mr. Elmhurst was given the bugle when he was in Germany in World War I," she began quietly. "He was only eighteen when the Germans were being driven back past the Hindenburg Line north to the Argonne forest. Separated from his troop, he joined up with an American company, all puffed up about how they were there to end the war. They had camped on the outskirts of a bombed-out village and, when Joseph was alone for a few minutes, an old woman slipped up to him, begging for food." Grandma Cannington paused and put the bugle on the table beside her.

Jason stared at the horn. The First World War. And it came all the way from Germany.

"I remember," she continued, "Joseph telling me how shocked he was when she said she had no food for her children, and that she was probably no older than his German-born mother in Canada. Joseph was young, battle weary, and homesick, and he gave the woman most of his supper rations, not expecting anything in return. To his surprise, she pulled this bugle from inside her cloak and shoved it at Joseph, saying *Vunderhorn* over and over." Gran smiled at Jason and went on.

"Joseph didn't tell the American soldiers or their officer, knowing it was against regulations to even talk to strangers. Anyone could be a spy. Anyone could plant a bomb. Joseph hid the bugle under his uniform and, the next day when they were attacked, he claimed it saved his life. The shrapnel dented the horn instead of killing him, although he had shrapnel in his shoulder for the rest of his days."

Grandma Cannington smiled and patted the arm of the chair. "I think we could use some more tea," she said, a little too quietly. She steadied herself on the settee's arm as she stood, as if telling this story had worn her out.

"What does *Vunderhorn* mean?" Jason asked after she had put the empty glasses onto her serving tray and left the room. His great-grandmother was German, but he didn't know any German words.

"Ask Gran." Charlotte replied, staring at the bugle.

Grandma Cannington reappeared with fresh tea and lemonade. Jason and Charlotte waited while she poured and dropped in a sugar lump. "In German," she said as she stirred, "the 'W' is pronounced like an English 'V.' *Wunder* means something that is a wonder, a miracle." She smiled briefly. "Joseph said the 'miracle' was that the *Wunderhorn* saved him from shrapnel. The 'wonder' came later when he claimed it was magic."

29

Jason watched Grandma Cannington stir. He knew from experience that when adults had something important to say, it often took them forever to get at it. *Wunder,* he thought to himself, and then he remembered the piece of paper he found with the bugle...*Wunder____* and *19__*.

"When he returned to Canada after the war," Grandma Cannington began finally, "Joseph was restless. The war did that to people."

"Excuse me," Jason cut in, "what year would that have been?"

"The armistice was signed November 11, 1918," Gran replied.

"Remembrance Day?" Jason couldn't believe it.

"That's how it all got started," Gran said quietly. She stared out the window, long enough to make Jason feel uncomfortable. "Joseph didn't make it back to Canada until February the following year," she finally continued. "He was shipped off to a British hospital, first, to recover from shell shock." She sighed and stared out the window again.

After another silence Charlotte cleared her throat. "It was a circus he joined, wasn't it, Gran?" She glowered at Jason as she said it, clearly telling him not to interrupt again.

"A travelling sideshow, but not right away. He came back here to his family home. I remember my mother saying he had suffered mild amnesia but seemed to recover. He couldn't find any kind of work in this area and, that August, he made his way to the Toronto Exhibition, the bugle tied to his belt. My mother said they didn't hear from him for a year after that. His mother was beside herself, figuring he'd fallen in with bad company or gotten killed somehow.

He was ahead of me in school and had a reputation for being wild. Even though we lived almost next door, I never would have spoken to him in those days. By this time, I'd gone off to the Conservatory to study music. I had a different life."

As Jason opened his mouth to ask her more about the Conservatory, he saw Charlotte glower again. He swallowed hard and said nothing.

"The following August, Joseph drove into the Elmhurst yard in a beat-up Model T Ford with a couple of scruffy looking friends, all excited to tell his parents he'd found his calling in a sideshow called 'The Seven Wonders of the World.' He said they had travelled from the Exhibition in early September, down through Chicago, across the mid-prairie states, and into California. He was all tanned and handsome, a charmer, so my mother said.

His quiet, church-going parents weren't charmed one bit. They barely spoke to his flea-bitten friends and were horrified by his bragging manner, as he told them he opened and closed the show with his dazzling bugle performance.

He only stayed home that one night, leaving early the next morning before his weeping mother and disapproving father were up. His father never saw him again and his mother only after she had her stroke and couldn't talk, almost thirty years later."

Mrs. Cannington stopped and sipped at her tea. Jason noticed one of her hands was shaking slightly and he wondered, again, if they shouldn't have asked, if telling this story was too hard for her. She looked up and smiled.

"You might wonder why I had any interest in this vagabond," she said. "Well, I certainly didn't, not for quite some time afterward. Life stirs us up and then, eventually, it settles us. I had grown up here, and after Dr. Cannington and I were married, we came back to Cobourg and ended up in this very house." She caught her breath and stared out the window. "Years later, after I was a widow, Joseph returned home to nurse his old mother."

She stood slowly, and walking over to the piano, played part of a sad-sounding melody. "Joseph was such a storyteller," she said without turning around. "I always believed him while he was telling this next part, but afterwards..."

"The next part?" Charlotte repeated carefully.

"He said that he became so clever at this bugle playing that they made him the Seventh Wonder of the World – a disappearing act with the bugle where dry ice gas engulfed him, in a fog, and he was swallowed up. 'Lucky seven' he always said, and that was why it was such a great hit." She sat back down on the settee and carefully ran her finger along the length of the bugle.

"He discovered, so he said, that he actually *could* disappear if he played *just the right notes.* They were in Chicago the first time it happened, sometime in the twenties before the Great Depression really hit. Joseph was bored with this sideshow and restless. He had been adding more notes, making the bugle sound better than it was, more like the trumpet he so desperately wanted, and this particular night, something went wrong with the dry ice machine. It went plain *kafluey,* that's how he put it..." She laughed and patted her hair as if looking in a mirror.

"Joseph said it pumped out twice as much fog as it usually did. Everyone backstage got so excited they forgot to open the trapdoor and drop him below the stage, so he just kept playing louder and longer until he felt a thump and found himself, so he swore to me, back in the rehab hospital in England where he was sent at the end of the war." Mrs. Cannington stopped and shook her head. "I always went along with it. He made it sound so real."

"How did he get home?" Jason asked, staring at the bugle.

"Played his way back on some rich people's ocean liner."

"And then?"

"He caught up with the same sideshow the following year at the exhibition."

"It sounds pretty far-fetched to me," Charlotte added.

"Of course it does, dear. When I tell it. But not when Joseph did."

"Did it happen again?" Jason asked.

"Several times, and each time he went further back in time, reliving, so he told me, a number of terrible war experiences until, in fear and disgust, he quit the sideshow and put the bugle away forever. He might have been imagining it. Shell shock did things to the mind."

She handed the bugle back to Jason and stood up again. "He told me he sold it before he moved back here, but obviously he didn't." She smiled again and looked past them. "I never really believed his stories, you understand, but now, looking at the horn, it all comes back. When I knew him years later, he was so dignified, white moustache and clothes just so. We met again in the Cobourg Kiltie Band. By then he had his trumpet."

She turned toward the kitchen. "I think we could use some cookies." Her tone of voice told them clearly that the story was over and there were to be no more questions.

"What did your gran play?" Jason asked quietly after she left. He couldn't help wondering about the bugle. Joseph travelling back in time.

"Flute," Charlotte replied, but Jason wasn't really listening.

After cookies and more lemonade, Charlotte curled up on the settee to read a book. Grandma Cannington began patiently showing Jason how to press his lips against the mouthpiece, how to blow the right amount of air through the horn to get one clear note and then two. Jason was surprised at how easy it was. He concentrated and found a third note and then a fourth.

While he worked on the notes, Grandma Cannington opened the lid of the piano bench and rummaged through a thick pile of music stored there. A few moments later, she pulled out a yellowed book called *Duets for Trumpet and Piano.*

"Joseph and I used to play duets," she said, smiling. She sat down at the piano and pulled a loose piece of music from the back of the book. "The Bugle Call," it said at the top. "You should be able to play this if you practice. Try it."

Jason took a deep breath and, haltingly, began. At first, he could only play part of the first line. Gran encouraged him, patting his shoulder when he got it right, playing a note for him whenever he was stuck. Soon his lips were swollen and sore.

"That's enough for the first time," she said. "You need to toughen up that mouth of yours."

Jason nodded. "I'd better be going," he said. "And thanks."

"Come over any time and practice," Gran replied, running her fingers up and down the keyboard at breathtaking speed. "You're a born bugler."

CHAPTER FIVE

I T WAS THE SECOND WEEK HE'D COME OVER ALMOST EVERY day to work on his bugle playing at the big stone house. His mom had barely come home before she was gone again – she was doing more teaching somewhere out of town. Jason was almost glad. His mom would be asking questions if she were home.

He was catching on quickly, and today Charlotte joined in on the silver flute. Gran was at the piano, thumping out grandiose chords while Jason stumbled through "The Bugle Call." Charlotte was trilling an extra part, making it up as she went along, something she'd told him she had always been able to do.

They had almost finished their third run-through of "The Bugle Call" when a loud, rat-a-tatting echoed down the front hall stairs into the living room.

"Keep going," Gran said, throwing in a few extra chords at the end of the last line. "We'll go through it one more time."

Squid proudly marched through the doorway in perfect

time, the drum on the yellow cord around his neck. In spite of the tinny loudness, Jason couldn't help being impressed by Squid's dexterity, the rat-a-tat-tats doubling and tripling in time to Gran's chords. He had obviously done this before.

At the end of the piece, Squid, of course, kept up his drumming, marching around the couch, la-la-la-ing Jason's bugle line at the top of his lungs.

"Time to stop," was all Gran had to say. Squid plopped to the floor and pulled the drum's cord over his head. "It's almost four," she went on, "and Jean Barton will be here for her music lesson." She opened one of the French doors. "How about a practice, outside? Like a marching band."

"Gran still teaches piano," Charlotte explained.

"A band, a band," Squid echoed. He grabbed the drum again and hammered away.

"Oh boy," Charlotte said. "This should be fun." She rolled her eyes.

"Only for forty-five minutes," Gran added, "and stay off the highway. One of those Lake Ontario fogs is rolling in from the lake. I noticed from the upstairs window a while ago. You won't be able to see any further than the end of your nose once it hits the highway." She gave Squid's nose a little poke. "Stay on the path by the fence and come back when you reach the Cobourg town sign." Squid giggled and ran for the French doors.

"But we won't have you on the piano," Jason protested. "It won't sound right without the piano."

"Try it," Gran said, literally shooing the two of them out after him. "Just try it."

Charlotte took over the melody line and, with Squid leading, they marched out the spruce-lined lane toward the highway and path.

"Hold it," Charlotte commanded even before they reached the highway. "Hey, Squid, it won't be any fun in the fog. Let's go back up into the loft."

"No way," Squid said, stomping his foot and rat-a-tat-tatting. "I want to be a band."

Charlotte took a deep breath and stared hard at her little brother. Jason could see a standoff looming. He stepped back and waited.

Charlotte grinned and snapped her fingers. "I know," she said. "Why don't we take Jason for a boat ride? You could row."

"No, no, no," Squid said defiantly, "and I'm going to tell if we don't be a band. So there." He started a drum roll and marched on the spot.

"Might as well try it to my house and back, then," Jason suggested. "Forty-five minutes isn't that long." He checked his watch. It was three fifty-five. What he intended to do once they got to his house was make an excuse to call it a day. Sibling squabbles he could do without.

Charlotte rolled her eyes and started to play again, marching on the spot. "Okay," she said between notes, and they turned onto a path Jason didn't even know was there – Squid in front, then Charlotte, with Jason bringing up the rear.

Something happened then, something none of them clearly understood, even afterward. The fog Grandma

Cannington warned them about started rolling in, a thick, wet cover, eliminating everything but a small section of the path ahead. Jason felt his playing grow stronger and stronger and he added extra notes.

Cars drove past, their headlights like two yellow spots dilating into solid discs, and disappearing behind. Each time, Squid paused and, in perfect time, twirled a drum stick in the air. Jason moved out in front, lifting his head higher so that his bugle notes poured ahead of him into the fog. Charlotte was following him now, with Squid lagging a bit behind. The sound wrapped around them, pulling them forward, bugle and flute notes growing louder and stronger, driven on by the urging of Squid's relentless drum.

They must have marched right past Jason's house; none of them even noticed. They were good – they were better than good, they were professional, like his mom. He was sure of it.

Across the highway, the New Lodge Farm sign slid in and out of sight almost as if suspended in air. As they came close to the Workmans' chicken farm where his mom bought eggs, Jason thought he heard sheep bleating. He didn't know the Workmans had sheep. The fog rolled back, momentarily, and instead of the house, Jason saw someone with a long wooden crook herding a flock of sheep across the road. He blinked and they were gone. Droplets of water formed in a ring on his bugle and the instrument glimmered almost like a beacon in the fog. Any minute now and they'd see the Cobourg town sign and it would be time to turn back. It was then it occurred to Jason that no cars were passing now, that it seemed very still.

The path had become a dirt road, a strange road, and as if by some signal, they all stopped, Squid's drum playing dwindling down to an occasional nervous *tap-tap*.

CHAPTER SIX

"WHERE ARE WE?" CHARLOTTE WHISPERED.

Jason turned to stare at her. She was pulling nervously at the ties of a long cloak she was wearing. Underneath, he glimpsed a roughly woven, ankle-length brown skirt. Squid's T-shirt had grown into an oversized drab-looking shirt belted at the waist by some frayed rope, his sturdy legs covered by coarse grey stockings. Jason looked down, amazed to see himself dressed like Squid. All wore rough sandals tied on with ragged strips of leather.

"Why are we wearing this stuff?" Squid asked, looking more than a little puzzled.

"I...I'm not sure," Jason replied, "but it's something pretty weird."

"I don't understand what's going on," Charlotte whispered again, looking at Squid and then back at Jason.

"We've transported somewhere," Jason replied, nervously, "to some other time." He looked around. "Maybe to some other country."

"These stupid stocking things are itchy," Squid complained, dropping the drum onto the dusty road. "Who stole my jeans?"

"Look at your flute, Charlotte," Jason said, staring at the instrument in her hand.

Charlotte ran her hand over it and inhaled sharply. "It's...it's more like a *recorder,*" she said in a barely audible voice. "A funny, old-looking recorder." She put the instrument to her lips and produced a series of rich-sounding notes. Her eyes took on a surprised, almost frightened look and she stopped in mid-phrase. "This is bizarre," she added. "Almost like we slipped through a time warp."

"No way," Squid chimed in. "We didn't slip, Lottie. No way."

"Well, whatever happened," Jason said, staring at the horn, "didn't change the bugle much." He turned it over in his hand.

"It's shinier," Charlotte said, touching it lightly. "Polished, like gold."

Jason held the horn at arm's length. "Maybe it's just the light or something."

Squid shrugged his shoulders and started playing again, a deep, resonating rat-a-tat-tat. He seemed unconcerned that the drum was no longer tin, rough leather strands replacing the yellow cord, its brownness blending in with his drab shirt and stockings.

Jason put the bugle to his lips, hoping it would sound the same. He began "The Bugle Call" and the notes ran ahead of him, different notes, better notes. Charlotte took a deep breath and added her harmony to the group.

Squid shouted, "Company march!" and they started off again along the strange new road. Ahead, in the distance, Jason thought he glimpsed the outline of a castle up high on a hill. A mirage, he thought; either that or he was dreaming.

Squid stopped when they came to the rickety bridge. To say it was poorly made was an understatement, its roughly cut boards unevenly spanning two steep banks with a glass-clear stream gurgling over rocks and through clumps of long, spiky grass beneath. "I'm thirsty," Squid shouted, dashing down the bank and splashing into the water.

"Oh boy," Charlotte muttered, racing after him. "Don't get any wetter than you have to!" she called.

Jason wrapped one arm securely around the bugle, using the other to steady himself down the bank. Charlotte had skidded to a stop at the water's edge. She was bending down, holding the folds of her cloak in one hand, scooping up water with the other, as if she'd done it all her life. Squid was splashing about in the knee-deep water, stockings and thick shirt rapidly becoming soaking wet.

"Get out, Squid," Charlotte demanded, after he'd splashed her twice, the first time accidentally, the second with a suspiciously deliberate gesture.

"You're going to freeze if you don't get out," Charlotte cautioned, moving part-way back up the bank. "Wet rat Squid, drippy little kid!"

Squid lunged past Jason, spraying water like a wet dog. "I'll get you, Lottie," he yelled, pounding up the slope. Jason scrambled up after them.

The sound of squeaking wheels and clopping feet silenced

the three of them. They stood uncertainly by the side of the road as a cart, pulled by two lumbering oxen, slowly approached.

When the man sitting in the cart saw them, he cracked his whip, his leathered face menacing. *"Was machen Sie?"* he snapped. *"Sie junge Diebin?"*

"What are those funny words?" Squid asked, moving closer to Charlotte.

"I don't know," Charlotte faltered.

The man cracked the whip a second time and Charlotte cried out, clasping the back of her hand.

"Wait a minute," Jason yelled, jumping in front of her. "We can't understand you. We..." He felt the butt of the whip in his stomach and instinctively raised his arm, the bugle still in his hand. The whip end pinged off the shiny metal. *"Heim der Diebe. Heim."* The man spat on the road and cracked the whip again, this time to spur on the oxen.

Jason stood rigid, anger and fear racing through him as the cart, one of its wheels noticeably wobbling, rumbled on down the road. *"Diebe,"* he whispered. "We're not thieves." He realized, then, that he understood what the man had said. He had ordered them home and called them thieves.

When he turned, Charlotte and Squid were standing absolutely still, her arm and part of her cloak protectively around his small shoulder. As she turned toward Jason, he could see a large red welt on the back of her hand. "I understood too," she whispered, stroking Squid's head with her other hand. "We're speaking some other language, Jason..."

"What an idiot," Jason cut in, still trembling. "What did he think we were going to steal?"

"I...I don't know," Charlotte faltered.

"We should have punched him," Squid said, his face still in the folds of Charlotte's cloak. "He was mean and dirty and he had black teeth."

Jason took a deep breath. They were in a strange country, speaking a strange language. If he was still up in the attic at home, he would wake up soon – feel the rough floor, his arm around the bugle.

Squid pulled away from his sister's cloak. *"Ich bin bange,* Jason. I'm afraid."

"Squid's doing it, too," Jason said, staring at the child. "We're all talking some other language."

"Heim," Squid said, starting to cry. "I want to go home."

"It's all right, buddy," Jason said, squatting down beside him. "We'll get home again, I promise."

This seemed to satisfy Squid, who rubbed his eyes and started drumming again.

"Look," Jason said, jumping up to check both ways, "the road's deserted."

Charlotte stared at him. "So where are we going?" she asked.

"I'm cold," Squid announced loudly.

Jason squatted down beside Squid and put his arm around the boy's waist. "Hey, buddy," he said, "you're shivering." He looked up at Charlotte. "We need to get Squid's clothes dried out. Maybe if we walk further down this road, we'll find someone who will take us in."

"We'll have to make sure they don't think we're going to rip them off," Charlotte said, pulling her cloak about her. A cold breeze rustled the grass along the road.

"Oh, come on, Charlotte, do we look like we are?"

"I don't know." Charlotte said, staring at him.

"We could start a fire," Squid said, jumping free of Jason, almost knocking him down. "Find sticks and start a fire." He looked about and, seeing trees further along the stream bank, tore off in their direction.

"Squid," Charlotte shouted. "Get back here."

"We'll all go," Jason added, running after the child.

A few steps along the bank, Squid tripped, falling headlong onto the rough ground. He lay flat out, howling either from anger or pain or both. Charlotte caught up and pulled her brother to his feet. His chin was bleeding and his hands were covered in dirt.

Charlotte crumpled down into a sitting position, pulling Squid onto her lap. She wrapped her cloak around him and hugged his shaking body. Jason joined her and they sat huddled together, listening to water gurgle over rocks, the occasional trill of a bird.

"Do you think," Jason asked quietly, "that the bugle had something to do with this?"

"Because of what Gran said?"

"Partly." Jason stopped and took a deep breath. "Do you think we might be in Germany?"

"What if we are?" Charlotte asked, rocking Squid, whose crying had turned into hiccups. "Will it make a difference?"

"Not right now," Jason said. "Right now, we need to find some place warm, someone who will give us food.

Squid snuffled and Charlotte put her hand gently on his cheek.

"It'll be all right, Octavius," she said softly.

"I'm cold..."

"Let's go," Jason said, jumping up. "It'll be dark soon. There must be a house further along this road."

"As long as it's not that cart driver," Charlotte replied quickly, pulling Squid to his feet and starting off.

Jason watched them and when he accidentally put his hand on the horn, the tingling ran from his wrist to his elbow. What if he had the same power as his great-uncle Joseph?

"If you want," he called, running after them, "I'll do the talking."

"It's okay," Charlotte replied quietly. "We'll manage, together." She squeezed his arm.

"It's almost as if when I played *the right notes,*" Jason said as they walked along, "we travelled back in time. Like Joseph. But instead of dry ice, it was fog."

"Well," Charlotte said, not sounding convinced, "you might be right."

Jason's mind raced ahead. "When we do find a house," he said, "we'll have to tell them something, why we're out here wandering along a strange road. Some really good alibi."

"Wh-what's an al-i-bi?" Squid chattered. He took a step back and performed his dog shaking routine again, showering them with wet, wool-smelling water.

"Take that thing off," Charlotte demanded. "We're going to wring it out."

"I'll freeze," Squid protested.

"Octavius, do as you're told."

Jason carefully laid the horn on the ground.

Her tone of voice silenced Squid and, when he couldn't easily undo the rope sash, he yanked at the shirt and wriggled himself out of it. Then he ran in circles around them, skipping over the horn each time, until Charlotte and Jason had twisted as much of the water out of the shirt as they could manage.

Squid pulled the shirt back on and made a face. "It hurts," he said, pulling at the rough material. He stared up at Jason, his bottom lip trembling.

Jason picked up Squid's drum and looped the rope over the child's head. "You know what?" Jason asked, undoing the rope knotted at his waist. "I'm going to be like you, Squid. Carry my bugle with a rope."

"How are you going to tie it, Jason?"

"Watch," Jason said.

"Can I help? Can I, Jason?" Squid yanked the rope from Jason's grasp.

"Squid," Charlotte said crossly, grabbing at the rope and missing.

"Squid's helping Jason," Squid shouted, flailing the rope back and forth.

"Time out," Jason said, stepping back. "Whoa there, little buddy. Here, you hold the bugle."

Squid solemnly took the horn and held it while Jason tied the rope at each end.

"You're a good knot tie-er," Squid said, watching Jason. "Show me how? Will you, Jason?"

"Next time, buddy. Right now we need to find a place to get you warm."

Squid nodded and raced ahead down the road.

"You're pretty good with kids," Charlotte said quietly. "Sometimes he drives me nuts."

"I surprised myself," Jason said, smiling. "Guess I'm a fast learner."

As they walked in silence for the next few minutes, Jason felt the horn banging against his back. The new horn, the different horn. "Remember," Jason said suddenly, "how your grandma said Joseph travelled back to the rehab hospital and then further back into the war?" The sun was low on the horizon now, a red ball far ahead of them.

"I remember how she said he got home again," Charlotte replied. "Who'd believe that?"

"But if he didn't have dry ice, he'd have to find another way, wouldn't he?" Jason asked.

"Mr. Elmhurst was shell shocked. I don't think Gran ever believed the story in the first place."

"But if he did go back, wouldn't you think there might have been a reason? Like maybe he wanted to talk to someone at the hospital, or help someone who was wounded on the front lines?"

"Did anyone ever tell you," Charlotte cut in, "that you have a wild imagination?"

Squid roared back between them. "Are we there yet?"

"Isn't that the outline of a castle?" Jason asked, changing the subject. It wasn't his imagination that had brought them here. It must have been the horn.

Charlotte shaded her eyes and look straight ahead. "Where? I don't see anything."

"More to your right, off in the distance."

"Wow, maybe it is. Look, Squid, see that big castle?"

Squid stopped and squinted ahead. "Nothing," he said, kicking at the road. "Nothing, nothing, nothing."

Jason could see Squid was near the end of his tether, as his dad would say. "How about a piggyback ride?" Jason suggested. "You'll see better." He handed the horn to Charlotte.

Squid slowly pushed his drum around behind and looked dubious. "You strong enough to carry me?"

"Of course I am," Jason answered, grabbing the little guy's sturdy legs. At least he hoped he was. "Now sling the horn over both of us," he instructed Charlotte.

"I see the castle," Squid said into the back of Jason's neck after they'd been walking a few minutes. "A real castle with knights and an alligator moat and..."

"We don't know that yet, Squid," Charlotte snapped.

She was a little ahead of Jason, her shoulders slumped forward, her knuckles white, clutching the recorder. Squid wasn't as heavy as Jason had expected. The child had put his head on Jason's shoulder, the quick rhythm of his breath beating gently against Jason's bare neck. An overwhelming feeling of responsibility washed over Jason. If they were in Germany, they must be further back than 1918. The rough wooden bridge, the rickety cart that man was driving. Mr. Elmhurst had managed to get home again, so it would be Jason's responsibility to get the three of them safely back after...after what? He had no idea, but he was sure that they had to be here for some reason. They would simply have to wait and see what it was.

Not long after they left the bridge, the sun disappeared. A brief glow lit the horizon and then it was gone, the dark hills rapidly closing in around them. Sharp white stars twinkled overhead and Jason wished he had paid more attention to the star map his dad had given him a few Christmases ago; a person could tell a lot from the stars.

"There's Orion," Charlotte said, stopping for a moment and staring upward. "Maybe he'll protect us."

"Orion, Orion. Dumb old Orion," Squid piped up, not even looking at the sky. He was walking again, his hand holding tightly to Jason's.

"It's a *star* constellation, Octavius," Charlotte said. "The sky warrior Orion."

Jason stopped and squatted down beside Squid. "Up there, buddy." He pointed to three bright stars close together. "We could use a warrior, that's for sure," he added. "You think we could be warriors, Squid?"

"Girls make brilliant warriors," Charlotte cut in. "I've got two new computer games with…"

"No, no, no!" Squid said, flinging himself against Charlotte. "No more talking. Let's go." He grabbed Jason's hand, pulling him so he had to jump to his feet.

Jason was amazed. "Guess we'll have to talk about computer games later," he said.

"I think so," Charlotte replied, grabbing Squid's other hand and grinning. "Let's keep going. There must someone living along this road."

The breeze was even cooler now and they walked in silence, their sandals scuffing the road with a steady sound.

"I see something," Charlotte said. "Look. Way up there to the right."

It looked almost like a fallen star flickering in the blackness ahead.

"It's sure not an electric light," Jason added as they plodded on. "We must be back in time, way back."

"Knights and castles," Squid chimed in.

"Medieval," Charlotte said, grabbing Jason's arm.

"That's it!" Jason said excitedly. "We're in medieval Germany."

"And you think we've been sent here for a reason?" Charlotte said in her older sister voice.

"It's more like...like I feel it, somehow."

Charlotte snorted, and grabbing Squid's hand, strode ahead.

Jason watched them and felt a familiar wash of loneliness, of not being understood. How could he explain it? He couldn't. They continued in silence.

They smelled the house before they actually saw it. Charlotte was sure it had to be a barn, but it wasn't. And it was.

"Yuk, smell that, would you," Charlotte said as they moved out beyond a small grove of trees.

"Stinky poo, good for you, stinky poo..."

"Shh, Squid, someone might hear us."

They stopped and stared toward the light, several lights, actually, wavering ahead. Jason made out the outline of a rough-edged building with a steep, scruffy-looking roof.

"It must be a barn," Charlotte whispered finally.

"Medieval," Jason muttered mostly to himself, remembering one of his computer games. "Medieval. I think they all lived together."

"Who?"

"Medieval people and their animals."

Charlotte stared at him. "You know what?" she said. "I think you're right."

"In the same house?" Squid chimed in. "Cool!"

They approached the building cautiously, Jason in front now, the other two right behind. They all saw the outline of the cart at the same time. Squid whimpered and Charlotte grabbed Jason's arm, her fingernails pressing sharply into his skin.

"We'll find another place," she whispered. "Come on, before that man finds us here."

Jason tugged at Squid and motioned for him to be carried. They backtracked to the road and tried to walk quietly past, but Jason was tired now and Squid seemed twice as heavy. Just beyond the house, Jason stumbled on the rough road, catching himself before he fell. Squid, feeling him stagger, cried out. A small black-and-white shape hurtled out from under the cart and came yapping toward them. The dog circled them, herding them together, barking for all it was worth.

Charlotte clung to Jason. Squid quietly hiccuped between sobs. The door of the house opened, revealing a large, burly-looking figure.

CHAPTER SEVEN

THE FIGURE HELD HIS TORCH TO ONE SIDE, PEERING toward them. *"Wer da?"* he called out. The dog quieted, sitting a way off, obviously satisfied he had done his job.

Wer da? Jason thought and, a moment later, "Who is it?" he said aloud.

"It's all right," Charlotte whispered. "It's not the same man."

"Lottie help, Lottie help," Squid kept saying, his salty tears making a clammy wet spot on the shoulder of Jason's shirt.

"Relax, little guy," Jason said, lowering Squid to the ground and squeezing his hand. "Nothing bad is going to happen." I hope, Jason thought as pushed the horn farther around his back so it was mostly out of sight.

The man approached cautiously. It was obvious they usually didn't let anyone in after dark. He held the lantern up to each of them in turn, pausing longest at Jason, inhaling sharply and fixing the lantern's glow on Jason's face. Even though he couldn't properly see the man, Jason sensed a strong reaction. Fear? Disbelief? Maybe this was a big mistake.

Jason squeezed Squid's hand and considered bolting.

"Kommen Sie," the man said brusquely. "Come." He led them to the rough dwelling and held open the door, motioning them inside to a small, dimly lit room. Light and smoke drifted over a rough partial wall, ahead. Voices from this second room, quieted as soon as they entered. In front of them, on thick straw, a cluster of sleepy chickens clucked intermittently and a tethered ox stood dozing.

As he opened the half-door, the man turned to Jason. *"Ich bin der* Wolfgang," he said brusquely. Then, without giving time to reply, he ushered them into a room pungent with cooking smells and woodsmoke. Wolfgang's family stopped and moved closer together as the strangers entered, Jason in front holding Squid's hand, Charlotte close behind.

A woman, obviously the wife and mother, gasped and stepped toward Jason. "Hubie?" she whispered, inhaling sharply, her hands crossing over her heart. Jason stared at her. She had the same eyes as his mom, almost the same cheekbones.

A boy and younger girl pressed in beside her, staring, and an old couple, likely grandparents, looked at each other, bewildered. "Hubie?" the old man echoed, leaning hard on his walking stick.

"They mean you," Charlotte whispered right behind him. "You have to say something."

"But I can't speak German," Jason faltered.

"Maybe you can," she said. "You have to try. Tell them who we are."

Jason took a deep breath. "I am...*ich bin der*...Jason. And my friend...*meine Freundin*...Charlotte." I'm doing it, he thought. I'm finding the words. "And Charlotte's brother...*ihr Bruder...*"

"Octavius," Charlotte cut in. She gave Jason a nudge and he nodded. It did sound better than Squid.

"Mein Bruder fell in the *Wasser,"* Charlotte said, looking at the mother. "He is so cold."

Jason was amazed that he understood these words. He barely noticed they were another language. What a relief, he thought, that all three of them could talk to these people.

"I am Petra," the mother said kindly. "And you have eaten nothing, I can tell. *Kommen Sie,* come." She took Squid's free hand and gestured them toward an open fire, like a campfire, in the middle of the room. Over it, on a wooden tripod, a blackened metal pot hung from three heavy chains. Whatever was simmering there smelled incredibly good. Squid followed the woman toward the warmth without a word, his wet clothes leaving a trail of dark spots along the dirt floor.

After Charlotte and Jason had dropped to sit cross-legged in front of the fire, the boy and girl and the old couple slipped over to the opposite side, peeking through the pot chains to look at the bugle now lying across Jason's lap.

"Wunderhorn," the boy whispered. *"Nicht gut,* not good."

"Ja, ja," the girl added. "Forbidden. Dangerous."

Before Jason had time to think about this, Wolfgang moved in beside them. "Elsa *und* Karl," he said pointing to the children. "Karl is my eldest son now," he added, inhaling sharply.

"I'm ten," Karl cut in. "Old enough to do a man's work."

"I am the eldest girl in this house," Elsa said, staring at her brother.

"You're only seven," Karl snorted. "A baby."

"Enough," Wolfgang said sternly. *"Oma und Opa,"* he added, turning and acknowledging the grandparents. They nodded shyly while Wolfgang stood, arms crossed, scrutinizing the strangers as Petra undressed Squid.

Amazing, Jason thought. These kids act just like Charlotte and Squid.

"Tunic. Stockings," Petra said, nodding at Elsa, who hurried over to the far wall where clothes hung on rough, wooden pegs. Squid stood surprisingly still while she dressed him in a larger and quite worn set. *"Danke,"* he said, smiling up at her.

Jason stared at the smoke rising from the flames. He knew he would have to say something about the horn, but he had no idea what. Where would he begin? How could he explain...any of it? The horn's shiny surface reflected fire and torch light, standing out in the drab surroundings of the rough little dwelling.

He put his hand on its surface and felt the tingling again. It was telling him something, he was sure. Something important. Without fully understanding why, he stood up and, grasping the horn, heard himself say, "We're so grateful for your kindness, taking us in and everything...if there's anything we can do to repay you..."

No one in the family reacted. Charlotte looked up at him questioningly. It was the least they could do, he thought, nodding and giving her a quick smile. She nodded back and Squid, now dressed again, plopped himself into her lap and promptly closed his eyes.

"Hubie," Petra said, staring at Jason. "I apologize, but you look so much," she sighed, "like Hubie."

"Hubie's gone, Petra," Wolfgang cut in. "Buried with the rest of them trying to better things."

"Hubie was your son?" Charlotte asked, looking up.

"Our eldest son," Wolfgang replied gruffly. "He didn't see his twelfth summer."

Squid rubbed his eyes and sat up. "My tummy hurts," he complained, starting to cry. "I'm hungry."

"Opa, Karl," Wolfgang said, striding to the far side of the room. Karl's hair was the same colour as Jason's, but his shoulders were broader. He swaggered ahead of his Opa, who shuffled, leaning heavily on his cane. Even with their backs turned and whispering, Jason knew what they were doing. Deciding whether the three of them could stay or whether they would be pushed back out into the cold night. Jason wanted to ask what was going on here. Why was Hubie killed?

Charlotte's hand closed on his arm and he looked up to see her frowning. "Don't butt in," she whispered. "Wait."

When Wolfgang motioned them to one of two wooden benches in front of a rough plank table behind the fire, Jason figured they must be in.

"You will share a meal with us," Petra said, smiling. It seemed to be a signal, as everyone set to work. Elsa shyly handed them bowls and, with Squid keeping close to Charlotte, everyone lined up as Petra ladled stew into each bowl.

"Meat from our neighbour's pig," Petra said, smiling, "with our potatoes and turnips in good gravy sauce."

As Squid held up his bowl, Jason noticed how red the child's cheeks were and that he was still shivering.

Karl and Elsa stood together at the end of the table, gesturing to Jason and Charlotte to squeeze in beside Oma. Wolfgang and Opa sat opposite, leaving space for Petra at the end. Obviously reluctant to talk to strangers, Karl and Elsa elbowed each other for room, giggling as Jason moved the horn around behind him and Charlotte pulled Squid up onto her lap.

"Octavius," Charlotte whispered, putting her hand on his forehead, "you're so hot."

"Squid's not hungry now," he said, pushing his face into Charlotte's cloak. "My head hurts, Lottie."

Petra, smelling pleasantly of woodsmoke, bent over them and ran her hand across Squid's forehead. *"Fieber,"* she said, straightening up. "He needs hickory tea." She hurried into the shadows at the back of the room and returned with twigs and an earthenware mug.

"I'll pour hot water on this," she explained, showing it to Charlotte. "It quells the fever. Do you think he'll take it?" Charlotte nodded and Petra moved back to the fire, quickly ladling steaming water into the mug from a second blackened pot at the edge of the fire.

"No, Lottie," Squid said, pushing at it when Charlotte first held the mug up to his lips, but she persisted, and eventually he drank most of the liquid.

"You must eat," Petra said to Charlotte. She lifted Squid into her arms, all the while chanting some little song to him, the tune comforting and familiar somehow. Charlotte nodded.

"Do you recognize that?" Jason whispered between mouthfuls.

"What?" Charlotte whispered back.

"That tune. That song she's singing to Squid."

Charlotte listened. No one at the table was talking and the tune filtered through the old man's raspy breathing, everyone's slurping and chewing. "It...it sounds a bit like 'Brahms' Lullaby,' but it couldn't be."

"Why not?"

"If we're here when you say we are, Brahms hasn't even been born yet."

"You're sure?"

Charlotte nodded and frowned. Jason couldn't tell whether it was because she was nervous talking about it or because she couldn't believe Jason didn't know when Brahms was alive. Why would he? His mom used to sing him a lullaby that sounded something the same. What if this lullaby was some old song Brahms had heard when he was little? Weird or what? This same tune could be here hundreds of years before his life at home.

"Would you like more?" Elsa stood beside him.

Ja...Danke, Jason said, handing her his emptied bowl. These people don't realize we're from another time, he thought. They have no idea. And they've taken us in. How can we ever repay them?

Jason was so busy eating, he didn't notice the others slip from the table, but when he finally looked up, he was alone with Wolfgang and Karl, and Opa puffing on a roughly carved wooden pipe.

"You should know what is happening here," Wolfgang said, staring at him, "and why it is dangerous for the three of you to be wandering alone on these roads, especially with that horn."

"In the afternoon," Jason said, "when we were back at the bridge..." He stopped, not sure what he should say, if perhaps the man who yelled at them was a neighbour, a friend.

"Go on," Wolfgang said.

"Someone passed us," Jason went on. "A man with oxen pulling a cart. For no reason, he...he hit us with his whip. He shouted at us as though we were going to rob him."

"What did he look like?" Opa asked.

"A big man," Jason began. He wasn't good at this, describing someone. "He...had a hard face."

"His cart?" Wolfgang asked. "What was it like?"

Jason tried to think. The man's anger. It was easy to re-member that. "It...was much like yours, outside," Jason said, shivering a little. "He had logs in it and a barrel."

"Anything else?" Karl asked. They were all staring at him now, as if whoever this man was, he might be important somehow.

"The wheel," Jason said, remembering. "The one wheel on his cart wobbled back and forth, almost as if it might come off."

"Gustav the Miller," Wolfgang said, a little too quietly. "Did he see the horn?"

Jason nodded. "He hit me in the stomach," Jason went on, "with the butt end of his whip. I held my arm up like this." Jason demonstrated. "I know I was holding the horn."

"He is not to be trusted," Wolfgang replied. "Neither he nor his loud-mouthed brother."

Petra and Elsa interrupted, placing small pottery jugs on the table, one for each of them. Jason turned to see that Oma was rocking Squid, his head against the old woman's shoulder. Charlotte was standing by the fire, her profile outlined in ember light. She had been listening; Jason could tell.

"We should tell the lad," Opa said, adding more tobacco to his pipe bowl, tapping it with a short stick.

Wolfgang nodded. "You have arrived here at a difficult time," he said. "Trouble is brewing, much trouble."

"And it's going to get worse," Karl added, frowning.

"You see," Wolfgang went on, "our *Graf* Friedrich, Lord of the Veste Coburg, is young and idealistic. He follows in the footsteps of his honoured, father, Heinrich."

"And now Heinrich's brother, Otto," Opa cut in, "the town *Bürgermeister,* thinks he should be Lord."

"Otto is the mayor of Coburg now," Jason said, trying to grasp the situation, "but he wants to be Lord of the castle?"

"He claims he was first-born," Karl said, as if that explained everything.

"You see," Opa continued, laying his pipe on the table. "Lord Friedrich's father, Heinrich, and Mayor Otto were twins. I remember when they were born. Such a to-do at the castle." He chuckled and was soon coughing. Elsa rushed up with a mug and Opa drank and wiped his mouth. "So much celebration. Fireworks for days."

"Young Friedrich's been in power less than a season," Wolfgang added, "and here's his uncle, Otto, demanding he step down, that Otto should rule the people."

"Burden the people is more like it," Kurt said. "Fatten his

own household by our sweat."

"But why?" Jason asked. "Why didn't Otto speak up about this long ago? Why did he let Heinrich become Lord in the first place?"

The conversation stopped and they all stared at him. "I...I'm a stranger here," Jason said, feeling out of his depth. "I don't know..."

"Within the court," the old man continued, "a first-born twin is automatically heir to the castle. Everyone assumed," he added, "that twin was Heinrich."

"Only now," the father added, "Otto insists he was first-born. Tells anyone who will listen that he is the rightful heir."

Wolfgang raised his jug to Jason. "To our Lord Friedrich, the true heir," he said, jumping to his feet. Jason followed with the rest. "To our Lord Friedrich," they all repeated, the two men draining their jugs without stopping, Karl taking short sips, his shoulders squared, head held high.

Whatever it was tasted awful. Jason managed a couple of gulps and then had to stop.

"More ale, Petra," Wolfgang called, sitting again.

"Someone must know who was first-born," Jason said, holding his jug close to his mouth so he wouldn't be given more.

"The midwife who delivered them, but she is long dead," Opa said, wiping his mouth with his sleeve. "But she did enter their names on a Royal Parchment, and the first-born would be listed at the top."

"So where is the parchment?" Jason asked. This was getting more and more complicated.

"Hidden somewhere in the castle."

"And no one has ever found it?"

Each one solemnly shook his head.

How big could a castle be? Jason wondered. The parchment would have to be somewhere. Besides, he and Charlotte and Squid were smart. It would be a matter of getting to the castle.

"What if," he asked, impulsively, "I were to find the parchment?"

Kurt snorted and turned away.

"The fire needs wood," Wolfgang said, waving to Kurt. The boy jumped up, obviously amused by Jason's strange offer.

As new wood crackled on the fire, Jason waited for an answer. Wolfgang stared past him and, after a few minutes, even Elsa and Oma stopped chattering to Charlotte. In the silence that followed, Jason waited, feeling more than a little apprehensive.

CHAPTER EIGHT

"Because you seem determined to help and because you arrived here with that horn," Wolfgang said finally, "it is time to tell you the legend."

Petra set the large pottery jug on the table and stood behind her husband, her hands on his shoulders. Oma hummed to Squid; Kurt returned to his place at the table. Jason watched Elsa and Charlotte slip in beside him. The room was unusually quiet.

"It begins a long time ago," Wolfgang said, "before the time of the holy church we know today." He stopped and Jason watched as they all nodded and crossed themselves.

"In those early days," Wolfgang went on, "the wandering German tribes believed in many gods and goddesses. One of the mightiest was Donar, god of war but also patron and protector of peasants, humble folk like us." He stopped and drank more ale.

Everyone leaned forward a bit, waiting. It was clear they had heard this story before and knew it well. "Donar had a special herd of sheep," Wolfgang continued, "that he kept high in the mountains. One day, two of the largest rams fought on a narrow ledge; the weaker one eventually fell to his death in the valley below."

"These rams grow fiercer," Opa said, laughing and slapping the table, "with each telling."

Wolfgang held out his jug and Petra refilled it. "Many years later," the peasant continued, "when gods and goddesses had retreated and Christianity was just beginning, a shepherd boy with white-blonde hair found one of the horns. It was larger than any horn he had ever seen." He paused and they all nodded. "The boy wrapped the small end of it with a strip of leather and taught himself to play. Now each day when the boy played, the horn would turn to gold, and each night when he left it on the floor of his hut, it turned back into an animal horn."

"Word of this magic horn reached the king," Kurt broke in excitedly, "and he summoned the shepherd boy to his castle."

Wolfgang smiled and continued. "The shepherd soon became a knight who rode into battle playing his golden horn, and for several years, the king claimed victory after victory. The shepherd knight gained much influence in the King's court and, remembering his humble beginnings, advised the Royal Treasurer to improve roads and wells and reward peasants who worked long and hard."

"Because of this," Opa said, "the kingdom thrived and crops were good. The shepherd knight with his golden horn became a hero to the peasants."

"The king, too, was pleased," Elsa said shyly, "so much so that he offered the shepherd knight his daughter's hand in marriage."

Jason listened, amazed not only by the story itself but also how they took turns, almost like it was a play and each had a part.

"Three days before the wedding," Wolfgang went on, "a great enemy from the north unexpectedly attacked the castle." He paused, and everyone shifted a bit. Opa laid his pipe on the table and Kurt leaned forward, the frown on his face already indicating the story's outcome.

"Now, ever since he had arrived at the castle," Wolfgang said, "the shepherd knight had kept the horn securely fastened to his belt, but during this fierce battle, it was knocked from his hand."

"When the enemy was finally driven back," Opa said quietly, "the king was horrified to find his shepherd knight among the dead. The golden horn was gone."

Kurt jumped to his feet. "The grieving king," he announced, "put out a decree to find the horn and execute the culprit."

"This legend eventually became law," Wolfgang went on. "A law that stated that a golden instrument was always and forever the exclusive property of royalty or the church."

"Anyone else caught with one," Opa added, "would be considered a common thief."

"Is that law still in effect?" Jason asked.

"Not officially," Wolfgang said, "but Bürgermeister Otto would most certainly use it against you."

"Lottie?" Squid had wakened and was frightened being on Oma's lap. Charlotte scrambled from her seat. "I'm here, Octavius. Charlotte's right here."

Petra moved over to face Jason. "Otto would use this law against anyone," she said, catching her breath. "Especially anyone who looks like you." She dabbed at her eye and turned away.

Jason's head was spinning. "Because I look like Hubie?" He looked from one to the other, hoping for a better explanation.

"One year ago this very month," Wolfgang said hoarsely, "we were on our way home from a meeting. Late at night. There was fog, thick fog." He stopped and cleared his throat. Jason watched him clutch the edge of the table. "Hubie was carrying a scythe we had loaned to a neighbour." At this point Elsa sobbed and ran from the table. Petra followed her into the shadows.

"We stayed close to the stream because it was difficult to see. The so-called soldiers, Otto's men, appeared suddenly, shining lanterns and demanding to know who we were." With every word, Wolfgang's voice grew fainter, until he spoke in a tight whisper. Jason leaned forward, straining to hear. "Hubie was a bit ahead of the rest of us, you see, the scythe blade gleaming, his blonde hair flying in his face. I called him back, but it was too late. One of the soldiers threw a mace." Wolfgang stood abruptly and turned away.

"That's terrible," Jason said, horrified that such a thing would happen. "What did they think he was holding? A sword?"

"These men don't think, lad," Wolfgang said fiercely, turning back. "They're paid to kill, nothing else."

"Ah, yes," Opa added, "but there's more to it than that."

"What Opa means," Kurt broke in, "is that Otto's men had a convenient excuse."

"As if they needed one," Wolfgang muttered.

"From time to time," Kurt went on, "people still claim to see the shepherd knight."

"Like he was a ghost?" Jason asked.

Opa nodded. "But only on a foggy night," he went on. "Before our neighbour, old Gerhard died, he swore up and down that one night he heard the sound of a horn outside his cottage. He lived not too far from here, down close to the stream." Opa puffed on his pipe and stared past Jason.

"And...?" Jason asked.

"Well, when Gerhard opened his door and held his lantern up, he claimed the shepherd knight appeared out of the fog. Just for a moment, he said, and then he was gone."

"He's not the only one," Kurt added. "Others have sworn they saw him."

"So the soldiers thought Hubie was the shepherd knight?" This was getting more and more far-fetched.

"They might have," Opa said.

"It was convenient," Kurt snapped. "They probably knew you were at a meeting."

Wolfgang nodded and sat heavily. He stared at the table, his shoulders slumped.

Jason felt anger, indignation. Otto must a be an evil, controlling man; his soldiers, scum, nothing but low life. "This has to be stopped," he said, impulsively. "The three of us will go to the castle. Somehow, we'll find the parchment and silence Otto."

"An ambitious task for a boy," Wolfgang said, looking up.

"You'll take the girl and child?" Kurt said, trying not to laugh. "What good will they be?"

"We'll talk about this in the morning," Wolfgang cut in, getting up. "Grass to be harvested tomorrow, Karl." The others followed quickly. "Make sure the scythes are ready."

Everyone scattered and Jason squatted down beside Charlotte in front of the fire. Squid had fallen back to sleep.

"Did you hear that?" Jason asked.

"Most of it."

"Am I crazy? Saying we can find it?"

"Probably," Charlotte replied quietly. "And I might have protested, except for Karl's comment."

Jason shrugged. "Medieval ways. Women and children stay home."

"That's what they think," Charlotte snorted.

"Don't worry," Jason added, "we're in this together. So how's Squid?" he asked, deliberately changing the subject.

"A little better, I think," Charlotte said. "Oma says I'm to leave him here by the fire tonight. She and Elsa will take turns watching."

"All night?"

"Apparently. We're to sleep out there with the animals."

"That's okay." Jason lowered his voice. "I'm sure this horn has special powers. It will help us, somehow."

"What do you mean?"

"The horn brought us here to get something done," he whispered excitedly, "and now we know what that is." He grabbed Charlotte's arm. "It's better than any computer game."

"It could also be a lot more dangerous," Charlotte said darkly.

Wolfgang and Elsa arrived, carrying blankets.

"We offer you a place to sleep. Out there," Wolfgang said, pointing.

"We're ready," Jason replied, jumping up. "*Danke.*"

Wolfgang strode toward the door without answering. Charlotte carefully laid Squid on one of the offered blankets, wrapping part of it over his sleeping body. Once in the outer room, Wolfgang stood awkwardly, waiting until Charlotte found a pile of clean straw beside the ox.

"One more thing," he said quietly. "About you and the horn."

Jason nodded, folding his arms, hoping it made him look casual...confident.

"If that horn is what it seems to be," Wolfgang said quietly, "then I think you might have a chance finding the parchment. Our elder girl is at the castle now..." He stopped and turned away, clearing his throat. "She can get a message to someone who can talk to Lord Friedrich, tell him you are here. He will want to see the horn, I am certain."

"Can I trust him?" Jason asked. He was only beginning to understand the bugle's power and didn't intend to have it taken away.

"The Lord, yes," Wolfgang said, turning back. "But many others, like Gustav," he grasped Jason's shoulder, "would make fodder of you, lad." He turned and strode to the inner door. "I will see what I can do," he said, turning back, "about getting you an escort."

"It's that dangerous?" Jason asked.

Wolfgang nodded. "I should be able to send a message to the castle tonight," he said, his voice lowered. "I take word to a checkpoint and it goes on from there. I hope we'll have an answer by dawn." He turned abruptly and was gone before Jason could reply.

"Did you hear that?" Jason said, dropping down onto the straw a short distance from Charlotte.

"Something about getting word to the castle?" Charlotte asked.

"For an escort. To take us safely there." He pulled the blanket over his knees.

Charlotte was silent for a moment and Jason wondered if she was having second thoughts about the whole thing.

"Charlotte, we can do it."

"Because of the horn?"

Jason nodded.

"You think you're the shepherd knight?"

"They seem to think I might be," Jason said, clutching the horn.

"I'm beginning to hope you are too," Charlotte said, staring at him. "We're going to need more than luck to find this parchment." She snuggled her back against the sleeping cow.

"Good night, then," Jason said, tucking the blanket around his chin. The shepherd knight, he thought, as his eyes closed; Hubie; the legend. Too many details.

How had he gotten into all of this?

CHAPTER NINE

J ASON WOKE WITH A START. IT WAS STILL DARK, THE animals still sleeping. He could just make out Charlotte's huddled shape in faint light from a small shuttered window near the roof. She was crying.

"Charlotte?" he asked quietly.

"I'm worried about Squid."

"What about that drink Petra gave him?"

"Hickory bark tea?" Charlotte sat up. "I don't know if it will help."

Jason stared at the unfinished interior of the darkened room. They were in medieval Germany, or so he thought. He had to keep reminding himself. Get used to it. Get over his time-travel jet lag.

"He'll be okay," Jason went on. "He's a tough little kid."

"I hope so," Charlotte replied, wrapping her arms around her knees. "I sure hope so." She turned and Jason could see her face wet, her eyes blinking. "It's so different here, so hard." She turned away.

"What do you mean?"

"Oma told me that Wolfgang and Karl work a small strip of land behind the house," she began, "and they have to give part of what is grown each season to the Lord. Last year when there was a drought, their older daughter, Bettina, was bonded to the Lord as a serving girl. She was only thirteen."

"Bonded?" Jason asked. "Like a slave?"

"Not exactly," Charlotte said. "But she must stay in his service for five years."

Charlotte shivered. "And...they say it will be God's miracle if Squid gets over his fever. Two of their children died before they were his age."

"As well as Hubie?"

Charlotte nodded.

"He was almost the same age as me," Jason said quietly.

"I know," Charlotte whispered.

"We'll be fine, Charlotte. We'll have an escort."

"I hope so." Charlotte stared at him, long enough to make him feel uncomfortable. "Maybe you should cut your hair," she said, finally. "Wolfgang and Karl have short hair. So did that man on the road."

"Are you kidding? No way. You sound like my mom."

"Sorry."

"We'll manage," Jason said, not knowing what else to say. "Hey, look at it this way. I don't know exactly what century we're in, but we're about five hundred years ahead of everyone else here. That should count for something."

"I guess you're right," Charlotte replied, rubbing her eyes. "And we'd better get some more sleep." She curled up again, pulling the blanket around her.

Jason moved the horn to one side, laying it carefully on the straw. Moonlight filtered in through the little window, its beams highlighting the shiny metal instrument.

"Maybe you should cover it up," Charlotte said, watching him through half-closed eyes. "Just in case."

"Good idea." Jason untied the rope from either end and pushed the horn into the straw until it disappeared. "See you in the morning." He pulled the scratchy blanket over himself and closed his eyes. Tomorrow, he thought sleepily. Tomorrow we'll...

WHEN JASON AWOKE, both the ox and Charlotte were gone. He pushed the blanket back and stood stiffly, shivering and watching his breath form a thin cloud in the morning air. Voices and woodsmoke filtered through the half-door to the living quarters.

"Morgen," Petra said brightly when he appeared. She was stirring a pot over the fire, porridge-like smells rising from it. Charlotte was close to her, holding several bowls.

He hated porridge, but there obviously wasn't going to be a choice. He nodded and looked around for Squid until he spied two small feet under the table. He was banging sticks together, obviously feeling better, and arranging them into what looked like a teepee.

Jason noticed right away that Wolfgang was missing from the table. He assumed the man was not back yet and hoped nothing had gone wrong. He thought of asking, but hesitated. Charlotte handed him his bowl and went ahead to the table.

"Morgen. Morgen." Everyone nodded and smiled as Jason slipped in between Charlotte, with Squid on her lap, and Opa. The porridge was grainy and there was no milk or sugar, only a little honey. So many things didn't exist here. Their lives were all pressed into this one room: no TV, no school, and they all had to work, even the kids.

He looked at these adults and tried to imagine how old they might be. The parents looked old and worn, but they couldn't be much older than his mom and dad, who were in their late thirties. This family had two children at home, six people all eating and sleeping in this one small room And what about, Bettina, the older daughter? Would she ever come home again?

Jason kept glancing toward the half-door, hoping Wolfgang would appear. He wanted to ask about the Lord's men coming from the castle. When would they arrive? How long would it take to get there? The bugle. He'd left the bugle buried out in the straw. He gave Charlotte a nudge. *"Das horn,"* he muttered while slipping out from his spot on the bench.

"Das Horn," Charlotte said. Petra nodded and Elsa, at the end of the table, giggled as she watched him go. He was beginning to be a celebrity here.

Jason knelt down and rummaged about in the half-trodden straw. The ox had huge feet and might have stepped on it. In his panic, he threw handfuls of straw back and forth with no systematic approach, creating a hole here and a pile

there. Something that looked like part of a leather halter appeared and he pulled it out, hoping the horn might be beneath.

What he held in his hand looked familiar, yet totally altered. The instrument was made of a large animal horn, the small end wrapped round and round in leather to form a mouthpiece. As he held it, he felt a jolt not unlike a mild electrical shock, and as he stood motionless and disbelieving, the horn slowly changed.

It wasn't obvious at first. The room was dark except for the small shuttered window, and only a few stray light beams mottled the straw-and-dirt floor, but as he watched, something glinted on one side of the instrument. Thinking it might be a metal band clamping the wrapped leather to the horn, he moved into a lighted area for a better look. The shininess rippled along the top, melting outwards from his grasp like a pool of liquid poured onto a floor. He felt warmth and a slight tingling sensation, and by the time he turned the instrument over once in his hand, it was entirely brass again.

A shiver ran down his spine and his hand shook. How did this happen? And why? He apparently looked like Hubie, who must have looked like the shepherd knight. Did that mean that he, Jason, was the shepherd knight? That wasn't logical. It didn't make sense. The horn gleamed in his hand. He turned it over once more to make sure, and then tied it quickly to his belt.

"You okay?" Charlotte whispered in his ear when he returned to the table.

"I'll tell you later," Jason whispered back, taking a deep breath..

Petra leaned over him, her hand on his forehead. *"Fieber?"* she said softly and hurried off, returning with a mug of liquid Jason recognized by smell as the hickory drink from the night before. He drank it without question, hoping he didn't look as pale as he felt. Maybe he'd just imagined it. He put his hand on the horn. Brass and solid.

How much later he wasn't sure, the outer door slammed and Wolfgang appeared. Jason was still staring at his half-filled bowl of porridge, unaware that the girls and women had again left the table. Squid, definitely back to normal, galloped around the table and the fire pretending to be a knight on his horse.

"Lord Friedrich sends his greetings," Wolfgang called. "You and that *Wunderhorn.*" He was standing inside the half-door, looking tired but pleased. Petra rushed to him, taking his heavy outer cloak, giving his arm a squeeze.

"Good," Jason replied. "When will the Lord's men be here?"

"Before midday." Wolfgang sat at the table and Petra hurried over with a steaming bowl of porridge. When he had finished, Wolfgang pushed the bowl back.

"It went all right, then?" Jason asked hesitantly.

"Good men and fast horses," Wolfgang replied. He stared at Jason, tapping his fingers, nervously, Jason thought, on the table. Was there something else? Some other complication?

"My good wife," he said, after a few moments, "thinks we should tell you about Frau Wölfin." He looked embarrassed somehow.

Everyone flocked to the table again except Kurt, who stood by the fire. "It's a made-up story," he said, kicking at the glowing embers. "Even more far-fetched than the ghost."

"Woodcutters have seen her," Opa said, lighting his pipe.

"They claim they've seen her," Kurt said. "Like those sky-high trees they've felled."

Squid detoured under the table, bumping everyone's legs and his own head when he stood up too soon. "Knights don't cry," he whimpered, burying his head in Charlotte's lap.

"Why don't you take young Octavius outside," Wolfgang suggested, staring at his son. "Show him where the chickens hide their eggs."

"Here," Petra said, handing Squid a basket. "You help Kurt find us some nice brown eggs."

Squid raced to the door carrying the basket. "I'm going to get eggs, Lottie. Come on, Kurt. Hurry up."

Kurt grinned and followed him through the half-door.

"My brother is what you call active," Charlotte said, rolling her eyes.

"A dear boy," Oma said. "Kurt will keep him busy."

Petra sat across from Jason and smiled. "Many do not believe Frau Wölfin exists." She glanced coyly at her husband and went on. *"Opa und Oma* remember her mother, the mid-wife..."

"You mean the midwife who delivered the twins?" Jason asked.

Opa nodded. "And the midwife had a daughter. She would have been old enough to remember everything, the royal babies, the parchment."

"It seems reasonable," Opa added, "that this child would

know where the parchment was hidden. She may well have been the one to tuck it away somewhere."

"But why did they hide it in the first place?" Jason asked.

"No one knows that," Petra said. "The castle was attacked many times. Perhaps they feared it would be stolen."

"The story goes," Oma continued, "that some years after the midwife died, her daughter, now a wise woman..."

"A witch," Wolfgang interjected. "The woman became a witch."

Petra shook her head. "Even as a young woman, she was skilled with herbs and cures," she went on, "and at some point she left to live in the forest."

"Probably chased out," Wolfgang said, leaving the table to stand in front of the fire. Jason could see the man was not comfortable with this story.

"A witch, maybe," Opa said, "but whenever a family had a sick child, where did they go?"

"Into *den mysteriösen Forst,*" Petra said in a hushed tone, "to find Frau Wölfin."

"The strange forest," Jason repeated. "And the daughter is Frau Wölfin?"

"The wolf woman," Opa said, smiling. "Because later on and even now, so they say, she is guarded by a pack of fierce wolves."

"So how does anyone get help from her?" Jason asked. He was beginning to side with Kurt. The whole thing sounded ridiculous.

"The town apothecary and his wife visit *den mysteriösen Forst* two or three times a year," Petra said. "The hickory bark I used is from there."

"So they visit Frau Wölfin?" Charlotte asked suddenly. Jason had almost forgotten she was there.

"They claim they do," Wolfgang interjected. His skepticism was obvious.

"They are honest people," Petra said. "You know they are."

"Then you think this Frau Wölfin would know the whereabouts of the parchment?" Jason asked.

"She should remember," Oma said.

"Eggs," Squid shouted from the doorway. "I found eggs." He walked slowly toward them holding out the basket. "Eggs break ve-ry easily," he said, putting the basket on Petra's lap.

"*Danke,* Octavius," Petra said solemnly. "You are a big help."

"Are we going soon?" Squid asked. "Are we, Lottie?"

"As soon as the soldiers come to get us," Jason said. "It won't be too much longer."

Wolfgang walked over to the table and cleared his throat as if to announce something.

Not another complication, Jason thought. We have enough already.

"The children...Petra and I," Wolfgang began, "we were hoping you might play."

"Before you leave us," Petra added, smiling.

Play for them. Of course they would. Should. It was the least they could do. "Charlotte? Squid?" Jason called. "Come on, we're going to play for them."

"Wouldn't it sound better outside?" Charlotte asked, taking the recorder from her pocket.

"Outside," Squid repeated loudly, grabbing his drum. He

began his rat-a-tat-tat and marched through the doors held open for them, everyone following, even Opa and Oma. Once through the doors, they turned to face the family and broke into the now familiar "Bugle Call." The family were soon tapping and humming along, Elsa loudly clapping her hands, Opa tapping his walking stick on the packed ground.

When the last drum roll faded, Petra and Elsa rushed forward, showering the children with hugs. "*Sehr gut,* so good," Petra kept saying.

Elsa slipped away and was back, momentarily, to give Charlotte a cloth bag. "*Brot,*" she said shyly and Charlotte opened the bag to find two loaves of dark bread, still warm. Karl came forward to awkwardly hand her a leather water flask and quickly retreated.

"*Danke,*" Charlotte said, holding both up and smiling. "Thanks so much."

Petra pulled a piece of yellow braid from her pocket. It was knotted on each end and tightly woven. "*Für das Horn,*" she said, handing it too Jason. "To keep it safe."

Jason put the horn down and tied the rope to it with a flourish. "*Danke,*" he said, smiling broadly. With this new piece of rope, he tied the bugle securely onto his rope belt, using several knots just to make sure.

"*Bitte.* You're welcome," Petra replied, giving each another hug.

"Listen," Wolfgang cut in. "I hear them coming."

Everyone quieted and, over the morning sounds of chirping birds and rustling leaves, hoof beats could be heard. Moments later, three solders came into view, the Veste

Coburg emblem visible on their tunics, even from a distance.

"Friedrich's men," Wolfgang said, with a broad smile. "Your passage to the castle is ensured."

"*Morgen,*" one of the soldiers shouted as they approached. The horses stopped abruptly in front of the peasant house, foam on their bits, sweat sleek on their backs.

"You've had a hard ride," the father commented, looking up at them.

"No time to waste," the closest said, dismounting. "The children?"

"Here we are," Jason replied, stepping forward with Charlotte and Squid. "Three of us."

Without replying, the soldier lifted first Squid and then Charlotte to sit in front of the two mounted men. "This one," he said, looking at Jason, "he has the horn, *ja?*"

"Yes, I have the horn," Jason replied. Isn't it obvious? he thought. The soldier quickly mounted and motioned to the father to help Jason into position.

"Godspeed," Wolfgang said, giving Jason's arm a squeeze.

"We'll send word back," Jason replied confidently. "When we get to the castle."

They took off abruptly, with no time to call *auf Wieder-sehen,* the horses prodded immediately into a fast gallop. Jason clung tightly to his horse's mane, hoping Squid and Charlotte were doing the same.

CHAPTER TEN

THE SOLDIERS GOADED THE HORSES WITH THEIR HEELS, shouting back and forth to each other, *"Ja Otto, ja Coburg."* Jason figured they must be mocking the Bürgermeister as they carried their charges to the castle. The slap, slap of the horn against his side reassured him. They were safely on their way.

Jason wondered how long it would take to get there. The sun, behind them, looked halfway to noon. Since Wolfgang's family had given them food, Jason figured the journey to the castle would take several hours.

The rolling countryside was not unlike home, except the trees were denser, wilder looking. They kept within sight of the stream, sometimes on the road, sometimes cutting through open fields, the castle always in the distance, its outline slowly coming into view against the sky. Jason adjusted his grip on the coarse mane; tightened his legs against the horse's sides. Even if he'd wanted to talk, conversation was impossible.

After what seemed at least an hour, Jason's muscles ached, and his hands were numb. The riders with Squid and

Charlotte were behind him. How were they managing? He wished he could reassure them, especially Squid.

The sun was almost overhead now, and Jason's stomach told him it must be nearly lunchtime. They had been veering farther and farther from road and stream and, as they approached another clump of trees, Jason's rider slowed suddenly. The other two reined in to a trot, then a walk. The horses seemed to know the way, moving easily through the trees, stopping when they came to a small clearing.

"You need a rest, *ja?*" Jason's soldier said, jumping down. The others quickly followed and, when the three children were on the ground, the soldiers pulled out leather flasks and drank noisily.

"To *das Wunderhorn,*" one said, grinning and slapping his thigh.

"*Ja Otto,*" another replied, slapping his side and belching loudly.

Jason's rider gestured to the other two and the three men strode off a distance to carry on a discussion, something interspersed with *ja* and *nein* and much pointing at the clearing and surrounding trees.

"I don't like it," Charlotte said, looking worried. "Something's not right."

"But they're Friedrich's men," Jason replied, giving Squid's shoulder a playful cuff. "What could go wrong?"

"My soldier held me so tight," Squid said, pulling at Jason's arm. "He's a strong guy. Like superman."

"They're rough, somehow," Charlotte said. "And why aren't they taking better care of the horses? Look at the poor things. They need a drink."

Jason noticed, then, that under the tunics, the men were poorly dressed, their hair and beards matted and unkempt. A twinge of uncertainty ran through him.

"This is where we must wait," Jason's rider said, striding up to the children. "For our replacements."

"Replacements?" Jason repeated. It didn't make a lot of sense.

"We're just the bottom rank guys," one of the other soldiers piped in. "We have to wait for the big shots to take you to the castle."

This set off gales of raucous laughter and Jason's rider pulled a wineskin from behind his saddle. "A toast," he said, "to the Lord in the castle." The other two held out their flasks for another round.

"But how long...?" Jason asked.

"Hey," one of them cut in, slumping his bulk down against the nearest tree, "don't get ruffled, kid." He slapped his sheathed sword. "As long as you stick by us, you're safe." More gales of laughter, and the other two sat with their companion. One of them pulled out what looked like a pair of dice, and after clearing a patch of ground, they set to playing some boisterous game, drinking heartily after each toss.

"Now what?" Charlotte whispered. She had pulled Squid closer to her. Fascinated by the game, he kept straining to see and, once or twice, tried to pull away for a closer look.

"Don't," Jason said firmly, putting his hand on Squid's arm. "Not a good idea."

Squid sat then, folding his arms and pouting.

"We'll wait it out," Jason whispered.

"What do you mean?"

"They'll fall asleep," Jason added, squatting down. He motioned for Charlotte to sit beside her brother. "Trust me."

"Then what?" Charlotte asked.

Jason pointed toward the far side of the clearing. "We're out of here."

The game became more and more rowdy, and twice a fight almost broke out. At one point, Jason's rider turned to wave at them, but basically, the men seemed to forget they were there.

Finally, when all three were snoring loudly, Jason motioned to Charlotte and Squid to leave.

Charlotte took Squid's hand and they tiptoed back toward the trees.

"Stay inside the ring of trees," Jason said, following, "so we can watch for anyone coming into the clearing."

"What a pathetic bunch," Charlotte said. "Do you really think they were waiting for someone?"

Jason shrugged. "It doesn't matter," he said, speeding up. "All that matters is us getting away from them."

"And if we had waited," Charlotte said, checking behind them once again, "who do you think would have showed up?"

Jason looked grim. "Someone to take me," he said.

"Just you?" Charlotte asked. "What would have happened to us?"

"I don't know," he said quickly. "I don't want to know." This wonderful, safe plan hadn't worked. Something was drastically wrong.

"Well, anyway," Charlotte whispered, "I guess it is you

they want. You and the horn."

"We going to be at the castle soon?" Squid stared up at them.

"We'll be there," Charlotte said, putting her hand firmly on her brother's shoulder, "as soon as we can." She stared at Jason. "For sure, those were not the Lord's men."

Jason nodded and put his hand on the bugle. He was hot property. The sooner they were inside the castle, the better. "But their tunics," he said, remembering.

"Stolen," Charlotte replied. "And we need to make tracks."

Squid grabbed her hand. "Come on, Lottie, let's go then."

They skirted around the clearing out of sight but inside the ring of trees, Charlotte first and Jason close behind. Stolen. Of course the tunics were stolen. Why hadn't he thought of that?

Squid kept getting sidetracked, wanting to stop and investigate some stone or twig.

"Squid, cool it, will you?" Charlotte said, grabbing his hand. "We don't have time."

As they left the clearing behind and moved carefully through the trees, they hoped in the general direction of the castle, Jason wished he had a compass. His dad had one. A wave of homesickness swept over him. He stopped momentarily.

"You okay?" Charlotte asked.

"A bit homesick," Jason said, walking past her. "How long do you think we've been gone?"

"I don't know," Charlotte replied, catching up. "I hope not as long as it seems. It's almost like a dream, isn't it? Maybe it is a dream."

"I don't think so," Jason said. "It's too real."

"We'll get home," Charlotte said, not too convincingly,

"I like it here," Squid cut in. He was right behind the two of them.

"Sure you do, buddy." Jason laughed, and reached back to give Squid's shoulder a little cuff. "I was thinking about a compass," he continued, "hoping we're heading the right way."

"I'm hungry," Squid announced, tugging at Charlotte. "When's lunch?"

"We can't stop yet," Charlotte said, looking behind them. She reached into the bag and tore off a piece of bread for her brother. "Here," she said, handing it to him. "Eat this while you walk. We'll stop later when we're farther away."

Without asking, she tore off another piece and handed it to Jason. He stopped, momentarily, the sun warm on his back.

"Come on, Jason," Squid said, pulling at him. "Lottie says we can't stop."

As Jason turned to follow, his hand brushed the bugle. The tingling ran up his arm again. "This morning," he said, remembering, "when I went back out to get the bugle..."

"You looked like you'd seen a ghost," Charlotte replied, waiting for them. "What happened out there?"

"It's...it's hard to explain."

"Tell me while we're walking," Charlotte replied as she took Squid's hand.

"When I found the bugle in the straw this morning," Jason began, following her, "it didn't look anything like this." He ran his hand over the shiny instrument. "It was an animal horn," he said, shakily. "Sheep, maybe. I couldn't tell exactly. Whatever it was, the end of it, the mouthpiece, was wrapped in leather."

Charlotte stopped and stared at him.

"Like my drum," Squid added. "My drum's different now."

"Are you sure?" Charlotte asked Jason, her eyebrows raised.

"You don't believe me?"

"It seems, I don't know, impossible," Charlotte replied.

"I picked the animal horn up and watched it change. Right in my hand."

Charlotte turned away, arms folded.

"Let's trade instruments then," Jason said, shoving the horn at her, "and see what happens." She handed him her recorder and began walking again.

"I'm first," Squid said, pushing in front of her. "Squid's the leader." He marched ahead of the other two.

"Quiet," Charlotte snapped, hurrying after him. "Try to be quiet."

Jason followed, his hand tightly around the recorder. The trees were thinner here, the sunlight stronger. This will prove it, he thought, staring ahead at Charlotte. One way or the other. Maybe I was imagining it. Maybe...

"The castle," Squid said, pointing. "Look Jason, the castle." Ahead of them, across several hills, it was suddenly there, its towers and walls reflecting the bright sun.

"We'll have to be even more careful now," Jason said, turning slowly in a circle.

Charlotte shaded her eyes. "Still lots of trees," she said, pointing in the castle's direction. "As long as the coast is clear, we should be able to make it to the top of that next hill."

"Okay," Jason said, checking once more, "let's go." He waved Charlotte and Squid ahead, hoping they weren't being watched. Luck, they needed luck.

Every few seconds, it seemed, Squid piped up. "Is the bugle different yet, is it?" Jason forced himself not to look, to keep his eyes on the back of Charlotte's head, the castle outlined against the sky. Even without looking, he could see it, though, swinging back and forth, Charlotte's nervousness kept at bay by the swagger of her step.

The hill was steeper than they'd thought, and all three stopped for a break, just before entering the clump of trees at its peak.

"Listen," Jason said, leaning forward a little. "Do you hear something?"

"Horses," Squid yelled suddenly. He grabbed Charlotte's skirt. "Run, Lottie. It's those bad bad men."

Jason grabbed Squid's one hand and Charlotte the other, and they sprinted for the trees, pulling Squid off his feet, dragging him the last few steps and flopping down into low brush just as two horsemen galloped past, their hoof beats muffled by the rough terrain.

Jason had fallen so that his face pressed into damp earth at the base of some thick bushes. He breathed in the smell and kept his eyes closed until he could hear again over the sound of his pounding heart. When he sat up, Charlotte was tousling her brother's hair.

"Did you see them?" Charlotte asked, catching her breath.

Jason shook his head.

"Knights," Squid announced, brushing dirt from his drum. "Knights looking for a dragon."

"More likely looking for me," Jason whispered. He felt sweat prickling the base of his neck.

"The bugle," Charlotte replied, falling to her knees and rummaging through the long grass. "I must have dropped it."

CHAPTER ELEVEN

T HEY ALL HUNTED, BACKTRACKING CAUTIOUSLY DOWN the slope, stopping to listen at almost every step. What if the horses had trampled it? What if a horseman had seen it? But then he would have stopped. Jason kicked at the grass as he walked, looking ahead for anything with a familiar brass glint.

"What's this?" Squid said. He was ahead, of course, and picking up something, held it out for them to see.

Charlotte gasped and ran a finger along its animal horn surface.

"See," Jason said, handing Charlotte her recorder, "I was right."

Squid, his eyes twice their normal size, gave Jason the leather-tipped instrument and watched as he put the altered horn to his lips.

Charlotte looked as though she had seen a ghost.

Jason managed a few squeaks from the instrument, but even as he held it, the familiar electrical tingling ran the length of his arm. The rippling followed like golden syrup or honey pouring slowly over its surface, dissolving the animal horn back into brass. With his next breath, the instrument was restored to its original solid form.

Charlotte and Squid stared at him, their faces simultaneously reflecting disbelief and belief.

"Maybe you are the shepherd knight," Charlotte whispered.

"It's magic," Squid said, looking as though that solved everything. "Jason's got a magic bugle."

"The *Wunderhorn,*" Jason replied shakily. He stared at Charlotte. "You see, we will be okay," he said quietly. "As long as I have the horn." He tied it securely to the rope at his waist.

"The castle, the castle," Squid broke in excitedly. He had run ahead and could see beyond the clump of trees.

"Even if we were picked up by the wrong men," Jason said, catching up to Squid and holding him still long enough to check the direction of the castle for himself, "Lord Friedrich's men must be out there looking for us."

"Maybe that's who just passed us." Charlotte sounded close to tears.

"When we get to the castle," Squid said, excitedly, "Jason kills the alligators, the big ones in the moat."

"Button up, Octavius." Squid pouted at his sister but kept quiet.

"We're nearly there, Charlotte," Jason said, squinting in the direction of the castle. "Let's go."

By late afternoon, one more hill had turned into three. The woods on this hill nearest the castle were peaceful, birds

chirping, sunlight filtering through the leafy branches.

"I guess we'd hear anyone coming," Jason said. "I don't know about you, but I'm starving."

Charlotte nodded and led them to a sunny spot between two trees. They sat wolfing down the rest of the loaf, all of them hungrier than they'd realized.

"It's not just water," Charlotte, said passing Jason the flask. "Petra called it *Wasserale*. I guess we'll have to get used to it."

Jason took a swallow and made a face. "Water with a bad aftertaste." He took another swallow and handed it back.

"My turn," Squid said, with his mouth full. Charlotte glowered as she handed him the flask. *"Gut,"* he said, after taking a long drink. "I like it lots."

"Should we save any?" Charlotte asked, ignoring her brother.

"Let's finish it," Jason said. He was still ravenous. Charlotte divided the second loaf and they ate in silence. For one thing, Jason felt less and less confident of rescue, especially as darkness was setting in. Where could the Lord's men be? Had even their kind family deceived them?

"You're sure Lord Friedrich is expecting us?" Charlotte asked again after they passed around the water flask, with Squid draining the last of it and complaining he was still thirsty.

"According to Wolfgang," Jason said quietly. "You were there. You heard what he said."

"I thought maybe he told you something else," Charlotte quipped, "when you were having all that guy talk."

"Two things," Jason said, determined not to get riled. "No, he didn't tell me anything else...and is that really fair? What choice did I have?"

"None," Charlotte said. "But it still bugged me."

"No fighting," Squid cut in, wagging his finger at the two of them.

"You tell us," Jason said, smiling and giving Squid a mock punch. Jason stared at Charlotte until she looked up and smiled a little. "We'll get through this. Okay?"

She nodded. "I did catch some of what they said," Charlotte added, shaking crumbs from her cloak. "The gist of it, but not all the details."

Jason motioned for Squid to piggyback again. "Let's get this show on the road, as my dad would say." As he stood, Jason shifted the child's weight and locked his arms through Squid's short legs.

Dusk filtered over them as they made their way down the hill next to the castle, and in the distance, lights from dwellings inside a walled town flickered like stars in an upside-down sky. This must be Coburg. Bürgermeister Otto's town. Jason shuddered. But ordinary families were inside, in front of warm fires, eating and sharing the happenings of their day. Not everyone in the town could be on Otto's side. Most likely many of them didn't even know what was going on.

Squid's small hands held tightly to Jason's aching shoulders. It was getting more and more difficult to see, and after he tripped for the second time, Jason lowered Squid to the ground and told him he would have to walk.

"Squid's tired," the child kept muttering.

"We're all tired," Charlotte cut in, taking her brother's hand. "Shh."

The castle walls lay black and intimidating ahead. High up in two of the towers, faint lights flickered. Once or twice, Jason thought he detected movement near the base of the wall, but it was too dark and they were still too far away.

"If we're lucky," Jason whispered, "a whole group of Friedrich's men will appear any minute."

"I sure hope so," Charlotte faltered.

What happened next took place with such speed and intensity that Jason, even later, was unable to figure it out. They were reasonably close to a road but protected by a cluster of dense undergrowth. Jason had spotted some taller trees ahead, and reasoning that they could stop for a break there, pointed in their direction. The moon had risen and they stood waiting for a passing cloud to darken the grassy area that lay between them and the taller trees.

The sudden clatter of hooves sounded as if from nowhere – several riders, one with a lantern swinging from his outstretched arm. "We're here," Jason called, waving at them, and then realizing too late who it was, he hissed, "go Charlotte, go. It's not Friedrich's men."

Jason dove toward the grove of trees, adrenalin charging through his veins, the bugle slapping against his leg. He heard Squid cry out briefly, then nothing but his own breath and heart, louder and louder, pounding and pounding until he could taste his own blood. A moment later, the pounding intensified and he felt a sharp blow to the back of his neck.

CHAPTER TWELVE

JASON OPENED HIS EYES AND CLOSED THEM AGAIN. WHERE was he? What was he doing slung over a moving horse, his throbbing head banging against its sweaty side? Kidnapped. He'd been kidnapped. A ragged cloth gagged him and his wrists stung from the rope binding them. He kept listening, hoping his captors might say something, anything to give him a clue as to what was happening, but all he heard was the clop-clopping of the horses' hooves echoing in the darkness.

The horsemen stopped, finally, and Jason could dimly see the outlines of buildings. Once dismounted, his captor dumped him onto a hard, stony surface, and when Jason managed to stand unsteadily, he realized he was on tightly packed cobblestones. He was in a town square with towering buildings on all four sides. When his eyes adjusted to the darkness, he could see that these buildings were brick, some darker, some lighter. All the windows and doors looked like gaping black holes, and when he turned, he thought he caught sight of a church spire.

One of the men hissed out instructions to someone in the shadows nearby. Jason was picked up like a bag of grain and toted inside, a heavy-sounding door opening and closing behind them.

From his inverted position, he counted thirteen stone steps as they descended into a candlelit room. His captor placed Jason on his feet again and someone pulled the gag from his mouth. He stood in front of an imposing white-bearded figure seated behind a wide plank table. From under a large velvet hat, the man's steely eyes swept over Jason, the lines on his face following the downward turn of his mouth.

"Bürgermeister Otto?" Jason asked, squaring his aching shoulders. It had to be the mayor.

"*Ja,*" the mayor replied, obviously surprised. "*Wie heißen Sie?*"

"Jason Carter." Jason had a fleeting glimpse of himself in the mirror at home and considered, but thought better of, saluting with "Private Carter."

"The boy smiles. Do you see that, Herr Hermann? He still thinks he has *das Horn.*"

Jason looked down for the bugle, his hands straining behind his back.

Otto leaned forward, keys from an elaborate gold chain clanking on the table. "You don't think you would still have it, now, do you?" His bushy eyebrows raised and he grinned, showing a set of uneven, yellowed teeth, his heavily ringed fingers drumming on the wooden table. The much younger Hermann sat scribbling incessantly with a quill pen, his thin sour face showing no emotion.

Jason noticed then on the table, at Otto's left, the bugle, half-buried in a piece of cloth scrunched into an open wooden box. He lunged for it and was immediately pinned on either side by burly guards.

"And just how did you acquire this horn, peasant?" Otto asked, lifting the horn and turning it in his hand.

Jason stared at the wall behind the man. What could he say? What could he possibly tell this tyrant that would make any sense to him?

"From some distant castle or cathedral?" Otto stood and loomed over Jason, his heavy robes falling across the table, his huge hands gripping its edge.

"No," Jason replied suddenly, "I found it in my attic, SIR, back home in Cobourg, Ontario, SIR, and I had no idea it was valuable."

Otto's face reddened, his nostrils flared. "No idea," he spat back at Jason. "Did you get that, Hermann? He had no idea it was valuable."

"Well, I didn't," Jason shot back. "And where I come from, they don't kidnap children and drag them off…" One of the guards smacked the side of Jason's head with his leather glove.

"You're plucky, but your inexperience shows," Otto said, eyes narrowing. "We will have to make an example of this lad. Don't you think, Herr Hermann?" He paused and Jason could see the man was enjoying himself, that this cat and mouse game was his entertainment.

"The law is clear," Otto continued. "This golden horn is obviously stolen property." He leaned forward again. "One wonders why you didn't keep it hidden." He paused and looked

Jason slowly up and down. "You don't appear to be stupid," he continued, "so there must have been a reason why you chose to flaunt it."

He sat heavily and picked up the horn, moving it back and forth from one hand to the other, smiling. "It doesn't matter now. We have confiscated it and consider you *schuldig,* guilty. A petty thief." Otto waved his hand in dismissal and the guards roughly escorted Jason along a dark corridor and into the dungeon, pushing him to the ground before shackling his leg.

He lay with his head against his arm and a heaviness closed his eyes. He didn't care where he was; right now he didn't care about anything...

JASON AWOKE WITH A START as something scuttled up the darkened wall and disappeared. His forehead throbbed and he put his hand up to feel a large lump on the back of his head. When he tried to pull himself up from the cold, dirt-caked floor, he remembered his leg was shackled and he tripped and fell back, scraping the palm of his hand. He had no idea what time it was, although from the light that filtered through a barred window high up on the wall, he figured it had to be the next day.

"*Morgen.*" An adult voice, behind him, but close by.

"*Morgen,*" Jason replied cautiously.

"*Wie heißen Sie?*" The voice was not threatening; rather inquisitive, hopeful.

"Jason," he blurted out. "My name is Jason Carter. Who are you?"

"Zhay-son," the voice said awkwardly. *"Ich bin der Rolf."*

As Jason's eyes adjusted to the dimly lit room, he made out the forms of six or eight other men – it was difficult to tell how many.

"Ein Ausländer," a second voice broke in.

"A foreigner?" Jason repeated. "That's for sure. And I'm in a dungeon, right?

"The Coburg dungeon, lad," one of them said. "Beneath the town hall."

"I thought so," Jason muttered.

The men went back to their own conversations then, ignoring Jason, or so he thought. He suspected they were debating whether or not he was the boy with the horn, that possibly as Otto had suggested, his reputation had arrived before him.

Would these men, then, be familiar with the legend? Not that his reputation was going to do him any good, not here, chained up like an animal. He moved slightly, hugging his one knee, stretching his shackled leg as best he could. The details of the past night replayed themselves like a video on the darkened wall.

And where were Charlotte and Squid? Not here, thank goodness. Maybe they'd managed to get away somehow. Maybe Friedrich's men had found them. Jason could only hope so. Charlotte was smart, confident, but, especially in this medieval time, she was vulnerable. And Squid? Mr. Optimism. Jason couldn't get over the way the kid looked up to him. He'd had no idea little kids were so trusting. Somehow, he had to get out of this place and find them.

Jason shifted his position on the cold dirt floor and shivered. Escaping from this prison was certainly not an option right now. Otto and his cohorts had his horn, and he was *schuldig.* Guilty. What about the men here? What had they done?

"So, *Zhayson,*" one of the men said quietly, "you've gotten yourself in for more than you reckoned, I'll bet."

"I...I guess so," Jason answered. He wasn't quite sure what he should say.

"There was no way you'd know, lad, that those men were most likely Otto's hooligans."

"You know what happened to me?" Jason found this hard to believe.

"News travels fast, lad. Otto figures if he rounds enough of us up, the castle will be an easy mark."

"But what about Lord Friedrich's men? And the castle, it has thick walls, good fortification?"

"It does and we know Otto will fail."

"But what we don't know," someone else cut in, "is how many of us'll get cut down before that happens."

Jason thought of Hubie and shivered.

No one spoke again after that, and Jason shifted position. His whole body ached, and he'd give anything for a cold drink of water. This felt like some awful nightmare, only it wasn't a nightmare, it was real. One thing for sure, the bugle wouldn't stay brass for long. Whatever Bürgermeister Otto did with it, for whatever reason, he would be soon be disappointed. Then what? He remembered Otto's cold disregard for him and sweat ran down the back of his neck. He curled into a sleeping position, his head on his outstretched arm, his eyes half closed.

Their singing began gradually. One voice, at first, quietly humming a tune Jason had never heard, then quietly singing, *"Die Gedanken sind frei."*

"My thoughts are free," Jason whispered.

A second voice added harmony as they repeated the line, until one by one, they all joined in, the tune hopeful and uplifting.

> *Die Gedanken sind frei*
> *My thoughts freely flower*
> *Die Gedanken sind frei*
> *My thoughts give me power*
> *No scholar can find them*
> *No trap ever bind them*
> *No man can deny*
> *Die Gedanken sind frei*

Although each man sang softly, the sound was full of power, as if the words lifted them beyond the walls of this dank place.

"You know this song, lad?" someone asked.

"No, but I like it," Jason said, sitting up. "Sing it again, and when I get my horn back, I'll play it." Jason turned, already knowing they were staring at him, that by mentioning the horn, he had confirmed the rumour.

The door lock creaked and the men fell silent, only the whites of their eyes visible in the half-light. All watched the slowly opening door, two dark figures appearing.

"Drink?" Someone was kneeling close to him. Jason gulped down the liquid, ignoring the aftertaste of ale. It was in a flask not unlike the one Karl had given them.

He could see the figure now, a boy, perhaps not much older than himself. *"Danke,"* Jason whispered gratefully. "Thank you."

The boy smiled and handed him a thick section of hard dry bread. Jason tore at it, great mouthfuls one after the other until nothing remained.

The boy stayed beside Jason, but there was someone else as well, moving between the shackled figures, someone taller, handing out food and water.

"More to drink, please," Jason blurted out.

The boy handed him the flask again and Jason drank until it was empty. "Who are you and how do you get in here?" Jason asked.

"Hindel," the boy whispered, gently squeezing Jason's arm. "My father and I bring what we can."

Before Jason had time to ask more, a bell clanged and the door creaked open, revealing a soldier, lantern in one hand, sword ready in the other.

"Auf Wiedersehen," the boy muttered, hurrying with the other figure to the opening. At the doorway, the boy turned back momentarily and Jason noticed a shiny metal cross hanging from a chain around his neck, its surfaces reflecting lantern light. The boy smiled briefly, then disappeared. A heavy bolt outside the door scraped into place.

"Auf Wiedersehen," one of the prisoners mimicked back.

Another snorted and kicked at the floor. Everyone was silent then and Jason heard the scuttling again. The men rattled their chains and the scuttling stopped. Mice, Jason thought to himself, or worse, rats. He shivered and listened to the others breathing, the occasional cough. How long had these men been locked up here?

He hummed part of the tune, trying to remember.

"Not too loud, lad," one of the men warned. "They may be still out there, and we're not supposed to sing, especially that song."

No singing. Nothing to eat or drink unless some outsider, someone who was free, came in with it. They could starve to death in here and who would know? Who would care?

Don't panic, Jason thought, rubbing at his shackles, it won't do any good. His mom was always saying, "Don't panic," when he was worried about some school assignment and especially when they moved. What a joke, worrying about school or moving. If he ever got himself out of this, he would never panic again. Starvation. Death. These were things to panic about. He looked at the men around him. Some were dozing, others staring into space. Everyone was quiet, calm. Was it terror, or had they actually learned to deal with this awful place?

"Excuse me," he said to the man closest. "Could I ask you something?" The man was humming quietly, tapping his finger in rhythm against his knee.

The man stopped. "Go ahead, lad. What is it?"

"How do you stand this?" Jason asked. "Aren't you worried about starving, getting sick?"

"There are worse things," the man said. "You've never been in the dungeon before?"

"Where I come from..." Jason started and then stopped. What was the point? None of it would make any sense to this man, to any of them. "I just wondered," Jason went on, "if, like in the song, you thought about other things, what it was like before..."

"My good woman's porridge," the man said, after a few moments silence. "Our new babe..." He leaned closer to Jason. "And Otto's death," he whispered. "Then we'll all be *frei* and have a better life."

Jason turned away. Otto's death? That didn't seem too likely, not in the near future. Freedom. He thought about home. Freedom there was being able to stay out as late as he wanted. No homework. Letting his hair grow longer. A joke compared to this.

He pictured his room, then, the secret opening in his closet, climbing the hill through the scratchy grass, the blue lake in the distance. It's true, he thought suddenly, my thoughts are free...

The door scraped open again and two burly soldiers appeared. Everyone, including Jason, tensed and waited.

CHAPTER THIRTEEN

"*Der Ausländer,*" a soldier barked, peering into the dimly lit room.

"*Ausländer, Ausländer...*" The words were passed from one prisoner to the next. The relief in their voices was obvious.

Before Jason had time to react, one of the soldiers was at his side, unlocking the shackle and dragging him to his feet. Jason felt the men's eyes follow him as he was roughly escorted from the dungeon. A faint *auf Wiedersehen* followed through the closing door. Wherever they're taking me, he thought, can't be worse than this.

Before he could catch his breath, one soldier held his shoulders while the other bound his hands behind him. They climbed the same stone steps and emerged into the morning air.

The sun, just visible above the top of the buildings, cast long shadows across the deserted cobblestone square. Compared to Wolfgang's small cottage, these buildings were magnificent, some of them four stories high. A few were brick, the rest had ground floors of roughly hewn rock with the upper floors made of rough plaster held in place by long vertical planks. Some of the second floor windows sported window boxes full of flowers. Although no one was in sight, Jason was sure that behind several of the partially closed shuttered windows, he saw eyes staring at them. Above him, not far away, a bell tolled. He counted as they moved through the shadows – five, six, seven. Seven in the morning.

The soldiers marched Jason through a narrow street off the square and under an archway where they were joined by three more foot soldiers, their chain mail vests clanking in steady unison as they strode along. Jason alternately walked or jogged, depending on their pace. He thought of asking them where he was being taken and why. He thought of yelling at them that Lord Friedrich's men would find him soon, that they were dead meat if they didn't let him go.

When he slowed momentarily, one of them cuffed him on the shoulder. "Keep the pace, peasant," he snarled, "or we'll have to drag you." Jason concentrated, then, on the cobblestones, on keeping up.

A crowd of townspeople was gathering, but their voices silenced as the group approached and passed by. The inquisitive faces, the stone wall they seemed to be following, the rough ground all blurred as Jason stumbled along.

When they turned and moved into an open space, he saw the rough platform ahead. The crowd that was following, spanned out around its base. Jason was pushed up steps and released to stand uncertainly by himself.

Someone pulled off his gag and he stared up at a single

upright and crossbeam fastened to the side of the platform. From the end of this crossbeam, a noosed rope swayed gently in the early morning breeze. Jason closed his eyes and tried to stop shaking. He was standing on a gallows scaffold.

He opened his eyes again and searched the faces below him, hoping Friedrich's men might suddenly appear or Wolfgang's family – someone, anyone to call to. Out of the corner of his eye, he could see a soldier's sword glinting in the sun. He was being guarded, on display, a petty thief. They were going to hang him for supposedly stealing the horn? Sweat broke out on his forehead.

Hermann approached, clutching a document, and puffing along beside him, a short, powerfully built man dressed more like a peasant, but with an air of power and authority. The executioner. Hermann waited while this man grunted his way up the steps to stand directly in front of Jason, staring as if sizing him up, his bushy eyebrows furrowed over a pock-marked face. Hermann examined the document several times and looked nervously about. The mayor, Jason thought, that's who they're waiting for. Bürgermeister Otto.

Jason kept perfectly still and stared straight ahead. He'd seen movie executions and that's what prisoners always did. He remembered asking his dad why. Why didn't they yell or plead? Now he knew. Numbness. Numbness and something else he couldn't quite get a hold of. Disbelief? His brain still telling him this wasn't really happening? He was shaking inside, his stomach knotting over and over. He stared at the wooden planks, aware only of his own breathing, of sweat collecting at the nape of his neck.

The crowd began muttering, and as Jason looked up, they pulled back, making a pathway. Bürgermeister Otto, flanked by two soldiers, strode toward the platform. Jason glimpsed the box held firmly in his large hand.

"So, peasant," he said, towering over Jason, "how do you explain this?" He opened the box revealing the dull animal horn with its leather-wrapped end, the yellow cord still in place. "Do you have an accomplice in my ranks, or is it a trick?" He was puffed up with anger, his face almost crimson. "Speak up, peasant, you don't have much time."

"It's not a trick, sir."

"Not a trick, you say? Then which of my men switched it for you? And where is it now?" He moved closer with each question until he was almost touching Jason.

"If you let me hold it, sir, it will change back."

A look of fear crossed Otto's face. He turned and held the horn up to the crowd. "The peasant claims he can transform this animal horn," he announced loudly, "into gold."

The crowd gasped. Someone shouted, "Let him do it, then."

"The peasant is a liar," the Bürgermeister replied loudly, returning the horn to its box. "A liar and a thief."

Jason wasn't sure how much longer he could remain standing. His wrists stung, his legs were shaking and, worst of all, he knew tears were close, that any minute he might lose it and start to cry.

"I don't know what they do with liars where you come from," the Bürgermeister continued, turning back to Jason, "but here we give them a taste of the whip. Liars who steal get the rope. Hermann, read the sentence."

Hermann stepped forward and cleared his throat. "Whereas in the month of *Juli, im Jahre* 1484," he began in a nasal monotone, "Jayson the peasant did steal one golden horn. He did, following his arrest and incarceration, by wits or magic, move or transport said horn to another location. Charged with theft, conspiracy, and possible witchcraft, Jayson the peasant has been found *schuldig* and shall hang by his neck until dead." He stepped back and swept his hand dramatically, signalling the executioner.

The word *Wunderhorn* was whispered back and forth through the crowd, who seemed, already, to know of Jason and his horn that shone like gold. Silence followed except for a dog yapping somewhere in the distance.

Out of the corner of his eye, Jason could still see one end of the yellow rope dangling from the box and he remembered Petra's face smiling at him, Wolfgang calling out, "Godspeed." Tears blurred the rest.

The executioner pushed Jason roughly toward the dangling rope. The noose wasn't in the right position and the executioner shouted for it to be lowered. A cranking sound brought the rope to rest on Jason's shoulder. He felt himself gagging even before the rope was pulled over his head.

"Halt."

The sound of hoof beats cut through the tense silence. A commanding voice had shouted in the direction of the platform. Jason heard the crowd exclaim – saw people hurrying out of the way, riders dismounting.

"Get on with it," Otto hissed to the executioner. "Ignore

them." Jason felt the man adjusting the rope, pushing it roughly against his neck.

"*Halt,*" the voice shouted a second time.

In spite of this, Jason still waited for the rope to tighten around his neck, waited for this to be over with, his heart pounding in his ears, louder and louder.

"Lord Friedrich of the Veste Coburg demands you *halt.*" It was the same commanding voice.

The rope was pulled roughly back over Jason's head, and he felt himself exploding, as if all the air had been knocked out of him. He crumpled to the platform and was immediately dragged to his feet by two soldiers.

The crowd muttered now, reacting to what had been said, what was happening. Jason watched two imposing figures stride forward, a group of soldiers, swords drawn, close behind. The Veste Coburg insignia on the soldiers' shields gleamed in the sun. A few seconds more and it would have been too late. Jason braced himself as his knees tried to buckle a second time.

The crowd cheered as the two men passed, some bowing respectfully. The taller man's green velvet robes swirled about his legs; his jewelled fingers held an ornate walking stick. Beside him walked a much younger, more plainly dressed man.

The taller gentleman removed his gloves, handing them and the walking stick to his servant. He stepped forward and spoke firmly, addressing both Secretary and Bürgermeister. "It has come to Lord Friedrich's attention," he began, "that Bürgermeister Otto has in his possession a golden horn belonging to this young man Jayson."

Jason squared his shoulders. His golden horn. But it wasn't golden now, and wouldn't be unless he could hold it again.

The mayor rushed forward, bowing as he came. "Kanzler Reinhard," he said, bowing again, "this peasant is a thief, a liar. Perhaps there has been a mistake?"

"But you do have the horn?" the Kanzler said, staring at the box in *Otto's* hand. "As Lord Friedrich's chancellor, I demand an explanation."

The Bürgermeister reddened and stepped back. "Yes, my Lord Chancellor."

"May I see it then?"

In the silence that followed, Jason watched a second group of Veste Coburg soldiers move closer to the platform and he counted. Twenty. They outnumbered Otto's men more than three to one. Jason glanced toward the Bürgermeister. Even if he threw himself forward, he couldn't reach the horn. Somehow he had to get hold of it.

Otto opened the box, revealing the animal horn.

"This is your idea of a joke, I presume?" Reinhard said, giving the animal horn a once over. "The golden horn, if you please?" He snapped his fingers impatiently.

"Yes, yes of course," Otto said, his face in a sneer. "Herr Hermann, what have you done with the horn?" He shoved the box into Hermann's hand.

Hermann paled visibly. He stumbled forward, stammering something and trembling. The document fell to his feet.

"Pick it up, fool," Otto snapped, "and get the horn."

This was it. His only chance. Jason shouted, *"Wunder-horn,"* and threw himself forward, ploughing into Hermann, knocking both of them to the ground. The horn and box clattered to the platform, and with his hands bound behind him, Jason rolled back and forth, determined to get his body over the horn, kicking Hermann first in the stomach and then in the leg. The man howled and thrashed and in the few seconds it took for the soldiers to pull them apart, the horn lodged momentarily under Jason's chest. He felt an electrical snap and knew the transformation was complete.

As two soldiers grabbed Jason, Chancellor Reinhard again shouted, *"Halt."* Jason, his face pressed sideways on the platform, his arms still twisted behind his back, watched the green velvet robes swish to his side. "A knife," he heard Reinhard say, and when his hands fell free, Jason grabbed the horn and, leaning on his elbow, raised the *Wunderhorn* over his head. The golden horn caught the morning sun as gasps and cheers rose from the crowd.

He scrambled to his feet to face Reinhard, who was smiling and shaking his head, amazement evident on his face. Otto and Hermann had shrunk back and were staring at Jason in disbelief.

Two Veste Coburg soldiers leapt to the platform, lifting Jason up between them. He raised the horn above his head and shouted, "Long live Lord Friedrich." The crowd cheered back, "Long live Lord Friedrich." As they carried him from the platform, Jason caught sight of Otto, shoulders visibly slumped, hurrying back toward town. The town soldiers and Hermann formed a straggly band behind him.

The next thing Jason knew, he was seated on one of the horses in front of a Veste Coburg soldier. Chancellor Reinhard rode beside him. "We go now to the castle," he said, smiling at Jason. "Lord Friedrich is eager to meet you."

All of this felt like a dream to Jason, his exhausted body going through the motions, his mind floating somewhere else. He nodded and tied the bugle's yellow cord onto his waist rope. When the crowd pressed closer, one of the soldiers on horseback shouted and they immediately melted back, leaving the dusty road ready for the procession. Above, on the hill, the castle walls and towers looked solid and reassuring against the skyline.

They moved slowly, at first, winding their way upward past groups of people who waved and cheered. The hill was higher than it looked and, once or twice, Jason looked back to the valley below, to the platform shrinking to a smaller and smaller square, to the town behind, its walls and archways peaceful in the morning sun. Jason shivered and listened to the steady clop, clop rocking beneath him. When his head nodded, a strong arm slipped around his waist.

He wanted to ask Chancellor Reinhard about Charlotte and Squid. Were they all right? Were they...?

Jason woke with a jolt when the horses stopped. They had arrived in front of the castle.

CHAPTER FOURTEEN

THE CASTLE TOWERED OVER THEM, ITS GREAT STONE WALLS so high that when they stopped in its shadow, Jason was forced to bend his head back as far as it would go in order to see the top. They faced an imposing tower, the highest of several Jason saw spaced around the castle wall at intervals. Between the front tower and the next one, a smaller projection stuck out from the wall. One of the soldiers waved what Jason assumed was a signal up to the nearest of these. Someone called down a reply, but Jason couldn't make out what was said.

There was no entrance at the front, and they proceeded around the castle to be met by several dozen soldiers standing at attention on either side of a heavy wooden door. The soldiers accompanying them dismounted and joined the others, forming two double lines spanning out in a "V" from the entranceway. Jason marvelled at their precision and speed.

One of the soldiers banged on the wide-beamed door with the hilt of his sword and it swung open, revealing a torch-lit tunnel. As soon as they entered, two soldiers lifted a heavy beam across the door and dropped it into place. Tight security, Jason thought, and again a feeling of relief swept over him.

He followed Chancellor Reinhard and his servant, the men's boots clicking on the cobblestones as they moved upward through the long, stone-arched tunnel toward light.

In the daylight again, Jason looked about. On the far side of this inner courtyard, a group of knights stood talking and joking as a boy pushed a hay-filled cart toward their tethered horses. Before Jason had much chance to look at the stone buildings, Chancellor Reinhard motioned him to follow. The door of the largest and most imposing structure swung open for them to enter.

Jason found himself in a low-ceilinged, torch-lit entrance-way where, as they marched along, everyone's shadows merged and separated on craggy stone walls. Yet another heavy wooden door opened and then they were inside a large rough-beamed room, sunlight pouring in through high narrow windows. In front of them, he saw three long wooden tables in a "U" shape, all draped with white cloths. Young pageboys scurried back and forth placing silver plates and jugs on each one.

A small bell tinkled and two servants rushed out through velvet curtains behind the farthest table. One of them whispered to Chancellor Reinhard. The Chancellor put his hand on Jason's shoulder. "Lord Friedrich will be with us soon and he is most anxious to see that horn of yours."

Jason nodded, his fingers tightly holding the bugle. What if Friedrich wanted to keep the horn? Everyone kept telling him how just and fair the man was. Any minute now and he'd find out. More questions pummelled his brain. When should he ask about the parchment? Should he mention Frau Wölfin? What had happened to Charlotte and Squid?

Lord Friedrich entered in a flurry with several servants hovering behind. He paused, momentarily, as one of them straightened the fur collar of his elaborate tunic.

Jason realized he had no idea how to greet a lord. "Chancellor Reinhard," he whispered, "should I bow?"

Reinhard nodded as Friedrich strode forward. Tall and muscular with short, white-blonde hair, he moved with energy and confidence. Jason watched the chancellor sweep his right arm parallel to his waist as he bowed, and Jason did likewise.

"My Lord," the chancellor said, "may I present Master Jayson and his horn."

Jason, his hand still on the bugle, looked up to see Friedrich smiling. "First let me say *willkommen,* welcome. Fraulein Charlotte and Octavius are likely in the garden with Bettina. They will all join us for the banquet, later."

Jason smiled and nodded. They were safe then.

"My uncle, Bürgermeister Otto, and I," Friedrich began, "have different ideas as to how things should be done. Let me assure you that you are all safe here."

"Thank you...sir," Jason replied. He wanted to tell the Lord of his intentions, of what he hoped to accomplish, but Friedrich was staring at the horn. Still a little suspicious of the Lord's intent, but seeing no choice, Jason untied the bugle from his waist rope and held it out.

He watched Lord Friedrich finger its shiny metal, wonder

and excitement so evident in his clean-shaven face. All movement in the room stopped, everyone watching.

"The *Wunderhorn,*" Friedrich said quietly, turning the instrument over in his hands. "We are honoured." He looked up. Jason noticed that his hand was trembling slightly.

"We...we will play for you, Charlotte, Octavius, and I."

"*Ja,* of course," Friedrich replied, handing the horn back, "after the banquet." He paused and looked at Jason. "Your unfortunate stay in my uncle's dungeon has left you somewhat worse for wear. Upstairs, in your quarters, I have ordered a change of clothing and a washing basin. And take your time. We won't be eating for a while yet." Friedrich clapped his hands and a young page appeared. "Stefan will show you the way."

"*Danke,*" Jason replied. He knew he must look dragged out, dirt from the dungeon and scaffold ground into his tunic. He followed Stefan up a set of narrow back stairs, their footsteps echoing on each stone step. Jason felt almost as if he were in a dream. He knew he must be very tired, that he had barely slept for the past two nights, but he couldn't sleep, not yet.

What if the parchment was hidden right here behind the rough walls of this staircase? It was too dark to see anything but the outlines of huge stones. He remembered looking up at the walls outside. The castle was at least two, if not three stories high. Finding the parchment was going to take longer than he thought.

Stefan bowed as he opened the door. "Your rooms, Jayson," he said. "Lord Friedrich hopes the tunic is suitable." He bowed again and hurried off.

Jason looked quickly around the small room. This sure beats the dungeon, he thought, flopping onto the end of the bed. Even a canopy. A fire crackled inside the stone hearth and on a cupboard shelf on the far side, he spotted clean clothes.

He climbed out of bed and inspected the room. On the shelf, he found a red velvet tunic, black stockings, and soft leather shoes with pointed toes. He looked down at his dirt-caked stockings and sandals.

In the wide window ledge, he saw a basin of cold water and some strong smelling soap. He quickly pulled off his tunic and stockings to scrub his face, hands, arms, legs and, finally, his smelly feet. He figured he could always dive for the bed if the door suddenly opened.

A few minutes later, as he was pulling on his new shoes, Squid and Charlotte burst into the room. Squid slammed the door shut and flung his arms around Jason; Charlotte grabbed both his hands. "We thought...we thought..."

"So did I."

"Lottie's got a bed like yours in the other room," Squid said, grabbing Jason's hand. "Come on, Jason. Come and see. I'm sleeping in the window ledge."

"I'm really whacked, buddy," Jason said, lying back with his eyes closed. "Maybe I could see it later?"

"You were in a dungeon?" Charlotte asked, sitting on the floor beside him. "The chancellor told us you'd been taken to the mayor's office for questioning."

"I was to begin with, then the dungeon." Jason felt himself drifting off.

Charlotte said something else and Jason forced his eyes open. "What?" he muttered. "What did you say?"

"Come on, Octavius," Charlotte whispered, "Jason needs to rest..."

IT SEEMED LIKE ONLY FIVE MINUTES LATER; Squid was on the bed, shaking Jason and calling, "Wake up, Jason. It's time to eat. Wake up."

Jason sat up and stared at Squid. "Where am I?" he asked groggily.

"In the castle, silly Jason." Squid giggled, and he jumped on Jason's legs.

"Off the bed, Squid," Charlotte demanded, coming into the room. "Sorry," she added, "he ran ahead of me up the stairs."

"How long have I been asleep?" Jason asked.

"A long time," Squid cut in, jumping off the bed. "We went to see the horses and the wagons and everything and then we got dressed." Squid looked older, somehow, in his velvety brown and green tunic.

"New stockings," he said proudly, "and they don't itch." Green stockings, Jason noted, and brown pointed shoes.

"We should go downstairs soon," Charlotte said. "The banquet will be starting."

Jason stared at her. "Wow," he said quietly, "you look... awesome." Her long silky dress was patterned with flowers and leaves, real flowers fastened into her hair, now in braids over her head. She curtseyed and looked pleased. "You're feeling better now?"

Jason nodded and relief swept over him. They were here. They were safe.

As THEY ENTERED THE GREAT DINING HALL, servants rushed back and forth, bringing dishes to the table – great urns filled with chunks of meat, large loaves of bread, platters piled with vegetables. Jason watched, feeling completely out of his depth, determined to behave as best he could in this unfamiliar situation.

Lord Friedrich was already seated at the head table and he turned to greet a beautiful young woman entering through velvet curtains. As she walked, her trailing brocade dress swished on the stone floor. Friedrich took her outstretched hand and kissed it as she sat beside him on one of two high-backed chairs.

Chancellor Reinhard dashed through a side entrance and quickly escorted Jason, Charlotte, and Squid to the head table.

"Lady Katherin," Reinhard said, facing her, "may I present Master Jayson." She nodded and smiled and Jason quickly bowed again. Out of the corner of his eye, he noticed Charlotte curtsey. Lord Friedrich motioned to the chair beside his. "For our guest of honour," he said grandly. Charlotte and Squid slipped onto a bench covered with a long, velvet cover edged in gold braid.

Moments later, two young children appeared, hurried in by a tall, slender girl who looked vaguely familiar. Her long dress was plain, her blonde hair in two braids fastened over her head. She looked at least a couple of years older than either himself or Charlotte. As she settled the children into their places, she noticed Jason and her eyes widened. She put her hand over her mouth, momentarily, then made eye contact with Charlotte and nodded.

"Bettina," Charlotte whispered, nodding back. "They wouldn't normally be eating here," she added, grinning, "but today is special."

The children, who both looked younger than Squid, giggled and whispered as soon as they spied Jason. Bettina tousled the boy's hair and playfully wagged her finger at the girl, obviously explaining who Jason was. They seemed impressed and were silent, but Jason noticed that they kept glancing toward him, shy inquisitive glances.

More men entered the hall now, the knights who were outside and a number of others. Hunger and apprehension began pulling Jason's stomach into a sharp knot. He had no idea how to behave here. He was so hungry, and worried he might make a fool of himself. He would watch Charlotte, assuming she had already figured it out. At home, he and his parents rarely ate a formal meal together. Everyone here, sitting so politely, reminded him a little of tea at Gran's.

"You must be starving," Charlotte whispered, giving him a nudge.

Jason nodded and watched as servants hovered up and down both sides of the table, bringing more food and more jugs of wine. Just before they began eating, two servants entered, one carrying a basin and linen cloth, the second a bronze, bird-shaped container, its long tail feathers forming a handle. Jason watched as the servant poured steaming water into the bowl. Both Lord and Lady dipped their hands in and out of the water, drying them on the towel. Flower petals floated in the warmed water.

A moment later, these servants stood between Jason and Charlotte with a similar bowl and towel. Jason carefully copied them and watched as Charlotte and Squid did likewise.

A round, red-faced priest in a plain black robe stood and chanted a blessing. Two young pageboys then moved from guest to guest, placing thick slices of bread in the bottom of each wide pewter bowl. Two more followed, ladling chunks of spiced meat onto the bread. More serving plates followed, heaped with a variety of vegetables. Jason watched Charlotte use her knife to stab each morsel, plucking it from the end of the sharp blade with her teeth. Hoping he could use the knife as effortlessly, he copied her, being careful not to cut his mouth.

"Don't eat the bread," Charlotte whispered. "They collect it, afterward, for the poor." Soggy, cold bread, Jason thought. Then he remembered the dungeon and wondered if that bread had been leftover from someone's meal.

The Lord's children and some of the men ate with their hands, and he noticed Squid copying them with gusto. As the wine goblets were filled and refilled, conversation grew louder and more boisterous.

Jason had never seen people eat so much food. He had no idea how long they continued, but after he had emptied his plate twice, he felt his eyes closing, his body drifting toward sleep. Luckily, the servants bustled in to remove the empty serving dishes. After a flutter of activity, two men servants appeared with an amazing iced dessert in the shape of a huge sleeping dragon. Everyone cheered and one of the knights jumped up and sliced it into many pieces with his sword.

Another knight stood, his goblet raised, and called out a toast to Lord Friedrich. The Lord stood and toasted back and everyone cheered again, stabbing pieces of the dessert with their knives as it was passed along. Jason found the dessert solid, like smooth fudge and overly sweet with a strange perfume-like flavour.

When Friedrich stood and raised his hand, everyone became silent. "We are honoured," he began, "to have yet another guest in our midst..." Charlotte nudged Jason who stood uncertainly. "Master Jayson has travelled a long distance to honour us with his presence and his magnificent horn."

A cheer rose and everyone jumped to their feet, raising their goblets. "To Master Jayson," Lord Friedrich shouted. "To Master Jayson," the guests echoed.

Servants appeared carrying lit tapers and moved quickly, first up and down the tables lighting candles, then reaching up to light lanterns hung along the walls. Jason hadn't even noticed it growing darker. He wondered how many hours they had been sitting here.

After the candles had all been lit and everyone had resumed talking, Jason turned to Charlotte. "I told Lord Friedrich we would play," he said. "Should we do it now?" He wasn't used to the spotlight and felt uncomfortable. At least when playing, he could concentrate on the notes.

"Yes," Charlotte replied, "follow me." She pulled her recorder from a pocket in her dress. A servant handed Squid his drum and they hurried over to a small platform close to the head table. Once there, Jason looked at Charlotte, unsure of how to start, worried that perhaps with everything that had happened, he wouldn't remember or, worse, that the horn wouldn't play.

Squid began with a quiet drum roll, grinning and unconcerned. Charlotte nodded to Jason and he put the horn to his lips. "The Bugle Call?" he whispered. She nodded and they began to play. Once he started, the notes were there and his confidence came rushing back. Playing made him feel that they would find Frau Wölfin and the parchment, that the rhythm of the notes would give them the rhythm for discovering how this would happen.

After the last note and drum roll, a cheer rose from the assembled group and the men rhythmically pounded the table with their fists until Lord Friedrich rose, raising his hand for silence. "Master Jayson, we thank all of you."

They bowed and the cheers and banging resumed until Friedrich again silenced them. "And so, good knights and honoured guests, more wine, more food." The crowd resumed their boisterous talk and Lord Friedrich turned to Jason. "You will continue to be our honoured guests," he said, "for as long as you wish to stay."

He waved and a heavy-set woman came forward, smiling and nodding. "It is getting late now. Liesa will show you back to your quarters." The woman giggled like a young girl, motioning them to follow, holding a lantern to show the way.

Jason stayed behind Charlotte and Squid as they walked along the passageway to the same damp, stone staircase. Their shadows magnified in the lantern light and Jason silently wished that their luck in finding the parchment would be as large as these shadows.

Liesa opened the door and hurried in to light lanterns in each room before curtseying. "Sleep well," she said, before closing the door.

Jason fell onto the bed. He was too tired to undress.

He didn't notice Squid scramble onto the bed and lie beside him.

"Can I sleep with Jason? Can I, Lottie?"

"No, Octavius."

What a kid, Jason thought, drifting off. He felt a blanket being pulled over him and vaguely heard Charlotte and Squid leave.

CHAPTER FIFTEEN

T HE NEXT MORNING, WHEN JASON FIRST AWOKE, HE HAD no idea where he was. Almost every part of his body ached and he realized when he rolled against his bugle that he was on a mattress packed with straw. He sat up and stared at light filtering in between two shutters. A window, he thought, and then he remembered. He was in the Veste Coburg. He was safe.

Liesa bustled in, unannounced, to add more logs to the fire. *"Morgen,* Jayson. Did you sleep well?" She opened the shutters partway, tossing the dirty water casually out the window before adding more from a large bronze pitcher.

"I think so," Jason said, sitting on the edge of the bed. "What time is it?" He wondered how he looked but certainly wasn't going to ask.

"Breakfast time," she replied. "Wet as a swamp out there today." She hurried into the other room.

"Is he up yet? Is he?" Jason heard Squid say from the next room.

A minute later, Squid was on the bed with Jason. "I don't have to take a bath every day," Squid announced. He held up one finger close to Jason's face. "Only once a week."

"I missed you," Jason said, tousling Squid's hair.

"Lottie cried," Squid said solemnly. "She said bad people were trying to hurt you."

There was a tap on the door and Liesa rushed past them to open it.

"Thank you, Stefan," she said briskly, taking the silver tray. The pageboy peeked around the corner. "Don't dilly-dally now," Liesa scolded, pushing him out the door. She slipped the tray onto a low table Jason hadn't noticed the day before.

"Charlotte will be joining you." Liesa curtseyed and hurried out.

"Squid?" Charlotte called from the other room. "Come and get your stool."

Squid jumped down and came back dragging a three-legged stool. Charlotte was behind him with two more.

"Master Jason," Charlotte said when she saw him. "You look...more awake."

"Not much privacy here," he said, taking a sweet bun and soft cheese. "Liesa walked in before I was even up." He was ravenous and reached for a second bun before Charlotte sat down.

"How long were you in the dungeon?" Charlotte asked, watching him.

"With nothing to eat?" Jason asked.

Charlotte handed Squid a bun and nodded.

"No supper," Jason said, "but then, in the morning, a boy and his father came in with bread and that water ale."

Squid looked up at him. "Were you scared in the dungeon, Jason?"

"You bet I was." Jason ran his hand gingerly across his neck. "But I'm here now. Right, buddy?" He gave Squid's shoulder a mock punch.

"Right," Squid replied, punching back.

Charlotte stood up and moved the tray back to the window ledge. "Bettina told me what was going to happen, what almost happened." She stared out the window, fidgeting with her hands. "She said there would have been full-out war if…"

"A war because of me?"

"Because of what you stand for."

"What seems weird to me," Jason cut in, "is that everyone knew so much about us, but still we were kidnapped."

"The men who met us were not even Otto's men," Charlotte replied quietly.

"In the dungeon, one of the men told me they might be."

Charlotte shook her head. "They were thugs, kidnappers. They heard about us and thought we were fair game."

"So they intercepted Friedrich's men and stole their tunics before coming to get us. Right?"

Squid stared at Jason. "You are a very smart boy," he said solemnly.

Charlotte turned back to the window, her shoulders shaking and Jason knew, that in spite of this serious talk, she was laughing.

"Whoever was supposed to meet us there in that clearing, didn't," she continued. "And that was lucky for us." She turned back to Jason. "You would have been held for ransom and, Squid and I...we...likely would have been sold." She took a deep breath and sat down again.

"But it had to be Otto's men who nabbed me," Jason said.

"Yes. And not long after, the Veste soldiers found us. Lord Friedrich said it was bad timing all round."

"Wow," Jason said. "This is better than any computer game."

"Easy to say now," Charlotte snapped. "Not so easy when you were in that dungeon." She disappeared into the other room and returned carrying a piece of cloth stretched over a small, round frame.

"Point for you," Jason said, smiling. "What's that?" He watched her begin sewing small, intricate stitches.

"Embroidery. Bettina showed me."

Jason jumped up and, going to the window, pushed the shutters completely open. The rain had stopped and everything sparkled. His room looked out toward rolling hills. Directly below, on a narrow strip of grass, a group of soldiers marched in single file. Just beyond, on the castle wall, Jason watched a sentry, the outline of his helmet reflecting the morning light.

"Bettina says Friedrich is sure Otto will attack the castle," Charlotte said, not looking up. "It's just a matter of time."

"He's certainly arrogant enough to think he will win," Jason said. He watched the soldiers turn in perfect step and march directly back from the direction they had previously been going. "These soldiers are amazing," Jason added. "Otto and his rag-tag bunch don't stand a chance."

"Let's hope not," Charlotte said. "I don't know what would become of us."

"Don't worry, "Jason replied. He stared out across the fields. "We're higher up than I thought, you know."

"If there's an attack," Charlotte replied, quietly, "we have to move to the inner rooms. All these along the outside become defence stations."

Jason ran his hand up and down the sides of the window ledge.

"What are you doing, Jason?" Squid said. "Can I do that too?"

Jason squatted down beside Squid. "Somewhere in this castle," he said, "there's a secret compartment, and inside that compartment, there's a special piece of paper we need to find."

"We could ask the soldiers to look," Squid said. "There's lots and lots of soldiers."

"The soldiers don't have time," Charlotte interjected. "Especially not right now."

The door opened then, and Bettina and the two royal children burst in. Squid jumped from his stool, yelling, "Can't catch me," and raced into the second room, the other two in hot pursuit.

"Bettina," Charlotte said, pulling her forward. "This is Jason."

Again, Bettina stared at Jason, catching her breath before speaking. "*Morgen,* Jayson," Bettina said. "You look...you look so much like my brother Hubie." She turned away, her hand shaking.

"Your parents," Jason began, not knowing what else to say, "told me the same thing." He laughed, feeling embarrassed. "It's weird, you know, having people tell you you look like someone else."

"It is good," Bettina, said turning back. She smiled and quickly wiped her cheek.

"Your family was so kind to us," Jason went on. "We're hoping we can return the favour."

"You think you can stop the war," she said, turning back to stare at him. "That's a big order."

"My horn will help us," Jason said.

Before Bettina had a chance to reply, Squid and the two royal children were circling the three of them, pulling at the girls' skirts and grabbing the bottom of Jason's tunic.

"Lord Friedrich says I'm to show you through the Veste," Bettina shouted over the din.

"Octavius?" Charlotte caught his arm.

The royal charges promptly hid behind Bettina's long skirt. "Friede, Hans," Bettina said, pulling them forward. "This is Jayson." The children looked wide-eyed and ducked behind Bettina again.

Once out in the hall, Bettina led the way, following along the shadowy candlelit passageway. They passed under an archway and down three wide stone steps to a large central landing. "Lord Friedrich's and Lady Katherin's chambers are here," she said, pointing to the opposite side of the landing. "And I am very lucky to have a small room adjoining, with the children. Most of the other servants sleep in the Great Hall."

Friede, Hans, and Squid tore down the stone staircase leading to the main floor. "What's above this floor?" Jason asked. He was sure he remembered three sets of windows, the topmost ones small and further apart.

"That's where grain and some of the vegetables are kept,"

Bettina said. "We can't go up there."

Once downstairs, they peeked into the big kitchen where pots were steaming on square stoves that looked like fireplaces with flat rocks on their tops. Chickens clucked somewhere out of sight and several women chopped vegetables on a large wooden tabletop.

"Another banquet today?" Jason asked.

"The main meal of the day is usually before noon," Charlotte said. "Yesterday was an exception."

Because of me, Jason thought, following behind the others. He wasn't used to being "the headliner," as his mom would have called it. At home, in some concerts, she was the headliner, and his dad was right after a book was published. It would be okay, he guessed, once he got used to it. He wondered, suddenly, if his dad had missed him and how long they had actually been here.

They were outside now and Bettina was explaining that the building directly to their right was the soldiers' and knights' barracks and, behind it was the stables. The tower, ahead, was the highest lookout, with the dungeon beneath.

"Do the prisoners eat regularly?" Jason asked.

Bettina looked puzzled and then amused. "There are no prisoners right now," she said. "Lord Friedrich granted them all freedom when he came to power. But if there were any, they would, of course, get pauper's bread."

"So who gets it then?" he asked, thinking of yesterday's banquet and the soggy bread.

"Lord Friedrich sends it to the poor outside town," she added. "Our Lord is most liberal and kind."

Jason nodded. Liberal and kind. Funny how words could mean such different things to different people. He stared at the tower. At home...and then he thought, there's no use comparing this place with "at home." I'm here in medieval Germany and I might as well make the best of it. It's not like we're going to be here forever. No way.

The others had disappeared around the far side of the tower and he ran to catch up.

"These are the gardens," Bettina was saying, leading them into a grassy area, "and it's lovely here, especially now in the summer." Squid and Hans ran ahead with Friede in hot pursuit. The flowerbeds, each one raised and neatly bordered with large square-cut stones, were in rows with cobblestone pathways between. Nearby on a raised grassy area, two knights sat playing a game that looked, to Jason, like chess.

"The younger one's Sir Lothar," Bettina whispered, suppressing a giggle. "He's out here almost every day trying to learn, but he has no patience for it."

"Your move," the older man said, as they passed by.

"You think you've got my bishop, don't you?" Lothar replied. His voice was high-pitched and nasal sounding. He looked up and eyed the children, staring at Jason for an extra moment. Something about his voice made Jason shiver.

When they were out of earshot, Bettina added, "He has a terrible temper, that Lothar. Last week he almost broke the board. He smashed it with his helmet."

"Are they really playing chess?" Jason asked. It seemed impossible.

"Yes," Bettina replied, giving him a look. "It's played at most castles."

When they came to a bench, Bettina and Charlotte sat down, pulling from their pockets the embroidery Jason had asked Charlotte about earlier. Squid and the two wild charges raced back and forth. Hans had a small soft-looking leather ball and the children were taking turns rolling it up and down various pathways.

"What's that ball made of?" Jason asked.

"Leather," Bettina said, not looking up. "And stuffed with bran."

"We've watched the lords and ladies," Charlotte added, "playing a sort of tennis game with it."

"Tenn-iss?" Bettina repeated awkwardly.

"It's a game people play," Jason said quickly.

"In our faraway country," Charlotte added.

Hans raced past, almost knocking Bettina's embroidery from her hand. *"Halt,"* she said sternly and then, *"Bitte,"* quite sweetly when he slowed to a walk.

"What's over there?" Jason asked, deliberately changing the subject. He pointed to what looked like a second garden, hidden by a stone wall. Over its top, ladies' pointed hats bobbed in and out of sight. Someone was plucking a stringed instrument and quietly singing. Jason listened, but he couldn't catch the words. The melody, though, was haunting, sad somehow.

"The knights' and ladies' courting garden," Bettina said, blushing and turning away.

Jason stared at her. Sometimes Bettina acted like an adult.

A courting garden, as if that explained it.

Squid roared up, his tunic wet, a trail of watery footprints behind him. "I found all these waterspouts," he said excitedly, waving his arms in a circle. "Coming out of a big dish sticking up out of a pond." Come and see, Jason. Come on." He grabbed Jason's hand and pulled.

"Oh dear," Bettina said, putting her embroidery down. "He's gone into the courting garden."

"They chased me out," Squid continued, still pulling at Jason. "Come on, Jason. They won't chase you."

"Octavius," Charlotte said. "Look at you. You're soaking wet. Again." She stuffed her embroidery into her pocket.

"It's time to go back anyway," Bettina said. "We'll be eating soon."

On the way back, Jason took a good look at the stone walls and towers surrounding them. Each of the towers along the wall had a door and several small slit-like windows. "Are those tower doors kept locked?" he asked casually, as they entered the main courtyard.

"I don't think so," Bettina replied. "Right now they're just lookout stations. But..." She stopped and caught her breath. "If there was an attack, they'd be swarming with soldiers." She turned abruptly and, taking each of the children's hands, marched them toward the main entrance.

Squid ran after them. "Octavius," Charlotte called. "Go and get your wet things off. I'll be right there." Squid raced through the big doors with Bettina and the children.

"She doesn't like to talk about attacks," Charlotte said quietly. "There've been a couple of minor skirmishes in front of the castle and it terrifies her. She says it's because of Hubie. She feels Otto was responsible and now he's going to attack the castle."

"Do you think we could ask her about Frau Wölfin?" Jason asked. "That is, if I don't find the parchment myself."

"We could ask her," Charlotte said quietly, "but not when the children are around. They repeat everything they hear to their parents."

"So what difference would it make? Lord Friedrich must know about Frau Wölfin."

"He does, but probably wouldn't want us to go into the forest," she explained.

"Oh good," Jason said. "So if I can't find the parchment, what are we going to do?"

"I don't know."

A group of knights passed them as they approached the Great Hall. Lothar was one of them. He stared intensely at Jason and, again, Jason felt uncomfortable.

"Lothar is one of Friedrich's most trusted knights," Charlotte said. "During a battle, he becomes second-in-command." She walked ahead to the door.

Jason thought of mentioning his reaction to Lothar, then didn't. So the man wasn't good at chess and stared at him. That shouldn't make him suspect. And of what? Jason didn't know, only that the knight made him feel uncomfortable somehow.

"Hey, daydreamer," Charlotte called, "you don't want to miss dinner." Jason hurried after her.

CHAPTER SIXTEEN

AFTER THE BIG MEAL, WHICH TURNED OUT TO BE ALMOST as elaborate as the day before, everyone seemed to take a nap. Bettina and the royal charges disappeared and Charlotte whispered to Jason that she and Squid were going back to their chambers for a quiet time.

"Maybe I'll go for another walk," Jason said, when Squid was out of earshot. "Do a bit of investigating."

"I want to come with you," Charlotte said. "I'm tired of being stuck in there with nothing interesting to do."

"What about Squid?"

"I'll see if Bettina will take him. I think they're going to a puppet show later."

Jason said nothing. How could they sneak around with Charlotte in that long dress? She wouldn't be able to run and what if someone saw her?

"You don't think I should come?"

"I don't know. What about your dress? How would you...?"

"I'll wear your old tunic," Charlotte said, "and a hat. If

anyone sees us, say I'm your page."

"Where will you meet me?" Jason asked. She was determined. He could see that.

"By the tunnel entrance," she said. "I won't take long." He watched her run for the great hall, holding her skirts up so she wouldn't trip.

Jason wandered across the main courtyard, slipping behind the soldiers' quarters to have a look in the stable. He found it empty and filthy with horse dung. He hurried back outside and, seeing no one around, made his way toward the tunnel entrance leading down to the outside doors. As he hurried along the wall enclosing the entrance, he heard footsteps approaching. He turned and deliberately sauntered over to the gardens, hoping whoever it was wouldn't call out, or catch up to him and start asking questions. The footsteps subsided as he entered the first garden and he turned to stand close enough to the hedge opening so he could still see the tunnel entranceway. No one was in sight.

Time dragged, and he thought again about home and how long they had been away. Maybe no time at all. Time travel was like that in books. Right, he thought. In books. This would make a good story, except no one would believe it.

He heard footsteps again and looked up to see a taller-than-average page in a floppy hat running toward the tunnel. He stepped out from the hedge and waved. Charlotte slowed down and they met alongside the closest tunnel wall.

"Wait till I catch my breath," she whispered, panting. "How do I look?"

"Okay," Jason replied. "Cool hat."

"Bettina found it."

"She knows, then?"

"I had to tell her," Charlotte said, "so she could take Squid."

"What did you tell him?"

"That you and I were going for a chess lesson."

Voices in the tunnel entrance silenced both of them. They listened, but couldn't make out all the words.

Jason thought he heard Lothar, he was sure it was the knight, telling someone that the Bürgermeister would take the castle. He looked at Charlotte. She was frowning and motioning them away. They tiptoed past the entranceway and stopped.

"As long as no one comes in sight," Jason whispered, "we'll make a run for it." He motioned toward the wall. "Over there, to that tower." He scanned the open area around the entrance and, when he was convinced the men weren't appearing, motioned Charlotte to follow. He was sure Lothar had said the Bürgermeister would take the castle. As if Lothar were in agreement. As if it were being planned.

Luckily, the door to this tower had not been properly closed. "Perfect," Jason whispered and, checking to make sure no one was in sight, pushed the door open just enough for the two of them to slip through. "Close call," he said, leaning against the door to close it. "Did you hear what they were saying?"

"Something about the Bürgermeister attacking the castle?"

"Yes, and the person talking was Lothar."

"Are you sure?"

"How could you miss him?" Jason said. He held his nose and continued, "The Bürgermeister will take the castle."

Charlotte giggled. "He didn't sound that bad."

"Almost, and I'm sure it was Lothar."

"But you don't know what he said before that, or what the other person might have said."

"Are you defending him?" Jason asked.

"Bettina said he was Friedrich's second-in-command," Charlotte went on.

"Second-in-command and first to betray," Jason added.

"I think you're jumping to conclusions," Charlotte said, "and, wow, is that steep, or what?" She pointed to the stone steps winding upward.

The tower interior was damp and cold in spite of the warm day. The steps wound up and out of sight, thin wall slits letting in small flickers of light, enough to see, but not well.

"I'll go first," Jason said. The steps were too narrow for his feet and he had to step up sideways, one foot crossing over the next. Spiders scuttled back and forth above him and he was sure he heard scratching on the wall somewhere. Charlotte was right behind, and when he began counting the steps as he went to keep himself going, she joined in.

They paused at thirty-five and looked up. More light. At the next turn of the staircase, brightness momentarily blinded both of them. Jason squinted and saw sunlight flooding down from an arched opening at the top. "Forty-nine," he said aloud, as his foot touched the last step.

"Okay," Charlotte whispered. "Now we're up here, where do we look?"

"If we can, we should go all the way around," Jason whispered back, "and check every place we can find."

From where they stood, Jason again counted six more towers around the walkway, the largest one at the front of the castle. "Look," he said. "See that smaller tower up ahead? I think it's about halfway between this big one and the next."

Charlotte took a deep breath. "Bettina called them turrets. I don't what they're like."

"Let's go," Jason said, motioning her to follow. He had no idea what he would do or say if they met someone. The walkway was wide enough for three men to walk abreast. Good for moving troops in a hurry, Jason supposed.

Barricade walls on both sides minimized their view. The outside wall was higher, over a metre high, protection, Jason assumed, for soldiers and knights in time of attack.

"Look," Jason whispered, pointing back toward the Great Hall, "can you find our window?"

"Second storey," Charlotte replied, counting. "It should be about there." She pointed in its general direction.

"I hope no one's watching," he added.

"I doubt it," Charlotte replied. "We can barely see the windows, so anyone up there likely wouldn't see us."

The turret was further away than it looked, and as they hurried along, Jason noticed floor slits at regular intervals, he assumed to let rain water escape. Whatever this turret was, it might be somewhere a parchment could be hidden.

The turret jutted out from the wall with a place inside

large enough for a man to crouch. A large slit at floor level would give a bowman advantage over anyone directly below. Jason peered inside, looking for a hiding place, but the wall was sealed and even.

"Out here," Charlotte whispered. "There's an opening underneath."

They both knelt down and Jason reached inside. Nothing. He lay on his stomach and tried again, reaching as far in as he possibly could. His outstretched fingers pulled out a few twigs and grass. "Part of a bird's nest," he said, throwing the twigs down. "Let's try the next one,"

The sun was well past its noonday position by now, its rays skimming over the walls, the walkway in total shadow. Curious as to where he was, Jason balanced on the edge of the wall to see over.

"What are you doing?" Charlotte asked. "Let's go." Jason heard her take off without him.

Pasture land and rolling hills spread in all directions, with many of the hilltops covered by trees. We were on one of those hills, Jason thought, grateful to be safely inside the castle. Looking directly down, he saw the path leading around to the castle entrance and he imagined the soldiers in their "V" formation, lined up at attention, waiting for some important event.

Without thinking, he grasped his horn and, leaning over the top of the wall, played for them. The horn shone in the late afternoon sun – the sound echoed out over the hills. Even while he was playing, he could hear them cheering, shouting "Jayson, Jayson..."

The arrow hit his bugle with such force that Jason was

knocked to the stone floor. A sharp pain reverberated right up to his elbow. He ran his hand over it, sure his arm had been hit, but it hadn't. He lay flat on the ground, his heart pounding, as several more arrows whizzed over him and down into the courtyard. When he realized the horn was gone, he panicked and jumped to his feet. He had dropped it.

A shout rang out inside the courtyard and Jason heard soldiers' boots clambering up the tower steps. Where was Charlotte? And what had he done? What *had* he done?

Jason turned full circle, looking for the horn once more. The end of it had caught the opening's edge. Jason grabbed it and ducked inside the turret just as the first soldier burst onto the walkway. But where was Charlotte? If she had made it to the next tower, would more soldiers find her on their way up? He scrunched down and waited, his heart pounding.

Soldiers sprinted past him, spanning out along the wall, bows aimed to the outside. They fired sequentially, in perfect rhythm, down the line. A cry rang out and they paused.

"We got him," one of them shouted. Jason's stomach heaved, partly from tension and partly from fear. He had caused this. So far, no one had noticed he was there. He thought of sneaking along back to the staircase, but if any of them heard the slightest sound, they would swing around and fire. At him.

Looking up, he watched the soldier closest to him reload his bow, the man's chain mail clanking, glistening in the late afternoon sun. He turned slightly and Jason saw an elaborate metal cross hanging on a chain from his neck. Even from this distance, Jason sensed his concentration. He was a tiger ready to spring.

The minutes dragged on and the soldiers remained in position, the only sound their quick breathing and the pounding of Jason's heart. His knees ached and his throat felt dry.

"End of watch," one of the soldiers shouted. They all relaxed, then, pulling their bows back to their sides, jostling each other and laughing as they marched past the turret and disappeared down the tower stairs. Jason climbed out and rubbed his aching knees. Had anyone seen him? If so, Friedrich would be told, for sure. Then what? How would he explain what he did? He looked the other way, hoping Charlotte would appear, but she didn't.

Jason tied the horn back in place. "Try not to be quite so impulsive next time." He could hear his mom saying it. Not likely Friedrich would be so forgiving. To begin with, a lot more was at stake. His life, for starters. Maybe Charlotte's too. He couldn't stop shaking as he retraced his steps down the stairs. He was sure someone would be there, waiting for him.

Jason peered out through the tower door, looking for Charlotte somewhere close by. The shadows were longer now and early evening dampness filled the air. He took a deep breath and raced past the tunnel entranceway, pausing beside the stable to look for Charlotte again. Where was she? When he reached the main courtyard, the soldiers were already there, some with their chain mail off, sweat visible on their tunics. They were passing around a flask and joking with one another. The soldier wearing the cross glanced at Jason but said nothing.

Jason slipped past them and raced through the deserted Great Hall to the stairway up to his quarters. The door was partly ajar.

"Lord Friedrich is sending a page for you," Charlotte said, as he entered. She had pulled her dress on over the tunic, her braid half fallen out, and she was sitting on her stool, close to the window, holding her embroidery, her hand shaking.

"Where did you disappear to?" he snapped. "I was so worried."

Charlotte stared at him. "You were worried? I thought you were right behind me. I stopped at the next tower and looked back to see you leaning out over the wall. And then you started playing the horn. How could you?"

"It was dumb, really dumb," Jason began. "I..."

"When the arrows started flying, I ran into the tower and reached the bottom in time to see soldiers disappearing up the other stairs." Charlotte jabbed the needle into her embroidery. "And there I was, stuck at the bottom, having no idea what had happened to you, whether you'd been hit or what. So I hightailed it back here..." She stopped and her voice broke, "hoping you were okay."

"Sorry," Jason said quietly. "I don't even know why I did it."

"You could have been killed."

"I almost lost the horn," Jason said, sitting heavily on the bed. He slumped over, his head in his hands.

This wasn't the same as getting caught hanging out the school window or discovering he could start a little fire with a magnifying glass, in the house. Why was he so impulsive?

A timid knock on the door brought him to his feet. "Master Jayson?" It was young Stefan. Jason followed him along the stone hall to the central landing and waited while the page knocked on the door opposite. The boy kept his head down and gave no indication of knowing why Jason was being summoned.

"Enter," a voice inside called. Stefan nodded to Jason and hurried off.

Jason closed the door behind him. Bowing low, he waited, uncertain what to do next. Large tapestries covered the walls and the bed's canopy was fringed with gold tassels. On a table near one of the two windows, Jason saw two hunting knives and a highly polished helmet. Lord Friedrich sat behind a second table, writing with a quill pen. He waved to an empty chair nearby. "Sit down, Master Jayson," he said, continuing his work. "Lady Katherin is at chapel, and I thought it a good time for us to talk."

Maybe he doesn't know, Jason thought. Maybe...

"The towers and the castle wall are available to you," he said, after a few moments silence, "but I think it best in future that you have an escort."

"It was a dumb thing to do," Jason blurted out. "I don't know why..."

"It is of no matter," Friedrich said, looking up. "In future, Sir Lothar will go with you. He has also offered to give you riding lessons."

Jason didn't know what to say. That Lothar gave him the creeps? That he was untrustworthy? "Thank you," he replied, hoping it didn't sound insincere. It would be great to learn to ride, as long as he ignored who would be his teacher. He thought of telling Friedrich, but what? He had overheard a conversation? It was too vague. He thought Lothar to be a hothead? Friedrich likely knew this.

"Lothar says he will have time for you tomorrow, most likely late afternoon."

"Thanks."

"I assume you have heard," Friedrich went on, "that my uncle plans to attack the castle?"

"Yes...yes, I..."

"I wanted to assure you that you and your friends are in no danger." Friedrich picked up a parchment. "This," he said, waving it back and forth, "is a letter demanding I abdicate my position as Lord of the castle." He stood up, slamming the paper onto the table. "He has the audacity to claim I am not the rightful heir."

"But there's a parchment proving you are," Jason blurted out.

"So I've been told from the time I was a child, by every nanny, every groom, even by Lothar." Friedrich walked to the window. "This is my home. I don't intend to give it up."

Someone knocked vigorously on the door. "My Lord? Are you there, my Lord?"

Friedrich hurried to the door and stepped outside. Jason heard a rapid-fire conversation, questions and answers, back and forth. It sounded important.

"You will have to excuse me," Friedrich said, reentering quickly. "I must cut our conversation short. There has been trouble in town."

"That's okay," Jason replied, bowing and hurrying to the door. "Thanks again, sir." He shut the door behind him and let out an audible sigh. Lucky or what, he thought, as he strode down the hall toward his quarters. No reprimand, no lecture, and riding lessons to boot. That his instructor would be Lothar was another matter. Maybe he would be called away with Friedrich and Jason would get someone else. He could only hope.

"You were lucky," Charlotte said when Jason finished telling her. "And he didn't ask about me?"

"He thought I was alone."

"Lucky for me, too, I guess," Charlotte said, smiling a little. She paused. "I'd love to take riding lessons."

"I could ask, but I think it would be sidesaddle," Jason said.

Charlotte made a face. "Don't bother then."

"I wanted to say something about Lothar," Jason went on, "but I just couldn't."

"Good thing," Charlotte said. "I think it's your imagination again."

"But I don't trust him, especially after hearing that conversation."

"Part of a conversation," Charlotte said, with a sigh. "We only heard part of it."

Jason stood up and went over to the fire. The embers were burning low and he threw another log on. Lothar had shifty eyes and Jason was rarely wrong about people.

"Have you asked Bettina about the parchment?" he asked, changing the subject.

"She says it's one of those stories everyone knows."

"And Frau Wölfin?"

"She has heard of her," Charlotte said. "She knew the old woman lived in *dem mysteriösen Forst.* She's considered a witch by many. That's why she hides out there. She'd be burned at the stake if they caught her." Charlotte shivered.

"No wonder she keeps a pack of wolves," Jason said. "I don't blame her." He jumped on the bed and sat cross-legged.

"Bettina says they're most likely stray dogs." Charlotte put the embroidery down and looked directly at Jason.

"She does know someone who occasionally meets Frau Wölfin."

"Someone we could talk to?"

"The apothecaries – Gunthar and his wife, Hildred. They have a shop right on the square in town."

"Oh good," Jason said, pounding his fist on the bed. "As if I want to go back there."

"There's a tunnel."

"A tunnel? From here down to the town?"

"Bettina says it comes out inside their shop," Charlotte continued. "She says she's been down it a number of times."

"Did she say why?"

"She was a bit secretive about it."

"Look," Squid said, bursting into the room, "a potato man." He held up a crudely made puppet, it's wrinkled potato head carved with a face. "The funny man gave it to me," Squid said, dancing his hand back and forth. "See my potato man. See my potato man."

"Hey, buddy," Jason said, jumping off the bed to squat beside Squid, "let's have a look."

Bettina appeared, looking somewhat frazzled, the two

royal brats also dancing potato puppets back and forth. "Be careful," Bettina said sternly to her charges. "If you're too rough with them, they will break." As soon as she noticed Jason, she caught her breath and whispered, "Hubie," again.

"How about a puppet play in the other room?" Charlotte suggested, jumping up to lead Squid in the right direction.

Jason stood and walked back toward the hearth. This Hubie thing was beginning to get to him.

"A puppet play," Squid shouted, dashing off. "I'll be the knight. Crash. Crash."

The other two disappeared after him.

"I know you are Jayson," Bettina said, blushing slightly. "I must keep reminding myself." She sat down, smoothing out her apron.

"It's okay," Jason said, turning toward her. "A bit weird, but okay. Charlotte said maybe I should cut my hair..."

"Oh, no," Bettina said, jumping up. "Don't do that. I want you to look like my brother. You could be...my adopted brother." She sat down, again, looking more embarrassed.

"Great," Jason said, not knowing what else to say. "That would be great."

"Charlotte says you were asking about Frau Wölfin," Bettina continued quickly. "That you wanted to meet her."

"Yes...yes, we do. The sooner the better." Jason knew she had deliberately change the subject, and he was relieved."

"It could be dangerous," she said.

"We don't care," Jason said. He perched on the edge of the bed, leaning forward sightly. "It's so important that we meet her."

"This is why you came here, then?" Bettina said, a certain awe in her voice.

"Yes, yes," Jason replied, jumping up. "Our purpose. Right, Charlotte?"

"I'd go along with that," Charlotte agreed.

"It would have to be done at night," Bettina said. "Lord Friedrich must not know."

"His head broke off," Hans wailed, running to Bettina, holding a potato part in each hand.

"We'll ask cook for another potato," Bettina said, getting up. Friede and Squid ran in, laughing and butting each other with their puppets.

"Yours will break too," Charlotte warned Squid. "Take it easy, for heaven's sake."

"We'll talk later," Bettina said, hurrying her charges out the door.

"Perfect," Jason said, doing a two thumbs up after she left, "I can't wait."

'We'll have to take Squid," Charlotte said, looking worried. "I couldn't leave him."

"Of course we'll take him," Jason said. "He's smart and he's...funny. We'll need that."

"Are you scared?" Charlotte asked, almost in a whisper.

"Maybe a little," Jason said, "but I just want to get going. Do something besides sit around here."

CHAPTER SEVENTEEN

FORTUNATELY, SQUID FELL ASLEEP RIGHT AFTER THEIR supper of buns and cheese brought on a tray by Liesa. Charlotte and Jason sat in Jason's room quietly working out a strategy for finding Frau Wölfin. If Bettina took them through the tunnel to the apothecary's, they still had to get to *dem mysteriösen Forst.* If these people could escort them, they still had to find their way to Frau Wölfin's house and get past the wolves. If Frau Wölfin knew where the parchment was, and was willing to tell them, they would still have to make their way back to the castle.

"A lot of 'ifs,'" Charlotte said.

"We'll manage," Jason replied. "Somehow the bugle will help."

"It didn't help you much on the turret," Charlotte said.

"I didn't get hit," Jason replied. "Just the bugle."

Charlotte said nothing for a few moments and then looked at Jason strangely. "Remember when Gran told us your uncle said the 'miracle' was that the *Wunderhorn* saved him from shrapnel?" she asked. "Do you think the horn saved you from that arrow?"

"It could have been luck, I guess," Jason replied. "But then again..."

A gentle knock on the door interrupted them. Jason jumped up to answer. They certainly weren't expecting anyone now. It was nearly bedtime. "Who is it?" he asked quietly.

"Bettina."

Jason opened the door and she hurried in, her walking cloak swishing from side to side. She carried a candle burning inside a hooded holder. "Lord Friedrich has left the castle and won't be back until tomorrow," she said. "Apparently he is seeing about reinforcement troops from another castle. There are reports that Otto is hiring more mercenaries." She hesitated. "I...can take you now."

"To the apothecary in Coburg?" Jason asked. This was sooner than expected.

"It's all arranged," Bettina said, looking flushed. "I...I hope that's all right." She put the holder on the table and adjusted ties on a small bundle tied in a blue silk cloth.

"Sure," Charlotte said, jumping up. "It's not like we have to pack."

Bettina looked a little puzzled. "I will take you part way through the tunnel. Hindel will meet us and take you the rest of the way."

"Hindel?" Jason asked, vaguely remembering the name. "The boy who brought food in the prison?"

Bettina nodded. "Oh, yes," she said enthusiastically. "He is most kind."

"We're sneaking off, then, without Friedrich knowing?" Charlotte asked, looking at Bettina.

"Lothar will be too busy to notice," Bettina replied, looking pleased with herself. She nervously adjusted the hood of her cloak. "Octavius will stay with Hans and Friede?" she asked.

"No," Jason replied firmly. "He'll come with us."

"He'd be frantic," Charlotte said, getting her cloak and recorder. "He goes everywhere with us." She ran into the other room and Jason heard her waking Squid and talking quietly to him.

A sleepy Squid appeared, the drum banging against his side. "He insisted on bringing it," Charlotte explained.

"In case we have to play," Squid said, rubbing his eyes.

"We'll have to be quiet," Bettina said, looking at Squid. "No talking and no whispering."

Squid solemnly put his finger against his lips and nodded.

"Good boy," Charlotte said, giving his shoulder a squeeze.

"What about a piggyback?" Jason suggested, squatting down. Squid climbed onto his back with no further prompting.

"Everyone ready?" Bettina asked. "We must go quickly."

They tiptoed along the hall, back the way they had come when they first arrived. At the bottom of the stairs, Bettina stopped and pulled open a narrow door into what looked like a storage closet. Once inside, she held up the candle, revealing buckets and mops and several wooden trunks. She pointed to a large trunk in the corner. "We have to move this," she whispered, "but it's not heavy."

Jason grabbed the end of the trunk and it slid with no

resistance, almost as if it was equipped underneath with rollers. A rope fastened to its handle lay along the floor, disappearing into the wall. The trunk had to be a camouflage.

Bettina squatted down and pushed against the wall section previously covered by the trunk. It swung in, revealing a narrow set of stairs, so steep that even as she shone the candle over them, they appeared to drop into darkness.

"I'll go first," Bettina whispered, "then you, Charlotte, and Squid. Jason, after you clear the door, push it back into place and pull on the rope knot. It pulls the trunk back." She bent down to show him where the knot was located, just inside the bottom of the door opening. "Ready?" she asked, holding up the light.

By the time Jason followed, the light was all but gone. He pushed the small door shut and felt for the knot. Bettina was familiar with this secret staircase, he was sure. The passageway must have been built for dwarves, he thought. After twice bumping his head on the low ceiling, Jason crept more gingerly, one foot at a time, bent over like a gorilla. He heard the others ahead, their breathing, the shuffle of their feet on the rough-hewn boards.

"Is everyone all right?" Bettina whispered once they were at the bottom.

"Where's Jason?" Squid whispered too loudly.

"Right here, buddy," Jason whispered back. "Behind you."

"Shh," Charlotte warned.

Bettina moved to a door directly in front of them. She opened it a crack and stood, listening. "It's safe," she said, beckoning them to follow. They hurried down this hallway, a faint light flickering ahead through an arched doorway. Bettina moved cautiously toward this light, stopping often to listen. At the doorway, they stood facing rows and rows of shelves filled with wooden barrels.

"The wine cellar," Bettina whispered. "The tunnel is on the other side."

They heard a shout, then a door slam, then silence.

"Who was that?" Jason whispered.

"Guards going off shift," Bettina replied. "Friedrich has the tunnel under guard."

"He uses it?" Charlotte asked.

"He sends Stefan to the apothecary for supplies once a month," Bettina replied. "Shh." She waited a few moments, then nodded, "all clear."

Jason took Squid's hand and they followed Bettina past rows of wine kegs, the barrels anchored with blocks of rough wood between. Jason counted four sets of shelves, although the top shelf had only the occasional barrel. He wondered how they were lifted up there? Did they have a pulley of some kind or just big muscle men?

Jason tried to see what was ahead. Bettina seemed familiar with the guards' routine, confident that the coast was clear. What would they would do if someone appeared unexpectedly? A servant sent to fill wineskins or, worse, one of the knights? He'd probably whip his bow into place and shoot.

"Are there dragons in the tunnel?" Squid asked, holding more tightly to Jason's hand.

"No dragons," Jason assured him. He squeezed the child's hand reassuringly, even though his own apprehension increased with every step. He was purposely going to Coburg again. The apothecary shop was in the town square, probably not far from the town hall and Bürgermeister Otto. It was owned by Gunthar and Hildred, whose son was Hindel. It appeared that Bettina knew Hindel. Puzzle pieces, but not enough to make sense of it all.

The wine cellar seemed deserted, the huge looming shapes of the wine kegs appearing and disappearing in their small ring of light. Squid moved closer and closer to Jason until he was almost glued to his side, the child's small sweaty hand gripping Jason's. No one spoke and their footsteps echoed momentarily behind them to be absorbed into the dark wood.

Bettina stopped suddenly in front of a wine keg in the wall. She put her hand on it and whispered, "This is how we get through."

Squid tugged at Jason's tunic. "Why are we stopping here, Jason? Where's the tunnel?"

"Shh," Jason said, "watch Bettina."

She twisted the keg's spout and the end of the barrel swung open, revealing a dark hole. Damp-smelling air rushed at them. The tunnel was on the other side.

"Cool," Jason whispered. He picked Squid up, putting his finger to his lips so the child wouldn't ask more questions.

"I'll go first," Bettina said, handing the candle holder to Charlotte. "After I'm through, pass me the light."

"I'll go next," Charlotte said quietly, "and then, Jason, you help Squid."

"There's a handle, here, on the inside," Bettina said to Jason. "To close it."

"No problem," Jason replied. He wondered how she managed by herself, holding the light and crawling through.

"It's not hard," Bettina said. "Watch." She hoisted herself up onto the shelf with the barrel and then, grasping the shelf above it, planted her feet inside the barrel, so she could slide along through on her back. They heard a soft thud as her feet landed on the ground inside. "The light," she whispered. Her voice echoed into the barrel.

Charlotte clambered up and was easily through, but Squid clung to Jason, his hands sweaty on the back of Jason's neck. "Too dark," he said, pressing his face into Jason's shoulder. "Not going. Too dark."

"Hold the light up," Jason said, "so Squid can see."

"Squid?" Charlotte whispered loudly. "It's okay, Lottie's right here. Put the drum through first."

Squid peered inside and caught his breath. "Lottie?" he said. "It's hard for me."

Jason helped Squid pull the drum rope over his head and held the child as he pushed the drum into the barrel.

"Got it," Bettina whispered.

"Jason will help you," Charlotte encouraged. "Come on, Squid, you can do it."

Squid nodded and Jason pushed his feet into the barrel. "Wriggle like a snake," Jason said. "Charlotte will grab your feet."

Someone shouted, then, on the far side of the cellar. Another voice answered. The guards were back.

"Hurry," Jason said, pushing Squid the rest of the way through. "Someone's coming."

He jumped up, grabbing the beam, swinging his feet into

the barrel, kicking it on both sides. The sound echoed down the rows of barrels. Another shout. Jason pulled the keg shut just as approaching lantern light scanned back and forth. He lay inside the dark barrel, afraid to move, heart pounding. Footsteps approached, pausing nearby to scan the light up and down.

"All clear," a voice shouted. "Try the next row." Jason waited until he could no longer hear the clump, clump of boots, then slid the rest of the way through.

The three of them stood huddled together in the tunnel's darkness, Charlotte with Squid wrapped inside her cloak. Bettina held up the light. "Close call," she said, looking relieved. "It's faster when I'm by myself."

Charlotte nodded, unwrapping Squid.

"Follow me," Bettina whispered. She waved them to follow and set off at a steady clip. Charlotte stepped in next with Squid in front of Jason.

We're in a secret tunnel, Jason thought, a tunnel from the castle all the way into Coburg. Its narrowness forced them to walk single file, the stone walls on either side damp and, in places, glistening wet.

"Does Bürgermeister Otto know about this tunnel?" Jason asked, a few minutes later.

Bettina stopped. "Otto thinks it's still blocked," she whispered. "One of the first things Lord Friedrich did when he came to power was open the tunnel again. It had been blocked for a very long time and took a whole season to repair." She beckoned them to follow and hurried ahead into the darkness.

"Lucky for us," Jason said, ruffling the back of Squid's hair.

"We going to be there soon?" Squid asked.

"It won't take long," Jason assured him.

Bettina marched confidently along, humming a tune somehow familiar to Jason. The courting garden. Courting. An old fashioned word for dating, well sort of dating. Bettina and Hindel, he thought. That explained everything. She meets him here in this tunnel. That's how she knows so much about the apothecary and his wife. They're his parents.

They walked upright most of the time but were occasionally forced to duck down, especially in sections where the rough log roof sagged or branches not cut closely enough jutted dangerously overhead. The tunnel appeared safe although the uneven dirt floor was ridged in places where the earth had sifted down between logs overhead.

Who had built this tunnel? Jason wondered. How long had it taken to excavate and bring in all these stones and logs? What if it went back to Roman times? This wasn't the time to ask. Would Bettina even know about Roman times? Not likely, unless someone at the castle talked about it. She had never been to school and most likely couldn't read. Jason concentrated on the rhythm of their footsteps, the sound of their breathing, saving up questions for later.

A faint light appeared ahead of them. *"Wer da?"* a male voice called. "Who goes there?"

"Hindel?" Bettina called out, sounding a little apprehensive.

Let's hope so, Jason thought. What they would do if it were someone else?

CHAPTER EIGHTEEN

"Ja, Hindel," the voice called back, confidently.

"Wait here," Bettina said, excitedly. She handed Charlotte her lantern and ran ahead.

They waited, the darkness close around them.

"Why are we stopping?" Squid asked, tugging on Charlotte's cloak.

"Bettina wants to talk to Hindel," Charlotte replied. "She won't be long."

"Romeo and Juliette is more like it," Jason said. He knew he sounded a little sarcastic. They didn't have time for this. They needed to keep going.

"Maybe," Charlotte said defensively. "But if they hadn't been meeting here, we wouldn't have this chance."

"Who's Romeo?" Squid asked.

Bettina and Hindel hurried toward them. They were holding hands. Hindel held up a large lantern. "Good to see you, Jason," he said, grinning. "My Bettina tells me you have been well looked after in the castle."

Bettina's blush was visible even by lantern light. "This is Charlotte," she said, "and her little brother, Octavius."

"We need to hurry," Hindel said. "The tunnel is unstable tonight." He gave Bettina a quick kiss on the cheek and motioned Jason and the others to follow.

Bettina turned to retrace her steps. "Godspeed," she called, her voice echoing into the darkness.

They walked steadily downhill now, and the tunnel turned slightly to the left as the incline increased. It grew damper and was definitely less secure than it had been earlier. More questions pummelled Jason. What was making the tunnel unstable? How long would the problem last? What would they do if it caved in in front of them?

A series of rumblings from somewhere overhead sent fine showers of dirt onto their heads and shoulders. The rumblings increased and, just ahead of them, a loud crack and groaning ended with one of the ceiling logs falling part way into the tunnel.

Hindel stopped and held up his lantern. *"Nicht gut,"* he whispered. "Not good."

They ducked under the fallen log and hurried on. The rumblings started again and Hindel paused, his face white in the lantern glow. "We'll have to run for it," he said tensely. "What about the child?" He pointed to Squid.

"I'm a fast runner," Squid said. "Watch me." He took off, Hindel after him with the lantern held high, Charlotte and Jason right behind.

It was difficult running in soft shoes, every lump and ridge cutting into Jason's feet. Charlotte kept the pace in spite of having to hold up her cloak and skirt. They were all panting heavily. Squid tripped a couple of times, but picked himself up and kept going. Finally, Jason grabbed the child's shoulder to slow him momentarily. "Piggyback time," Jason said. "Up you go."

"Hurry," Charlotte said, passing them. She was walking now, catching her breath before the next sprint.

"I wish I knew what was happening" Jason said, following close behind.

"It happens every so often," Hindel called back. He too was now walking. "Too many heavy wagons up top. We clean it out and make repairs."

Behind them, the rumbling increased to a roar, loud cracks and earth crumbling down. Jason held onto Squid's legs and ran, Charlotte close behind crying, "No, no. Please, no." Hindel's lantern kept them going, and as they pounded along, dirt and rocks poured into the tunnel behind them. They ran until Charlotte flopped onto the ground, holding her sides and gasping. "We have to stop...for a minute..."

"Bettina," Jason said, as he lowered Squid down. "Will Bettina be all right?"

"She'll be back at the wine cellar by now," Hindel said, wiping sweat from his forehead, "and anyway, it's this end of the tunnel that's the problem. More heavy carts and oxen down here."

"How long till we get there?" Squid asked, kicking at the dirt floor with his shoe. "I'm hungry."

Hindel pulled the blue silk bundle from his waistband. "Bettina gave me these," he said pulling a lumpy cloth-covered package from inside. "One for each of us." He handed it to Charlotte, who quickly laid the cloth on the ground, pulling back the folds to reveal four sweet iced buns, a little squished but still delicious.

"My Bettina is very thoughtful," Hindel said, squatting down. "We will marry in four years when her bond with Lord Friedrich is done." He stuffed the whole bun into his mouth and stood abruptly as if he had revealed too much. "We must keep going," he muttered brusquely. "Hurry."

Squid was still eating as Jason grabbed his legs and hefted him up into position. As they hurried along, Squid's half-eaten sticky bun pressed into Jason's neck. He was barely aware of it, however, the ache in his back and legs overpowering almost everything else.

When a low rumbling began both in front and behind, Hindel shouted and they all broke into a run. Squid, terrified, kept tightening his grip around Jason's neck.

The second cave-in seemed worse than the first – dirt and broken logs crashing down, showers of dust filling the tunnel. The sound echoed up and down so that it was impossible to tell if it was behind or somewhere in front, or both.

"We will walk," Hindel said, his chest heaving. He took Charlotte's arm and helped her. She was moving bent over, her cloak and skirts dropped and dragging on the ground.

Sweat dripped from Jason's forehead and his shoulders ached. Squid's face was pressed into his neck, the child's breathing rapid and tense.

We must be nearly there, Jason thought, hoping desperately they weren't trapped. Hindel was saying nothing.

Moments later, when Hindel held up the lantern, Jason saw that the tunnel in front of them was blocked. He lowered Squid, who ran up to the pile of earth and logs yelling, "Stupid tunnel, let us through," all the while kicking at the pile, stopping only when he stubbed his toe.

"Now what, Lottie?" he asked, changing his tack. "We need a bulldozer. Rrmmm, rrmmm..." He shunted an imaginary one back and forth, advancing and retreating from the dirt and logs.

Hindel looked amused and somewhat puzzled. "We'll have to dig our way out," he said, not sounding too perturbed. "When we do not arrive, my father will know what has happened. He will bring help."

Jason nodded, and sliding his bugle around to the back of his belt, knelt down to scrape at the loose dirt with his hands.

Hindel put the lantern on the floor and warned Squid to watch out for it. He took a short dagger from his belt and began prying at one of the larger rocks. Charlotte pulled off her cloak and found a stone to use as a scraper. Squid threw his drum onto the ground and went into a dog-digging imitation, twice almost putting out the lantern.

They dug and pulled and scraped until their hands felt bruised and sore. One of Squid's fingers was bleeding, but he was relentless and determined to do as much as the others.

"I'm out of breath," Charlotte said finally, stopping and wiping the sweat rolling down her forehead. "Is it just me, or is there less air in here now?" She took a deep breath and coughed from the effort.

"If the other end is blocked, too," Jason said, feeling his

heart pound harder than he wanted it to, "I'd say there'd be less air." If they didn't get out, they would suffocate. How long that would take or what it would be like, he didn't want to imagine.

"My father should be here soon," Hindel said, sitting on the end of a log they hadn't been able to budge. "He must have heard the collapse."

Charlotte caught her breath again. "I think we should take breaks and rest to save the air that is here," she said.

"I don't see what difference that will make," Hindel replied. He stood and pulled hard on the log.

There would be no use explaining this to Hindel. Jason moved close to him and the two of them pulled and yanked, but the log didn't budge. Hindel gasped, suddenly, and staggered to one side.

Jason put his hand lightly on Hindel's shoulder. "There isn't enough air left in this tunnel," he began, "for your body to work properly." Jason gave his own chest a few thumps. "Your lungs are inside, here, and they need air to keep you going. It would be a good idea if we took turns."

Hindel slumped to the ground and stared up at him. "Is it because of the horn that you know this?" he asked.

"Yes," Jason said quickly. It was, in a way.

Charlotte nodded and sat down near Hindel. Squid continued digging furiously with five-year old optimism that defied logic. "I'll go first," Jason said, ignoring Squid. He took the stone from Charlotte's hand and went at the dirt around the projecting log, scraping away until he could reach in up to his elbow. He stood up and tried to lever it back and forth, but it still wouldn't budge. Squid joined him and they pushed and pulled until neither had any breath and they both fell onto their backs to recover.

As Hindel jumped up to help, the lantern went out.

"Lottie? You got a candle?" Squid asked. "It's too dark in here."

"Now what?" Charlotte whispered.

"We'll keep working," Hindel said grimly.

Jason felt his apprehension even in the darkness. Where was Hindel's father? Where was this rescue he had so confidently predicted?

"But we...can't...see." Jason knew Charlotte was close to tears.

"It's okay, Lottie," Squid cut in. "Jason has a magic bugle. He'll save us."

Jason lunged toward the debris and found the log. Hindel moved in beside him and they pushed and pulled, Jason slamming his whole weight against the log over and over until his chest tightened and he was gasping for air.

"Stop," Charlotte called out. "Both of you, stop."

Jason slumped down and leaned against the log. He couldn't stop shaking.

"It's impossible," Charlotte muttered. "It's just impossible."

"No, it's not," Hindel insisted. He gasped for breath again and was forced to sit.

Squid started to cry and Charlotte tried to hum one of their tunes to him, but her voice kept cracking. Jason knew she was rocking her brother, her big sister spirit kicking in, in spite of everything.

Jason closed his eyes against the blackness and tried to think of something, anything that might help them. Something behind him moved slightly and he tensed. Rats? Snakes? Another shudder. It was the log he was leaning against.

"Someone is there," Jason said, jumping to his feet and pulling again on the log, "I felt the log move."

Hindel leaned against it. *"Vater?"* he called. "Father, are you there?"

"Maybe it's another cave-in," Charlotte whispered. "Maybe..."

"Shh," Jason said. "Listen."

A faint scraping sound filtered from somewhere inside the pile. A scratch, scratch, scratch and the log moved again. Hindel and Jason pushed, and the log gave just a little. "We'll be okay," Hindel faltered. "Father and his neighbours are digging us out."

"I told you," Squid said, cheerfully. "See. I knew they would come."

Jason had no idea how long they waited in the darkness, listening as the scraping grew louder, finally hearing voices with Hindel calling out that they were safe. The minute an opening appeared, Squid scrambled over the dirt and logs and wriggled through to the other side, Charlotte following closely behind.

When Jason stood, his legs buckled and he squatted down, feeling blood rush to his head. He came to with Hindel and another man pulling him through to the other side.

Hildred, Hindel's mother was waiting with a blanket. "You're safe now," she said, wrapping it around his shoulders. "You're all safe now."

CHAPTER NINETEEN

JASON SAT ON A WOODEN BENCH IN FRONT OF THE CRACKLING fire, his stomach full of good soup and bread. Gunthar approached holding a carved wooden goblet. "Hildred says you must drink this," he said, handing it to Jason and sitting beside him, "but I'll warn you. It's bitter tasting."

Jason nodded and took the goblet. The stuff smelled awful.

"We should have shored up that tunnel," Gunthar said, "especially at this end." He sat on the bench, his elbows on his knees, staring into the fire as Jason gulped down the liquid. The flickering light highlighted the man's angular face and prominent nose. He clasped his large hands together. "This wasn't the kind of welcome we wanted for you," he said.

Hildred bustled over, stirring something in a bowl. "Hold out those hands," she said, her eyes twinkling, "and I'll fix them for you." Jason watched as she gently applied what looked like a mixture of oatmeal and herbs moistened with water. It felt cool and soothing to his cuts and bruises. "We'll leave it on for a while," she said, turning his palms up, "then shake the excess into the fire. Your hands will be good as new by morning."

Gunthar stood, and Jason noticed how much taller and thinner he was than his wife. Hildred gave his arm a squeeze. "Hindel's waiting for you to help him," she said. "We always make up remedies before we leave," she explained to Jason.

After they both hurried off, Jason listened to Charlotte and Squid behind him. Squid was having a bath of sorts, the same as he had had a while earlier – a small amount of warm water poured over him while crouching down in a wooden tub, strong yellow soap, another dousing with cold water and a rough cloth for drying.

Jason was impressed that the experience in the tunnel hadn't fazed Hindel. At the table, he had eaten his soup and laughed, saying the tunnel blockage was only two arm lengths thick. He could remember one that had been five or six.

Jason's eyes opened and closed and opened again, but he caught himself before slumping forward on the bench. He wouldn't fall asleep, not here. He wrapped the oversized night-gown around his feet and stared at the flames curling across the blackened logs.

This house was grand by peasant standards. A wooden floor, a fireplace, cupboards, and a long table with two smooth benches. The dispensary where they kept the herbs and reme-dies was next to this room and Jason already knew there was an upstairs where they would sleep.

Gunthar had said he was born in this place and so, too, his children. Hindel was the youngest, with two older sons already knights at the castle, one daughter a nun, and another married to a merchant in another town. He said nothing about children who had not survived. Perhaps they had been lucky.

"You're falling asleep." It was Charlotte, setting a cleaner and nightgown-clad Squid on the bench.

"No, I'm not," Jason replied, straightening up again. Squid snuggled up against him, his black hair still damp.

"It's my turn," Charlotte said, disappearing behind them.

"You gonna marry Lottie?" Squid asked after they had stared at the fire patterns for a few moments.

That jolted Jason awake. "What?" he snorted. "Where would you get an idea like that?"

"Bettina's going to marry Hindel."

"That's different, Squid," Jason said, fast-pedalling his brain to come up with something. "At home you have to go to school and college and stuff before you get married."

"When are we going home?" Squid asked. "I miss Mommy." He pushed his face into Jason's arm, little sniffles breaking in between the words.

Jason put his arm around the child and tousled his hair as he'd seen Charlotte do. "As soon as we find the parchment for Lord Friedrich," he said, trying to figure out how to explain it. "Hans and Friede's daddy really needs us to find it. Then we'll go home."

Squid looked up at him, his bottom lip trembling.

"Honest," Jason said. "I promise."

"Hindel promised to find my drum," Squid said, trying to look brave. "He says it's still in the tunnel."

"Your drum?" Jason hadn't realized it was missing.

"Remember?" Squid said. "I put it down when I was digging."

"Right," Jason said quickly. "Then I'm sure Hindel will have it back here in the morning."

This seemed to satisfy Squid and his body slowly relaxed until his head slumped into Jason's lap. He sniffed a few more times and then his breathing evened out into sleep.

Marry Charlotte? Out of the mouths of babes, his dad would have said. He hadn't thought much about girls – well, maybe a couple in Toronto, but there were always bigger guys who were better talkers. Computer games were safer; you didn't have to talk to computers. Besides, he didn't think of Charlotte that way.

Charlotte was a friend, a pretty good friend at that. Someone he could count on, and right now, that's what they both needed. Going home? He didn't want to think about it. Once the parchment was found and the fighting stopped, they would make it happen. How, at this point, he had no idea. He'd take Squid's approach. When the time came, the bugle would get them home.

"He's fallen asleep," Charlotte whispered, sitting down beside Jason with her back to the fire. Her hair was wet and she bent over, twisting the long thick strands round and round until water ran out, making a puddle on the floor.

"He's homesick," Jason said quietly. "And the drum. I didn't realize..."

"Hindel's going back for it." She shook her head back and forth, running her fingers through her hair.

"That's what Squid said. That whole episode was something, wasn't it? We were lucky, big time."

Charlotte stared at the fire. "Are you homesick?" she asked finally.

"I have been, a couple of times. You?"

"Off and on," Charlotte said. "My dad travels a lot and mom usually goes with him. I'm used to looking after Squid and more or less being on my own."

"My mom is the one who travels in our family," Jason said. "My dad's alway there, but he's glued to his computer most of the time, so we don't do much together."

"So I guess we're both independent types," Charlotte said. "Lucky we're not always arguing." She grinned.

"I can't imagine being here without you and Squid," Jason said. "Not that we've had much time to think."

Charlotte caught her breath and stared straight ahead. "Gunthar and Hildred have worked out a plan for us," she began quietly. "Tomorrow we set out with them on their route through the countryside, selling herbs and remedies. Even though wagons have been robbed lately by Otto's men, they plan to take their usual route and go past the forest near night-fall."

"Will they be meeting Frau Wölfin?" Jason asked.

Charlotte shook her head.

"But I thought Bettina said they bought supplies from her."

"Not this time. Things are tense in town right now, and they don't want to leave Hindel here alone for too long."

"So we're on our own to get there." Jason had known there would be a catch.

"Hildred says Frau Wölfin lives on the far side of the

swamp. She says there's a path that goes directly to her cottage."

"We have to go through a swamp?"

"Around it."

"What about the wolves?"

Charlotte puckered up her nose. "They're going to give us pigs' feet to feed them."

"How many wolves are there?" Jason asked.

"Hildred says no more than five or six, so she's giving us each four feet, just to make sure."

Pig's feet, Jason thought. Probably rank and starting to rot.

"I know it sounds gross," Charlotte continued, "but it's what they do when they visit, and Hildred says it works like a charm."

"Better than being attacked, I guess," Jason said dully.

"There's one other thing," Charlotte said, staring at him.

"We have to learn how to howl too?" Jason snapped.

"What's with you?"

"I'm tired," Jason replied. "Maybe a little discouraged."

"But you shouldn't be, "Charlotte said, staring at him. "We're here and we have these kind people helping us."

They both watched the fire then, and Jason thought how excited he had been when they started down the tunnel. It seemed such a long time ago, but it wasn't, a couple of hours at the most. Time was so non-specific here. Wolfgang's family had no clocks. There was a tower clock at the castle. He'd heard it chime several times, but had never seen it. And...he remembered suddenly, there was a clock in the Coburg town square. He made a mental note to listen for it.

"You are both dry now?" It was Hildred behind them. "Come. I will show you where you will sleep. Not the castle, but comfortable enough, I hope."

Charlotte gathered up the sleeping Squid and they followed Hildred to a narrow wooden staircase, not unlike the secret one at the castle. At the top were two doors, facing one another. "We sleep in there," Hildred said, pointing to one side, "and you will be here."

Inside the room, Jason saw three straw mattresses with coverlets, a low table with basin and water jug, and luckily for them, a fireplace with glowing logs warming the room.

Charlotte gently lay Squid down and the child rolled onto his side, one hand flung over the edge of the mattress. She covered him with his cloak and moved to warm her hands by the fire.

"What about Hindel?" Jason asked. This had to be the children's room.

"He will sleep downstairs tonight." Hildred said. "By the fire."

"There's one other thing I need to tell you," Charlotte said, after they snuggled down on their beds. "When we go in the cart with them, tomorrow, we'll be disguised as mummers."

"Mummers?"

"Travelling performers wearing masks. Gunthar says it's the only way, as they never know when Otto's men will show up, demanding this or that."

"What do we perform?" Jason asked. He was terrible at acting and hated being on stage at school.

"We sing a song. Something easy. It's no big deal."

"'Three Blind Mice?'" Jason said. "'Mary had a Little Lamb?'"

"We could," Charlotte said, "but I was thinking of an old folk song. I think it may be even German."

"What's it called?" Jason asked.

"'I Love to Go A-Wandering.'"

"Never heard of it." Sing some dumb song? He hated singing.

"I think you have," Charlotte said patiently. "Listen...Val de re, val de rah, val de re, val de rah, hah, hah, hah, hah..."

She sang softly and Jason did recognize it. It was one of those boring songs with too many verses that they sang in music class. "I love to go a wandering..." Jason sang back.

"That's it," Charlotte said excitedly, "you do know it."

"Not all the verses."

"Don't worry about that," Charlotte said. "We'll practice on the way. Squid already knows the hah, hah, hah's."

"I'll bet he does," Jason said, smiling.

Charlotte pulled the coverlet up around herself. "Oh yes," she said. "And Hildred says not to worry. If anyone asks, she'll say we're relatives." The next moment she was asleep.

Jason lay watching the night sky through the window. Stars and more stars. Light travelling through space. Shining on them here and at home? Yes and no. Sequence. Order. Time. It was all too confusing. Too complicated.

A cloud slipped across the moon, darkening the room and the three sleeping children.

CHAPTER TWENTY

HILDRED FUSSED AND LOOKED AFTER THINGS LIKE ANY mom would. The next morning, before they ate, she came bustling into the room carrying identical brown smocks with stockings and well-worn soft shoes. "So no one will think you're from the castle," she said. She also produced the lost drum and Squid squealed with delight as soon as he set eyes on it, complaining loudly when Charlotte said he couldn't play until he was dressed.

Hindel and Gunthar were already in the dispensary when they arrived downstairs. Smells of freshly baked bread and frying sausages filled the air. Porridge steamed in bowls at each place.

"A special treat," Hildred said, bringing a small jug to the table. "Fresh *Milch*."

"Milk," Jason said. "Thanks. We haven't had any for ages."

Hildred beamed. "Gunthar mentioned you were here when he was buying eggs at Herr Bernhard's farm this morning. Bernhard was milking the cow. 'For your guests,' he said."

Once the table was cleared, Hildred brought four masks and laid them carefully on the table. "My children used these," she said a little wistfully. "They are old but will do well for you."

Jason's mask felt too tight and smelled mouldy. He twisted it back and forth, squinting and trying to see through the ragged eyeholes. He chose the bear and Squid, who immediately grabbed the donkey, proceeded to run back and forth hee-hawing and bumping into things. Jason was more than a little surprised that Charlotte chose the pig over the horse, but she said it was because of *Charlotte's Web,* one of her all-time favourites.

Hindel had worn one of these masks, Jason thought. It was hard to think of Hindel as a kid, and yet he was only a teenager, maybe fourteen or fifteen. Jason thought again about Bettina and Hindel, that they would marry in four years when her bond was up with Lord Friedrich. If Hindel became the apothecary, and it seemed he would as the other children had already left, Bettina would live here. Better than going home, although Jason supposed home was an okay place to her. She'd have a chance here, though, to make a better life. Funny, when he was at home, he never thought about things like this.

"The bear," Hindel said. "Good choice. It was mine."

Jason yanked off the mask and grinned. "A bit tight," he said, rubbing the side of his face, "but it will do."

"Father asks if you would like to see the dispensary."

"Sure," Jason replied, looking around for Charlotte.

"She is helping my mother," Hindel said. "Getting supplies into *den Wagen.*"

Squid marched into the dispensary right behind them, drum in high gear and, after he had almost collided with two separate shelves of glass bottles, Gunthar spoke quietly to the child and the two of them left.

A moment later, Squid, minus the drum, appeared at the doorway. "Gunthar says to tell you we're going to hitch the ox to the cart. He says I'm a lucky boy!" And he was gone.

Jason was staring at three covered glass bottles containing leeches when Hindel came up beside him. The small worm-like black creatures looked about as long as one of Jason's fingers. Each one had suctioned itself to a spot inside its jar, submerged in murky water. In two jars the leeches were thin and almost flat, while in the third, they were swollen like fat slugs.

"Leeches," Hindel said, quietly. "These two jars are the new ones."

"And these?" Jason pointed to the third jar.

"They've been used," Hindel said, in a matter-of-fact tone. "It will take about three months for their blood to absorb."

Jason shivered. "They're used to help wounds heal, right?" He remembered his dad telling him how leeches were placed alongside a healing wound to reduce blood buildup under the skin. The idea had totally grossed Jason out.

"These are for bleeding," Hindel said, staring at him. "I have not heard of using them for wounds."

Jason scrutinized the slimy creatures and tried to look nonchalant. "Well...it is to reduce blood building up," he replied. "But in connection with a wound that's healing."

"Are you sure?"

"My dad told me."

"I'll have to tell Father about this."

"My dad read about it in a *Buch*, I think." It might have been TV, but "book" would at least make sense to Hindel.

"Your father is a learned man, then?"

"He's pretty smart," Jason said. "He writes *Bücher* and..."

"We're ready! We're ready!" Squid stood at the doorway, jumping up and down, his donkey mask in hand.

"May you find what you need," Hindel said, solemnly offering Jason his hand.

"Thanks," Jason replied, "we plan to." Hindel shook his hand vigorously, then stepped back. *"Auf Wiedersehen,"* he added softly. "And Godspeed."

A SHORT TIME LATER, they were bumping along in the *Wagen*, Hildred and Gunthar walking ahead, one on either side of the lumbering ox. In a worn sack, Hildred had packed three warm cloaks for them. Charlotte had her recorder fastened inside her tunic sleeve and Jason had pulled his tunic to hang loosely out over the bugle and rope belt. They all sat on the back of the wagon, their legs dangling over the edge. Herbs and tonics and the two jars of leeches were packed in front, with the pigs feet in another sack, tied to the outside.

Squid soon climbed inside and began asking questions about each and every thing in the cart, especially the leeches. The third time Charlotte caught him trying to yank the cover off one of the jars, she pulled out two small wooden soldiers from under a bag. "These were Hindel's, a long time ago," she said to her brother. "Hildred says you can have them."

Squid was instantly lost in some game, toting the soldiers up and down the nearest bags, chattering away, half in English, half in German.

"So, if Otto's soldiers stop us," Jason said quietly, "who starts singing?"

"I will," Charlotte said, "and you and Squid can join in on the chorus."

"Does Squid know?"

Charlotte nodded.

Gunthar stopped a couple of times to show their wares – once to a man and his wife hand-pushing a rickety cart, and once to family walking, Jason guessed, into town. Neither group bought anything, but it gave the three of them the chance to practice singing and marching.

A soon as Charlotte sang the first line, everyone joined in, singing loudly to Squid's rat-a-tat-tat's. Jason was sure they must look stupid, marching more than a little carefully so the masks wouldn't fall off. Afterward, everyone clapped enthusiastically and the man in the family group threw them two sticks of wood from the bundle tied to his back. Hildred said that meant he was impressed.

"We going to be there soon?" Squid asked as soon as they were bumping along in the wagon again. "I'm hungry."

Charlotte pulled a cloth packet from one of the boxes and produced a small *Brot* loaf. "Snack," she said, tearing off pieces for each of them. "Some of this morning's fresh bread."

Otto's soldiers must have been waiting close by. One minute

they weren't there, and the next minute they were in front of the oxen, barking out questions to Gunthar.

"This is it," Charlotte whispered as they slipped off the end of the cart and stood waiting. Gunthar gave them his spiel about herbs and medicines, with Hildred pulling out samples from the front end of the wagon, both of them chattering and laughing. Jason hoped their mummer performance would be as convincing.

Charlotte was listening, waiting for the right moment. Squid stood, drumsticks poised, wound up and ready to go, unaware of any impending danger.

"Now," Charlotte said quietly, slipping off the back of the wagon. She started, "I love to go a-wandering," and Jason and Squid followed, joining in on the first verse, all of them feeling more confident. When they came to the chorus, Squid set it up with an elaborate drum roll. "Val de re, val de rah, val de re, val de rah, hah, hah, hah, hah..." And miracle of miracles, the soldiers joined in. Five verses later, the soldiers saluted and rode off, talking and chortling to each other.

As soon as they were out of sight, Hildred hugged first Charlotte and then Squid, while Gunthar solemnly shook Jason's hand. Gunthar said it was unlikely the soldiers would bother them a second time. They had passed the test.

WHEN THE SUN WAS HIGH OVERHEAD, they stopped at an inn tucked down between two steep hills. After the children jumped free of the wagon, Gunthar led the ox to a water trough beneath a huge oak tree. Hildred disappeared inside.

Jason and Charlotte sat on a shady patch of grass near the tree while Squid ran around in circles singing "Val de re, val de rah…"

"He needs more exercise," Charlotte said, watching him. "You were great, singing," she said to Jason, pulling at a piece of grass. "I don't know why you were worried."

"Thanks," Jason said. "I always hated singing in school." He laughed. "I remember when we learned that song. A folk song. Bor-ing."

"I know what you mean," Charlotte replied, "but it doesn't seem boring here, does it?"

"It fits right in."

"Kommen Sie," Hildred called, beckoning them into the inn. Gunthar held the door and they stepped inside to cool dimness, dark-stained wood everywhere. Paneled walls, rough oak tables and benches, even the ceiling was wood, heavy beams with planks between.

In one corner, a group of old men sat smoking and tossing dice on their table. They stopped and stared as the group entered. Jason worried that he might be recognized. He kept his head down and stayed close to Gunthar.

Hildred waved and one of the men waved back. *"Guten Tag,"* she called, smiling. *"Mein Onkel,"* she explained as they moved to a table on the far side. "He has seen five decades. God has been his provider."

Fifty, Jason thought as he slipped into a seat closest to the wall. The man looked seventy, at least.

The innkeeper's wife bustled in with a pot of soup and bowls. Hildred jumped up to help her. *"Gut, gut,"* she said, ladling a generous portion into each bowl. "Distant cousins from Bavaria." She nodded at Jason and Charlotte. Squid was under the table, investigating.

"*Ja, ja,*" the woman said, paying little attention to them. Jason felt relieved and hoped they wouldn't be stopping anywhere else.

Soon after they were back in the wagon, Squid fell asleep. "Thank goodness for small blessings," Charlotte whispered. "Finally, we'll get a break." She pulled out her recorder and began quietly playing.

"Where did you hear that tune?" Jason asked. He was sure it was the one the men in the prison sang.

"I heard Liesa singing it a couple of times."

"Men in the prison were singing it," Jason said. "*Die Gedanken sind frei,* my thoughts freely flower."

"You know the words?"

"Some of them," Jason replied.

Charlotte started again and Jason sang:

Die Gedanken sind frei
My thoughts freely flower
Die Gedanken sind frei
My thoughts give me power
No scholar can find them
No trap ever bind them
No man can deny
Die Gedanken sind frei

Clapping greeted them when they ended. "*Gut, gut,*" Hildred called back.

"A song of the people," Gunthar added, enthusiastically.

"Everyone knows this song?" Jason asked.

"All who love freedom," Gunthar replied.

"Men in the prison said the song wasn't allowed," Jason said.

"Otto has banned it," Gunthar said. He laughed and slapped his side. "That will, of course, ensure that it will live."

"Do you know any more words?" Jason asked.

"Shall we sing them another verse, Hildred?"

Hildred moved to the back of the wagon, her eyes shining. "Play for us, dear child," she said, "and we will teach you."

And if tyrants take me
and throw me in prison
my thoughts will burst free
like blossoms in season
foundations will crumble
and Otto will tumble
and free men will cry
die Gedanken sind frei

They sang it through several times, Squid waking and adding his lively drum beat. Jason concentrated on the words, remembering the men shackled in the prison, the scaffold, the arrow hitting his bugle. The tune and the words gave him hope. They would find Frau Wölfin and the parchment. They would return safely to the castle. They would return home.

No one else passed them, and when Jason looked up, he

was surprised to see they had left the main road and were on a narrow rutted path, *der mysteriöse Forst* ahead in the distance.

CHAPTER TWENTY-ONE

"STRAIGHT DOWN THIS PATH," GUNTHAR ASSURED THEM. "It's a snug little cottage, always open for travellers."

"You can stay the night," Hildred explained. "Get an early start in the morning."

Der mysteriöse Forst rose up in front of them, rays from the late afternoon sun casting long shadows out from the cart and ox. Each of them put on a cloak; each held a bag of pig's feet. Hildred gave Charlotte a second bag filled with *Brot* and cheese. Jason carried a large flask full of *Wasserale*. Squid stashed the wooden soldiers in the pocket of his cloak. Hildred persuaded him to leave his drum and promised she would keep it safe.

"We will be back this way late tomorrow afternoon," Hildred assured them. "We will wait for you here."

"*Danke,*" Jason said, summoning up as much confidence as he could. "We'll be back for sure."

"*Auf Wiedersehen,*" Charlotte called as they drove off.

"Godspeed," they heard Gunthar answer.

"Okay," Jason said, looking toward the thick underbrush bordering the forest. "Little cottage, here we come."

The forest was darker and more foreboding than Jason expected. The "short walk" to the cottage was on a narrow path that twisted and turned, huge branches towering overhead, blocking all but the faintest rays of light. And the farther they walked, the damper and colder the air became.

Jason stopped when they came to the fork in the path. "Gunthar didn't say anything about left or right, did he?"

Charlotte edged around him and peered at the two paths. "They both said to follow the main path," she said. "Wouldn't you know there'd be a fork."

"What's a fork?" Squid asked. He was behind the other two, pushing to see.

"Two ways to go," Charlotte said, letting him past.

"We should go this way," Squid said, pointing to the left.

"Really?" Jason replied, "how do you know?"

"'Cause," Squid said. "Way, way down there, I can see a roof."

"I can't see anything but branches," Charlotte said. "Are you sure, Squid?"

Jason squatted down so that he was the same height as Squid. "You're right. The path goes up a small hill, and from here I can see the thatched roof."

"Smoke coming out of the chimney too," Squid said, excitedly.

"There shouldn't be," Charlotte said, squatting down behind Squid. "Gunthar said no one was there."

"Maybe someone lit a fire for us...'cause they knew we were

coming." Squid stood up looking enormously pleased with himself.

"Nice thought," Jason replied, jumping up, "but not likely."

"So what should we do?" Charlotte pulled Squid to his feet. "We have to find somewhere to sleep."

"Why don't we stay on the path until we're close," Jason began. "Then you and Squid hide and I'll sneak a look at who's there."

"What if they're bad guys," Squid asked, "and they grab you?"

"I'll be careful," Jason replied. Charlotte looked worried, but said nothing.

High above them a bird trilled, two notes, three times in rapid succession. Without thinking Jason whistled the pattern back. The bird answered.

"I didn't know you could do that," Charlotte said, staring at him.

"I'd forgotten," Jason replied, smiling. "I tried it at home, the day I first came to your house. And you know what? It's perfect to use as a signal." He whistled again and again the bird answered.

"But how will we know if it's you or the bird?" Squid said. He puckered up his lips, practicing little whistle sounds.

"It doesn't really sound the same," Jason replied. "Listen." He whistled, and they waited. Nothing.

"Maybe you're not in the right key," Charlotte said, trying not to smile.

The bird trilled from a different location. Jason turned and whistled again.

"I can tell the difference," Charlotte said. "So what will this signal mean?"

"I'm okay," Jason said. "It'll mean 'don't worry.'"

They walked in silence, and when the roof came into view, Charlotte and Squid slipped past several big tree trunks and were gone. "I can't see you," Jason said in a half-whisper.

"Good," Charlotte whispered back.

It was dusk by now, and when he came close enough, Jason saw a faint light flickering inside the cottage. The fireplace, he thought. Good. With no other light, it would be easier to sneak a look inside. He circled around the small clearing, moving from tree to tree, until he was close to one of the two small windows. They were shuttered and he knew there would be no glass. He would peek through the crack; listen for voices.

He slipped under the side window. Two men were talking and one sounded familiar. A nasal-sounding voice. Lothar? Jason stood on tiptoe, trying to see through the crack where the two shutters met. The door creaked. They were coming outside. Jason slipped behind the house, his heart pounding. The men stopped and continued talking.

"Otto is strong. He knows what he wants." Jason was sure it was Lothar. What was he doing here?

The door slammed. "True, and it pays to be vigilant." This voice was gruff, harsh sounding.

"You are sure, then," the nasal voice went on, "that they will be coming through this way tomorrow?"

"My contacts are always reliable," the gruff voice replied.

"It should be fairly easy, then," the other said, "for us to nab them."

"Be fast and unexpected."

They're talking about us, Jason thought. They're going to kidnap me. Again.

Jason listened to the men stride toward the path. He slipped back along the side of the cottage so he could see them.

"Should we put the fire out?" the gruff-voiced man asked. He was rough looking with a scraggly beard, not unlike the so-called soldiers who had met them at Wolfgang's house.

The other was in full Veste armour and carrying his helmet. When he turned back toward the cottage, Jason flattened himself against the wall. It was Lothar.

"It's mostly smoke now," Lothar replied. "And I appreciate this information." He slipped a small bag into the man's hand.

"Part of my job," the man replied, slipping the bag into his pocket. "Things are rough in town these days, a lot of fighting in the streets. I'm going to lay low for a while."

"I know where to find you," Lothar added. "Has a time been mentioned?"

"I would recommend early."

"We'll be at the edge of the forest by dawn," Lothar replied. "It won't hurt to wait."

"Good luck, then..." The man offered his hand and Lothar grasped it firmly, then turned toward the path out of the forest. The informant took off at a clip through the woods, thankfully in the opposite direction from where Charlotte and Squid were hiding.

Jason stayed until he was sure Lothar would be past Charlotte and Squid's hiding place. He whistled and broke into a run to meet them.

"Someone has already squealed on us..." he began.

"A soldier passed us," Charlotte said, holding tightly to Squid's hand. "Back there on the path."

"Sir Lothar," Jason added, turning to retrace the path toward the cottage. "He's bringing men and they'll be waiting to kidnap us when we leave the forest tomorrow."

"How do you know?"

"I heard the whole thing," Jason went on. "The other guy mentioned Otto and he told Lothar we wouldn't be coming out of the forest before tomorrow."

"How would he know that?" Charlotte asked.

"I have no idea."

"Have you ever seen this man before?"

"I didn't really get that good a look at him."

"But you're sure it was Lothar?" Charlotte asked, pulling Squid along to catch up.

Jason stopped. "Haven't we had this conversation before?" he snapped. "It was Lothar, and he's obviously in cahoots with Otto."

Charlotte sighed. "So what do you think we should do?"

"We could leave now," Jason said. "Keep going on that road the way Gunthar and Hildred were heading. Hope we would find them."

"And not see Frau Wölfin?" Charlotte asked. "I thought that was the point of all this."

"It was...it is," Jason faltered, "but if they kidnap you and Squid..." He clenched his fists. "I'd want to kill anyone who hurt either of you."

Charlotte put her hand on his arm. "Nothing's going to

happen," she said firmly, "to any of us."

"I'll help you fight the bad guys," Squid cut in. "I'll help you, Jason."

"Sure you will, buddy," Jason said, smiling again, "and we'd better make tracks to that cottage. It'll be dark soon."

"Anyway," Charlotte said as they hurried along, "after we find Frau Wölfin and ask about the parchment, she can suggest another way out of here."

WHEN THEY STEPPED INSIDE, they found the cottage small but adequate, a good supply of logs in one corner and a bucket full of clean water nearby. After a brief discussion, they brought the pigs' feet in with them and hung the bag on a peg by the door. For safekeeping.

"You're sure," Charlotte said, a few minutes later. "Maybe he just looked like Lothar." She was putting another log on the fire.

"It was him," Jason said. He pulled shut the bolt on the inside of the door. "I couldn't mistake that voice. Besides, he turned and I looked right at him."

"You don't think they'll come back here, do you?" Charlotte asked. She slumped down on one of the two straw mattresses.

"No, because Lothar said he would come back at dawn and wait at the forest's edge," Jason explained.

"And the other man?"

"He said he would lay low...in town."

"How could someone from town know what we're doing?" Charlotte asked.

"I don't know," Jason said. "Maybe it was that man who sold Gunthar the milk." He was getting sick of this discussion. He was the one who had heard the conversation, not Charlotte.

Squid sat cross-legged in front of the fire, playing with his soldiers. "This is a nice place," he said, marching a soldier back and forth. "We going to eat soon?"

Charlotte grinned and pulled the *Brot* loaf and cheese from the bag. Jason dragged a mattress closer to the fire and they sat quietly eating bread and drinking *Wasserale*. Squid was asleep after a few mouthfuls, his dirt-smudged hand still holding a crust of bread. Jason carried him to the other mattress and covered him with his cloak.

"What about Gunthar and Hildred?" Jason said, sitting back down. "Tomorrow, they'll be waiting for us."

"If we stay on the same path until we're nearly there," Charlotte said slowly, "and then move into the trees, we should be able to hear them, if it's Otto's men."

"Hildred and Gunthar won't wait if a bunch of soldiers are milling about."

"You're right," Charlotte replied. "They'll know something is up."

"Well, as my mom always says, we'll have to cross that bridge when we come to it." Jason stood and walked over to where Squid was sleeping. "I'll sleep beside Squid," he said. "You stay by the fire."

Charlotte pulled her mattress back a distance and lay down. "Hildred said to keep the mattress back from the coals," she explained. "She said most cottage fires were started by sparks snapping onto dry mattresses."

Jason lay listening to Squid's rapid breathing. The child's hand twitched and his eyelids fluttered. He's dreaming, Jason thought. I hope it's a good dream. He pulled the cloak further over the child's shoulders and snuggled into the mattress.

Outside the moon had risen and an owl hooted in a tree above the cottage. Jason listened and thought about trying to copy the sound. His thought drifted into sleep as the owl flew silently away.

CHAPTER TWENTY-TWO

EVEN THOUGH THE COTTAGE WAS DAMP AND COLD THE next morning, they didn't bother to light another fire. After a few mouthfuls of cold *Brot* and *Wasserale,* they found the path behind the cottage and set off deeper into the forest, they hoped toward Frau Wölfin's cottage. Everywhere water droplets clung to leaves and stones; even the trunks of the great trees were wet with morning dew.

"It probably never dries out in here," Charlotte said, pulling the edges of her cloak together. "I can hardly wait to get to the swamp."

"How do we get through the swamp, Jason?" Squid asked. He was marching in front of them, his arms swinging back and forth.

"Well, if there's a bridge," Jason said, "we'll go over it."

"And if there's a tunnel," Charlotte cut in, "We'll go under it." She made a face at Jason and grinned.

"You two being serious or silly?" Squid asked. "'Cause I want to know."

"We won't know until we get there," Jason said, breaking a dead branch as he caught up to Squid. "Here, buddy. A walking stick."

"You have a walking stick, Jason?" Squid took the stick and inspected it as he walked.

"Be careful," Charlotte warned. "You could poke your eye out with that thing."

Jason found another longer branch, and after pulling the twigs off, walked with it, swinging his free arm. Squid copied him and when Charlotte picked up a broken branch the right length, the three of them marched along singing, "Val de re, val de rah...val de re...val de rah, hah, hah, hah,hah,hah..." until they stopped, laughing and exhausted, flopping down on the edge of the path for a rest.

A series of distant, roaring squeals brought them to their feet. The sound subsided as they listened. All normal forest sounds had stopped, almost as if waiting.

"What was that?" Charlotte asked, peering into the trees.

"I don't know," Jason replied. Squid pressed himself against Jason and said nothing.

The squealing resumed, louder and closer, followed by the horrific shriek of an animal in pain. Charlotte grabbed Squid's hand, and with Jason in the lead, they ran on down the path, hopefully away from the sound. Something was being killed, and the sound of its suffering ricocheted back and forth through the trees so it seemed to be on all sides of them. They ran until sharp pains cut through Jason's chest. Squid was gasping, Charlotte's face flushed. They needed somewhere to hide, somewhere away from this fierce predator. There was no cave, no cottage, only trees.

They were in a grove of old cedars now, their branches gnarled, some within reach. Jason stopped abruptly and grabbed Squid. "You're going up, little buddy," he panted. "Climb." And he pulled the child roughly up onto his shoulders.

Squid grabbed a branch and climbed. He was crying but scrambled up without hesitation. "Next," Jason yelled, motioning Charlotte to another tree. The squealing and snorting accelerated in pitch. He grabbed her around the knees and pushed himself to a standing position. "Okay," she called, hauling herself up. Jason ran at the next tree and jumped for the lowest branch. His fingers caught, but he dangled, momentarily, swinging his legs to get a foothold and push himself up. A shape hurtled toward him, squealing as it came.

Jason felt something sharp rake his leg below the knee, and as he pulled his feet clear of the ground, five or six more creatures crashed beneath, snorting and panting and tearing up turf.

Jason sat on the branch, hugging the tree trunk, his legs pulled up as high as they would go. He felt his stocking torn up past his knee, a welt stinging on the calf of his leg. He couldn't look down or even over to see if Charlotte and Squid were okay. He hung on and waited.

The creatures left as quickly as they had come. More snorting and pushing and they ran off, leaving the forest silent again.

"Jason?" Squid called in a quavery voice. "You okay?"

"I...I think so," Jason faltered. "What about you, Charlotte?"

"I'm terrified," Charlotte called shakily. "Other than that, I'm okay."

"Did you see them?" Jason asked.

"Pigs," Squid, said. "Ugly, awful pigs with horns."

"Wild boars," Charlotte whispered. "I remember Hildred saying there weren't any in this part of the forest."

"Well, she was wrong," Jason said, taking a deep breath. "Now what?"

"I don't know," Charlotte replied. "Are you hurt?"

"A gash on my leg. It hurts, but I'll survive."

"We were lucky." Charlotte sounded close to tears.

The forest was quiet then, with only the occasional bird chirping and a few insects buzzing nearby.

"We must be near the swamp," Jason said, running his hand along the rough tree branch.

"You're right," Charlotte added. She sounded less shaky now. "Big cedars like the ones by our pond at home."

"Good thing you both know how to climb trees," Jason added.

"I can climb higher than Charlotte," Squid called.

"Don't do it now," Charlotte shot back.

A new sound broke the silence. Yips and barks and crashing through the trees. Wolves close by, running in a pack. They circled beneath them, sniffing and yapping, then took off together in a rush. Moments later, a terrific din, barking and squealing, growling and snorting, the sound diminishing only as the boars finally retreated.

"You ridiculous furballs. What are you up to now?"

Jason looked sideways and glimpsed a figure on the path,

a small wispy person swinging a huge gnarled walking stick, a wild halo of grey hair almost covering her face. She gave a loud whistle and the wolves returned, racing back and forth between her and the trees where the children hid.

"What is it, my furballs? You've treed something?"

"Us," Squid announced loudly. "Jason and Charlotte and me."

"We have pigs' feet," Charlotte called shakily. She dropped her bag to the ground and the wolves ripped it open, growling and jostling each other.

"Pigs' feet," the woman chortled. "It's Hildred that's sent you, then."

"Yes," Jason replied, throwing his bag out as far as he could manage. One of the wolves pounced on it and trotted off a distance, only to be harassed by several more.

"Here," Squid called. He threw his bag at the woman's feet. She opened it and scattered the contents further away. Moments later, all the wolves lay gnawing contentedly, with only the occasional growl or yip.

"Come down then," the woman said, "and let me have a look at you."

Squid was down first and then Charlotte. Jason moved more slowly, the gash stinging, his whole leg throbbing. "My leg," he called. "It's going to take me a minute." He lowered himself slowly and then jumped. The next thing he knew, he was lying on the ground, everyone looking up at him.

"Jason?" Charlotte squatted down beside him. She put her hand on his forehead.

"I'm fine," Jason said, sitting up. "Just a bit dizzy."

"The pig got him," Squid said. He took a deep breath. "But your big dogs scared them all away."

"You're only children," the woman exclaimed. "In my cat's eye, you didn't look this young."

"What's she talking about?" Charlotte whispered.

"I have no idea," Jason replied.

The woman ignored them. "All morning, I watched you. Crashing along down the path. Singing." She looked briefly at Jason's leg. "You'll live, boy. I'll fix it up and you'll live."

It didn't make sense, that she said she'd been watching them. Jason stood and faced her. "We have been wanting to meet you, Frau Wölfin," he said. She was so tiny, not much taller than himself.

Frau Wölfin put her hands on her hips and stared at the three of them. "You're a tired looking bunch," she said. "And likely hungry too." She turned and strode off, beckoning them to follow.

The wolves scrambled after them, several pushing past the children to trot beside their mistress. Squid put his hand on one, but pulled back when the creature growled.

"Leave them alone," Frau Wölfin called, "and they won't bother you."

"They're wild wolves," Charlotte whispered to Squid, taking his hand. "Not dogs."

"They look like dogs," Squid insisted. "They bark like dogs."

The swamp was suddenly there, dank and misty, long reeds and wide grass blades in clumps across its surface. Frau Wölfin led them around its far side, sometimes on a path and sometimes over low-slung log walkways tied together with thick vines. She's built these, Jason thought. By herself, she's cut these logs and strung them together. The woman must be stronger than she looked.

When she stopped, Jason realized they were in front of a cottage. Even this close, it was camouflaged, two huge cedars draping branches over it, the log walls and thatched roof blending into the trees behind. The wolves disappeared through tree root openings at its base.

Frau Wölfin stood near the door, staring at Jason. "Where is your horn?" she asked sharply.

"Here," Jason said. "Under my tunic for safekeeping."

"Let me have a look at it, then," Frau Wölfin replied. She narrowed her eyes and stood squarely in front of the door.

"Are we going inside soon?" Squid asked, tugging at Charlotte's cloak.

"Shh," Charlotte said. "In a minute."

Jason could see it was a standoff. She wasn't going to let them in if he didn't hand it over. Reluctantly, he untied the yellow rope and handed Frau Wölfin the bugle.

She turned it over in her hands several times, but said nothing.

"I'll play if you'd like," Jason offered.

"That won't be necessary," she said, turning to go in.

Jason wondered if she could read their thoughts. He had to talk to this woman. "Thank you for rescuing us," he blurted out.

"Thank the furballs," she said, brusquely. Then she opened the door and waved them in.

CHAPTER TWENTY-THREE

IT TOOK A FEW MOMENTS TO ADJUST TO THE DIMLY LIT interior. Jason and Charlotte stayed close to the door with Squid squeezed between them. Frau Wölfin put the bugle down and added logs to embers glowing in a stone fireplace. They watched her swing an iron pot over the advancing flames. She didn't make them feel welcome or tell them to sit down and so they waited.

Everything inside was made from cedar logs. The table, covered with a thick, patterned cloth, showed ridges where logs were fastened one against the next. Two benches on either side of the table and a chair in front of the fire were all log, the hand-cut pieces tightly laced with dried vines.

Jason didn't notice the shelf overhead until Frau Wölfin reached up and placed the bugle on it. A huge cat jumped down from it onto the table, to be scooped up by Frau Wölfin, who slung the creature around her neck. "Dear Herr Prinz," she said in a singsongy voice, quite different from the one she used with the children. "We have guests, Herr Prinz, friends of dear Hildred." She stepped forward into the firelight, revealing the cat's large tabby face, its huge eyes watching them from one shoulder, its back feet and swishing tail resting on the other.

"Nice kitty," Squid said, running toward Frau Wölfin, holding up his hand. The cat sniffed his fingers and slowly licked them. "Ooh, scratchy," Squid chortled, holding his hand steady. "Your kitty has a very scratchy tongue."

Frau Wölfin bent forward and the cat leapt onto the table. "Ah yes, dear Prinz," she said stroking his head, "your eyes will tell me where these strangers started and where they will end up."

"His eyes?" Squid said, climbing onto the bench and staring into the cat's face.

"His right eye," Frau Wölfin began, "tells me the past and the left, at times, the future." She rubbed the cat's neck fur and he purred loudly. "I stare into my Herr Prinz's eyes every day," she replied, "sometimes the left, sometimes the right. It's fascinating what I see."

"You were watching us, then?" Jason asked. "That's how you knew the boars were after us."

"Lucky for you I was," she replied.

"Can you see where we're from?" Charlotte asked, almost in a whisper.

Frau Wölfin bent over her cat and stared into its right eye, chanting:

Strange sleek carts that race alone
Like magic, down a smooth black road
Two fancy castles made of stone, one
Near a pond with boat and toad.

She stopped and stroked the cat. "Good Prinz, dear boy," she whispered.

"Are you looking at my grandma's house?" Squid said, pushing in front of her. Herr Prinz mewed and rubbed against Squid's face.

Jason took a deep breath. "Can you see how we'll we get home?" he asked. Depending on the bugle was one thing. If she could tell them for sure, maybe everything else would fall into place.

For several moments, Frau Wölfin stared into the cat's left eye. Jason and Charlotte inched closer. The old woman hummed several notes and then, settling on one, chanted:

When the hillside fills with singing
When the night sky seems like day
When the fog leaps from the fire
You'll be marching on your way.

Frau Wölfin paused and Herr Prinz jumped heavily to the floor.

"Enough," she said and strode over to stir the pot again.

"Can you remember that?" Jason whispered.

"I'll try," Charlotte said, "but it doesn't make much sense."

The cat padded to Jason and stared up at him, his large yellow eyes piercing and direct. Jason remembered Frau Wölfin's comment about the wolves and hesitated to touch the creature.

"Herr Prinz is friendly to everyone," Frau Wölfin said, not turning around.

Charlotte reached over and stroked his back. The cat

purred against her, a loud rattling purr.

Jason had never seen such a large cat. He squatted down and it rubbed against him, pushing its nose onto his leg, sniffing the cut.

"Don't let him lick," Frau Wölfin cautioned, turning to scoop him up again. "It would smart like old Hades. Sit here," she added, pointing to the chair. "Let me have another look."

Jason winced when she touched his leg. "Poultice," she said and disappeared into a dark corner. Now that he was accustomed to the dimness, Jason noticed two windows, one on either side of the room. Covering each was cloth, oiled so that light filtered through. He glanced up at the shelf. His bugle was still there, still brass.

Frau Wölfin returned with a bowl, and after adding water from a jug near the fire, mixed the contents with her hands. Charlotte stepped forward to look at Jason's leg. "Shouldn't we wash it first?" she asked. She pulled at Jason's torn stocking.

"Wash it?" Frau Wölfin looked surprised. "Water will open the wound, girl. Make it worse."

Charlotte stood her ground. "Soap and water will clean it," she said firmly. "Do you have soap?" Squid knelt down by the fire to watch, Herr Prinz soon purring beside him.

Frau Wölfin produced soap and a small bowl that she filled with water. Giving Charlotte a cloth, she watched askance as the wound was cleaned. Jason winced but kept still, knowing it was crucial. Cover a wound without cleaning it? No wonder medieval people died young.

Frau Wölfin packed the squishy poultice onto the wound,

binding it round Jason's leg with a long strip of cloth. Water dripped down into his shoe and he pushed his leg toward the fire. "It will stick as soon as it dries," she explained.

"Thanks," Jason said. "It feels better already."

Frau Wölfin didn't answer and, with Charlotte on the floor beside Squid, they watched her stir the big pot, good smells rising up with the steam. She placed bowls on the floor beside the fire and pulled a loaf of bread from a shelf above.

Herr Prinz ran to her, alternately mewing and purring, shadowing her every move.

"You want a morsel," she intoned. "A wee bit of meat, is it?" She took one of the bowls on the floor and scooped into the pot with a large ladle, finally producing the required morsel. "It'll be too hot for you, you silly cat face," she said, putting the bowl on the mantle above the fire. "You'll have to wait." The cat mewed pitifully, then sat licking his paw as if not the least interested.

A few moments later, Frau Wölfin put Herr Prinz's bowl in the middle of the rough table and waved the others to sit. Herr Prinz leapt up, his long fluffy tail almost in Jason's bowl.

After drinking steadily for several minutes, Frau Wölfin put down her bowl. "You haven't travelled all this way for your health," she said, staring at the three of them.

Jason wasn't sure how to begin. "We have been guests at the castle..."

"Lord Friedrich's castle." Jason could tell she already knew. So why was she asking?

"Yes," Jason replied. "And we have been looking everywhere for the parchment..."

Frau Wölfin sat back in her chair and stared at him.

"Why do you feel it is your business to find the parchment?"

"Since we arrived here," Charlotte cut in, "many people, including you, have been more than kind to us. Bettina's family and Hildred..."

"You are?" Frau Wölfin stared at her.

"I am Charlotte, Jason's friend. We came here, all of us, not realizing there would be such turmoil. Such unfairness between town and castle."

Frau Wölfin shook her head and laughed, swirling her wild curls back and forth. "Life, my dear children, is turmoil and unfairness. You are too young to understand."

"Can I use my fingers to eat the rest of this?" Squid asked loudly. He belched and said, "Excuse me."

"We have not yet been introduced," Frau Wölfin said, staring at him. "You are?"

"My name is Octavius," Squid said solemnly, "because my daddy teaches history."

"Ah yes, history," Frau Wölfin mused, staring into space. "It is always easier to deal with the past, than talk of the present or think of the future."

"But we need the past," Jason said, "to help us solve the present and give hope for the future."

"Your words are older than your years," Frau Wölfin replied. "I know that you are impulsive and exceptionally brave."

"Lord Friedrich is in danger," Jason went on, "and we need to prove to Otto, for once and for all, that Friedrich's father Heinrich was first-born."

"And what makes you think I would know anything about that?" Frau Wölfin rose abruptly from the table, and scooping up Herr Prinz, sat beside the fire, her back to them.

"Now what?" Charlotte whispered.

"I'm not sure," Jason whispered back. He glanced up at the horn again, but it seemed to be gone. Feeling panicky, he jumped up and ran toward the shelf.

"What are you doing?" Frau Wölfin said sharply, turning to look.

"The horn," Jason said, taking a deep breath, "the horn has..."

Frau Wölfin rushed past him, dumping a surprised Herr Prinz onto the floor. She squinted at the shelf and then reached up with her hand.

"Aha!" she said, turning the animal horn over in her hand. "I wasn't mistaken, after all." She carefully handed the horn back to Jason and backed up a few steps to watch.

"It's going to..." Squid began.

"Shh, Octavius." Charlotte frowned at her brother and closed his mouth.

Jason felt the now familiar tingling and watched Frau Wölfin as the horn slowly transformed to its former golden self.

For the first time, the old woman grinned, exposing several missing teeth. "I'll bet this flummoxed that old swine Otto," she cackled, scooping up Herr Prinz. "I'll bet this set him back on his heels."

"He wasn't too happy," Jason said, grinning in spite of himself.

"It's no wonder," Frau Wölfin went on, sitting down by the fire again, "that he's put a price on your head."

"He has?" No wonder Friedrich didn't want him to leave the castle.

"So you want to find the parchment?" she said, her back to them again.

They listened to the crackling fire and to Herr Prinz's unbelievably loud purr. After what seemed like forever, Frau Wölfin's singsongy voice began,

Pussy cat, pussy cat where have you been
I've been to Coburg and much I have seen
The mayor he is wicked and wants to be lord
The Lord will survive if he lives by his sword.

"But he wouldn't have to," Jason said, jumping to run and sit in front of her. "If we found the parchment, it would be proof. Heinrich was first-born. You were there. You helped your mother deliver the twins."

Frau Wölfin gasped and Herr Prinz leapt to the floor. A growling and scuttling started up under the floorboards.

"Quiet, you furballs," Frau Wölfin called sharply. The noise ceased. She stood and walked slowly to one side of the room, muttering to herself, and then back, stopping in front of Jason, still cross-legged in front of the fire.

"I'll say it once and I'll not repeat, so listen well." She turned and stared into the fire again.

Jason crept to his feet and hurried to stand beside Charlotte. He looked at her and she nodded. Even Squid was giving it his full attention.

Frau Wölfin put another log on the fire, jabbing at it with a branch until the bark caught. Jason watched her body tense, her hands rise slightly, then fall to her sides.

Her voice, when it began, chanted the words slowly and deliberately.

In the castle in a vessel
Find where life and death both nestle
Seven steps times seven follow
Seven places round and hollow
Underneath, an urn holds fast
The heir's true bloodline from the past.

"You must go now," she whispered, without turning around. "And you must tell no one that I am here."

Jason beckoned the other two and they walked quietly to the door. He turned, wanting to say thank you, but somehow the silence held him back. Frau Wölfin stood statue-like, silhouetted against the fire, Herr Prinz's two great eyes staring at them from high on a shelf.

CHAPTER TWENTY-FOUR

JASON PULLED THE COTTAGE DOOR SHUT AND THEY STARED into the early afternoon sun.

"We didn't ask her about a different way out of the forest," Charlotte said.

"And what about those pigs?" Squid added. "What if they come after us again?"

"I don't know," Jason said, "but if we want to make it back in time, we'd better get going." He turned and walked deliberately away from Frau Wölfin and the cottage, trying not to think. Wild boars, Otto's men. Who knew what else lay in wait?

They walked in silence, back along the path and onto the first section of logs. What choice did they have? None, as far as he could see. The important thing was – did he remember the riddle? *In the castle, in a vessel, find where life and death both nestle...* which didn't make a lot of sense. Then something about steps and holes somewhere and an urn... "What's an urn?" he asked Charlotte.

"A container," Charlotte replied, "like a big vase." She was right behind him. "I was thinking about the riddle too." She took a deep breath. *Underneath, an urn holds fast, the heir's true bloodline from the past.*

"I can't remember the middle part," Jason said.

"Okay," Charlotte replied. "Let's start from the beginning. Together..."

In the castle, in a vessel
Find where life and death both nestle...

Squid piped up:

Seven steps times seven follow
Seven places round and hollow

"Way to go, Squid," Charlotte said. Three sets of voices carried on:

Underneath, an urn holds fast
The heir's true bloodline from the past.

"We breathe air," Squid said, looking puzzled, "but there's no blood in it. Is there Lottie?"

"It's a different heir," Charlotte said, trying not to giggle. "It's hard to explain. Jason, help me..."

A bark rang out. They were on one of the wooden sections in the swamp and they all froze. A dog shape hurtled past, then another and another.

"Hey now, you furballs," a familiar voice called out, "don't go racing off in all directions at once."

Jason turned to see Frau Wölfin striding toward them, her great walking stick thumping on the wooden logs. He wanted to run and hug her, to say thanks a hundred times. She stopped a few metres away and slung a bag she was carrying from one arm to the other.

"After you left," she said, coming closer, "I remembered Hildred needed more of these herbs." She strode past them, her cloak flying out behind. "Besides," she went on, "you could use company through *den mysteriösen Forst.*" Several more wolves circled round, then raced ahead into the trees.

"We're safe now, Jason," Squid said, catching hold of Jason's hand to keep up. "The big dogs will keep us safe."

Charlotte ran to catch up to her and Jason watched, hoping Charlotte was thanking Frau Wölfin. The next thing they had to worry about was safely meeting Hildred and Gunthar. Frau Wölfin slowed her pace slightly so that Jason and Squid could catch up.

"You're worried about Otto's men," Frau Wölfin said, when the two of them were close enough.

"Yes...I..." Again, he wondered if Frau Wölfin could read their minds.

"We'll cut through another way, then," Frau Wölfin suggested, "so we meet Hildred sooner."

A few minutes later, she turned abruptly and pushed through some bushes to a new path. Jason motioned for Charlotte to lift Squid up for a piggyback. Frau Wölfin picked up her pace again and they had to jog to catch up to her. Jason wondered how old she was. Her hair was grey, her skin weathered, and yet she had amazing energy. More than he did, he thought, scrambling to keep up. Charlotte was puffing too.

The path went down an incline, and at the bottom, turned sharply to the right. Jason looked up to see Gunthar's cart in a small clearing ahead, the ox standing, eyes closed, voices chattering close by.

"Hildred, you old sow's ear," Frau Wölfin called. "Come and welcome us."

Hildred and Gunthar appeared, both holding handfuls of shiny green leaves.

"Frau Wölfin," Hildred called. She thrust her leaves into Gunthar's hands and ran to embrace Frau Wölfin, the two women laughing and patting each other's backs.

Gunthar stowed the leaves inside the cart and returned to give Jason's arm a friendly cuff. Squid grabbed hold of Gunthar's leg and wouldn't let go.

When Hildred gave Charlotte a hug, Charlotte burst into tears. "We're so glad to see you," she faltered. "We..."

"The boars went after them," Frau Wölfin cut in. "Not far from the swamp."

"How awful," Hildred said, giving Charlotte another hug.

"And big dogs saved us," Squid announced, running back and forth between Gunthar and the cart. "Lots and lots of big dogs."

As they bumped along the rutted road back, Jason felt more and more apprehensive. If Otto's men attacked them here, what chance would they have? None of them had any weapons. If he stood up and played, would the bugle protect him? Was he, somehow, the shepherd knight?

"See?" Gunthar said, as they came to the main road. "The coast is clear. No one's going to bother us now."

"We'll do what we always do," Hildred said cheerfully. "Drive quietly into town. Hindel will take you part way up the tunnel and you'll be back in the castle before you know it." She handed them a basket with *Brot* and *Käse* and *Wasserale.* "Here," she said, "something for your hungry stomachs."

The two of them sat on the front of the wagon now, talking over their shoulders to the children in the back. Soon after eating, Squid was nearly asleep and Charlotte was softly playing her recorder.

But the tunnel is still blocked, Jason thought, unless Hindel has cleared it. And how could he? By himself. The riddle. I should concentrate on the riddle. He whispered it to himself, pleased that he could remember. When he came to "seven steps times seven follow," he stopped. The tower. He had counted forty-nine steps when he and Charlotte climbed the tower. The parchment, then, was hidden somewhere on the wall.

"Charlotte," he called softly.

"What is it?" she asked.

The wagon creaked over the brow of the hill, the ox straining and taking its time. A series of shouts echoed up toward them.

"The road is blocked," Gunthar called. "Just before the bridge. Soldiers."

"Why would they be doing that?" Hildred asked. "Should we turn back, Gunthar?"

"They've already seen us," Gunthar said, wearily, "and if it's more of Otto's hooligans and they want this cart or us, there's not much we can do."

"It's me they're probably waiting for," Jason muttered. This is what Lothar had been talking about. Troops to intercept him. He manoeuvred himself to the rear of the cart, ready to jump. "I'll slip off the back and hide somewhere."

"Wait," Gunthar said. "How do we know it's you they want?"

"It's me," Jason replied, thinking of Lothar standing in the clearing. "I know it." Just then, a smaller group of soldiers appeared from the woods at the bottom of the hill behind them.

"Hide?" Charlotte asked, staring at him. "Where would you go?"

"Nowhere," Jason replied, slumping back inside. "More soldiers are behind us." Lothar had to be in on this.

"Veste soldiers," Charlotte whispered, staring out the back of the wagon before kneeling beside Jason. "I can see the Coburg insignia."

"If Lothar's one of them," Jason muttered, "that won't mean much."

As the hoof beats grew louder, Gunthar steered them off the road. "We'll wait," he said tensely, as the wheels bumped over rougher ground. "There's sure to be trouble."

"Why are we stopping?" Squid asked, rubbing his eyes. "Can I get out?"

Charlotte grabbed him as he stood up. "Stay here," she

said, pulling him down beside her. "It's not safe."

As the soldiers galloped past, Hildred climbed in beside them. She shook dust from her cloak and smiled, giving Charlotte a hug. "Not to worry," she said, "those are Lord Friedrich's soldiers and they will take care of it." Jason noticed her face pale, though, her hand shaking slightly.

More shouting broke out at the bridge as soon as the Veste Coburg soldiers drew close. Jason had counted as they rode by and knew they were greatly outnumbered by the soldiers on the bridge. If reinforcement soldiers were coming from another castle, where were they? And where was Friedrich? Jason had to do something. Impulsively, he clambered to the front of the cart beside Gunthar.

They were too far away to hear what was being said, but the soldiers blocking the bridge shouted and gestured at the Veste soldiers. Jason put his hand on the bugle and felt its familiar electrical charge run up his arm to his shoulder. Swords were being drawn now as shouting continued. Without warning, one of the Veste horses whinnied loudly and reared, its rider falling to the ground.

Jason grabbed Gunthar's arm. "Hold the ox," he said, pulling the horn from under his tunic. "I'm climbing on his back." He scrambled along the cart's wooden shaft and jumped onto the creature. It snorted and pawed momentarily, but Gunthar managed to hold it steady.

Sword blades were flashing now, the sound of metal against metal echoing up the hill. Jason straddled the ox, clamping his legs around the creature's wide back. He lifted the bugle and notes soared into the air. He wasn't exactly the shepherd knight, sitting here on an ox still hitched to a cart, but it was the best he could do. It might help, somehow.

Moments later, Charlotte and Squid joined in from inside the wagon, and even though their sound was muted, it spurred Jason on, increasing his volume, his high notes trilling into the afternoon sun.

"More soldiers," Gunthar called suddenly. Out of the corner of his eye, Jason saw them on an adjacent hill, several dozen more with an unfamiliar flag flying overhead. Moments later, alongside, a Veste Coburg flag was visible. The reinforcements, Jason was sure. He hoped Friedrich would be there too.

When these soldiers charged down the hill, shouting and drawing swords, the Veste soldiers at the bridge shouted to them and cheered. The bridge defenders were thrown into confusion; several kept fighting while others turned abruptly and galloped off. Within a few minutes, all had spurred their horses to jump the stream and retreat.

A shout rose from the Veste soldiers: "Long Live Friedrich." A few followed the retreating soldiers a short distance then turned back, cheering.

Gunthar called, "Hang on, Jason. We're on our way down." The wheels bumped over rough ground again and back onto the road. Jason clung to the ox's yoke. It was considerably more awkward than sitting on a horse.

Ahead, at the bottom of the hill, two soldiers lay crumpled on the ground, several others bending over them. A few were leading their horses to the stream, while two others held a horse that whinnied and tossed its head. It's been wounded,

Jason thought. He could see blood on its shoulder.

Gunthar pulled the wagon to a stop just as Friedrich arrived in their midst. Gunthar removed his cap and bowed from his seated position. Jason slipped from the ox and did likewise.

"And so, Jason, it appears you have been off on an adventure of your own."

Jason clutched the bugle and straightened slowly. Would Friedrich be angry? How much did he know already? What should he tell him?

"I...I was getting information about the parchment, sir."

"From these good people?" Friedrich looked mildly puzzled.

"No, sir...from...from..." Frau Wölfin had warned him to tell no one.

"From the wolf woman?"

Jason nodded, feeling he had no choice.

"You went into *den mysteriösen Forst?*"

"Yes, sir."

"Alone?"

"With my friends, sir."

"My Lord," a voice broke in, "two knights have been wounded. They need transport."

"At your service, my Lord." Gunthar jumped to the ground. "Hildred," he called. "Men are wounded."

"And a horse, my Lord."

"Can it be saved?"

"I think so, my Lord."

Hildred appeared, carrying a basket and water flask.

"Tend to the men first," Friedrich said as she hurried by.

Jason looked back to see Charlotte and Squid standing uncertainly beside the wagon. He hurried over to them, glad Friedrich had been distracted. There would be more questions, but not now, not in the midst of this chaos. And Lothar? He was no where to be seen. Could Jason have been wrong? Could their being caught here be merely a coincidence?

Gunthar disappeared inside the wagon, making room, Jason assumed, for the two wounded men. Hildred was kneeling down beside one man, his groans audible even over voices and horse whinnies.

"Lord Friedrich says we are to take you to the castle." Jason looked up to see Lothar staring at him. Where had he come from? It was then Jason realized how many soldiers had surged down the hill. They were surrounded by soldiers now, many of the soldiers dismounting and talking to one another. No wonder the others fled.

Jason nodded to Lothar and watched as another soldier hoisted first Squid and then Charlotte onto waiting horses. Lothar pointed Jason to a horse beside his. A tired-looking soldier stood holding the reigns, steadying the horse.

Jason took a deep breath and thought about movies he had seen. Westerns. The hero always thrust his foot into the stirrup, patting the creature reassuringly with one hand and taking the reigns with the other. Then, effortlessly, he swung his other leg up and over. Jason mounted, heart pounding, and it worked.

Lothar nodded, taking the lead. As they trotted across the

bridge and broke into a gallop, Jason leaned forward, his legs gripping the horse's sides. It was certainly easier than riding the ox.

The ride back was fast and direct. Three additional riders galloped with them, and as the castle came into sight, Jason felt an overwhelming sense of relief. He looked over to Lothar who nodded and smiled briefly.

Jason realized he had to have been wrong about Lothar. Then it dawned on him. The man who met Lothar in the cottage must have been a spy coming to warn Lothar that Otto's men were waiting to capture Friedrich on his way home. The small group of Veste soldiers who approached the bridge was simply a decoy. The others must have already been there, waiting to come over the hill. Cool strategy, Jason thought. He looked over at Lothar again. The man looked tired, actually, like someone who had been up all night. If he had ridden to the other castle and back, he probably had.

The outside castle doors swung open without announcement, four men inside waiting to push the great beam back into its locking position. It was nearly dark and only a few torches lit the tunnel passageway. As soon as they entered the main courtyard, the horses were reined in and each child was rapidly lowered to the ground.

When the men turned to lead their horses to the stable, Jason stepped forward. "Thank you," he called to Lothar. "Thanks for escorting us."

Lothar looked over his shoulder. "If you chose to stay," he called, continuing to walk, "you would make a good knight."

They slipped inside the Great Hall. It was dark except for a faint light near the stairs. "Did you hear that, Jason?" Squid whispered, as they hurried up the stone steps. "You'd make a good knight."

Charlotte said nothing and Jason assumed it was because she was tired out. It had been a long day. As soon as she settled Squid in his bed, Charlotte returned to sit on a stool. Jason was in front of the fire, checking his bandage. Amazingly, it had stayed intact for the whole journey. "Did Frau Wölfin say how long I should leave this thing on?" he asked Charlotte. When she didn't answer, he turned to see what was wrong.

"The horse," she said in a whisper. "Was it going to die?"

"No," Jason said, coming to sit on the other stool. "It was going to be all right."

"And the soldiers?" She was crying now.

"I...I don't know. Hildred was doing what she could."

Charlotte nodded. "After we find this parchment," she said, sniffing and clearing her throat, "I want to go home."

"We will," Jason replied. "Even Frau Wölfin said so."

"Do you think she was making that up? Seeing all that stuff in the cat's eyes?"

"It was like she went into a trance or something," Jason said. "And she was right on about your house, even the toad."

"Chaucer," Charlotte replied, smiling a little. "Do you think Frau Wölfin will watch us after we're home again?"

"I doubt it," Jason said. "And hey, I thought I was the one with an imagination."

"It must be rubbing off on me." Charlotte took a deep

breath. "We'd better go over that riddle, don't you think?"

Before they had time to begin, there was a knock on the door.

"Who is it?" Jason called out.

"Bettina."

Charlotte ran to the door. "I was so worried," Bettina said, throwing her arms around Charlotte. "I heard about the skirmish, and I knew you'd end up right in the middle of it."

"Frau Wölfin was amazing," Jason said, as Bettina joined them.

"Did she tell you where the parchment was?" Bettina asked.

"She gave us a riddle," Charlotte said.

"A riddle," Bettina replied. "What good is a silly riddle?"

"We think we can figure it out," Jason added.

"Well, you don't have much time," Bettina said, clasping her hands together, "because there are reports of Otto's troops getting ready to attack. Probably by dawn."

"Troops?" Jason snorted. "What troops?"

"He's hired three or four mercenary bands and they're getting organized down in front of the town wall," Bettina went on. "They've even got a siege engine."

"What's a siege engine?" Squid asked sleepily. He was standing in the doorway, his eyes still half-closed. Charlotte jumped up to get him.

"It's like a giant slingshot," Jason explained, remembering from a computer game.

"And they pick the boulders up," Charlotte continued, scooping Squid into her arms, "and toss them back...into...bed." She disappeared with him into the other room.

"No, Lottie..." He was protesting, but not too much. "Shh..."

Bettina looked at Jason. "The men Otto has hired are ruthless," she whispered. "If they get inside the castle..."

Charlotte reappeared. "We'll have to be more quiet," she said, sitting.

"Friedrich has an army out there," Jason whispered. "From another castle."

Bettina didn't look convinced.

"We saw them," Charlotte said. "They chased off Otto's men at the bridge."

Bettina nodded. "I'd best be going," she said, "back to my charges. I hope we can talk in the morning."

"She's not too optimistic, is she?" Jason said, after she left.

"She frightens easily," Charlotte replied. "Ever since Hubie..."

"Shouldn't we get back at the riddle?" Jason didn't want to talk about Hubie. They had a job to do and they needed to get at it.

CHAPTER TWENTY-FIVE

J ASON HALF-WAKENED. WAS SOMEONE KNOCKING? HE WAS sure he had only just fallen asleep. He rolled over and watched the fire embers glowing faintly. The knock came again and Jason slipped out of bed, pulling on his tunic. A sleepy-looking Stefan stood at the door, holding a candle. "Lord Friedrich requests your presence," he whispered.

As Jason followed him down the hall, trying to collect his thoughts, the chapel bell chimed three. Three in the morning? No wonder he felt tired. Why did Friedrich want to see him now? He had already said too much. And how would he explain the riddle?

Lord Friedrich's uniform was dust-covered, his face drawn. The man had not been to bed, Jason was sure. Papers lay strewn over his table, the room well lit with extra lanterns. Friedrich did not offer him a seat.

"First of all, the horn was of great help," Friedrich said. "I commend you for your bravery."

"I wanted to get closer," Jason began, "but..."

"That would not have been a good idea." He shuffled his papers briefly. "You said you were in the *dem mysteriösen Forst*. Is that correct?"

Jason inhaled sharply. No beating around the bush, Jason thought. Wham. Right to the point. "Yes...yes, sir. We were."

"And the wolf woman?"

"She saved us from wild boars," Jason blurted out. "She was good to us..."

"I have no quarrel with her," Friedrich said with a wave of his hand. "My uncle Otto," he pounded his fist on the table, "is another matter, entirely another matter."

"Frau Wölfin...the wolf woman," Jason began slowly, "gave us a riddle to find the parchment."

"A riddle?" Friedrich looked almost amused. "She said there was a parchment?"

"I explained to her," Jason said, coming closer, "that Otto was demanding your place. I said she was there when you were born and she must know."

"And so she gave you a riddle," Friedrich said. "How like her."

"It was as if she wouldn't or couldn't tell us directly."

"Otto would like to see her dead."

Friedrich rose and moved to the window. "We are preparing to be attacked," he said, after a few moments silence. "For these last weeks," he began, beginning to pace, "I have been more than patient. First, there are reports of increased robberies on the roads. I have sent extra troops to patrol. The next thing I know, Otto demands a meeting in the town and when I send Chancellor Reinhard, Otto is angry and will not see the man.

Demands that I appear." Friedrich stopped pacing momentarily, and stared out the darkened window.

"That seems unfair," Jason began, feeling he must comment on the first statement before the second, while wondering if he was being asked for advice.

"Unfair," Friedrich spat out. "It is unheard of, ridiculous. And that nonsense at the bridge yesterday? That was the last straw."

Friedrich sat abruptly and gave the table a pound. "I have officially informed that uncle of mine that if he wants to attack, then to go ahead and attack. We are ready. He paused again, and stared directly at Jason. "From all reports, it appears he will attack at dawn."

Jason nodded and marvelled at the seemingly renewed energy of the man.

"The troops you saw at the bridge will be waiting in the woods, east and north of the castle. I have taken the liberty of telling their leader that a bugle call would signal their advance."

"I would be honoured do it, sir...your Lordship."

"Good. I'll send word when I need you. And Master Jason?"

"Yes, my Lord?"

"If anyone tries to stop you? Say you are sounding signal for Lord Friedrich."

"Yes, my Lord."

Jason closed the door and raced back along the hall. He and the bugle would sound the advance. Perfect. Then while the men were distracted, he would find the parchment. As long as he didn't worry about hitches, it was perfect.

A soldier passed him and then two more, all running. Jason hurried to find the door to their quarters open, Bettina and Charlotte waiting with a sleepy Squid inside.

"We have to move," Charlotte said. She handed Jason his shoes and another tunic and set of stockings.

"You going to fight too?" Squid asked, yawning and rubbing his eyes as Bettina's candle guided them along the passageway.

"Better than that," Jason said, striding ahead. The riddle, he was thinking. It's even more important now to figure out the riddle. He didn't notice Bettina enter an open doorway.

"In here," Charlotte said, grabbing Jason's shoulder as he was about to walk right by. "Where were you going?"

The room was small, with no window, the royal children asleep on a large bed in the corner. *In the castle in a vessel,* Jason said to himself, looking about, *find where life and death both nestle.* Where, up on the castle wall, would that be? Charlotte picked up Squid and bundled him in beside the others. The child snuggled down and fell back to sleep.

"Where is Lady Katherin?" Jason asked. It seemed odd to him that she was not with her children.

"She is at chapel," Bettina said, "praying for those going into battle." She sniffed several times as she lit the candle in her hand before blowing out the larger one hanging from the wall. She placed the holder on the table close to the door and sat on the bench beside it, her arms wrapped tightly around her waist. "They'll be bringing the wounded into the Great Hall," she said, staring at the floor. "Gunthar and Hildred are already there."

"I guess they couldn't go back to town," Jason replied. "Not now."

"If Hindel is killed," Bettina whispered, "I will give myself to the church." She hunched forward, her shoulders shaking.

Charlotte knelt beside her. "He won't get killed," Charlotte said, putting her arm around Bettina's shoulder.

"Hindel?" Jason asked. "Hindel is involved in this?"

Bettina looked up at him, her face drawn and wet with tears. "Anyone in town not for Otto," she managed to say, "is here to support Friedrich."

"How would they get here?" Jason asked.

"Through the tunnel."

"But it's blocked," Jason said.

"Was blocked," Bettina replied. "Hindel is with the troops already." She pulled a metal cross from inside her tunic. "He gave me this for safekeeping." She turned away from Charlotte.

Jason sat down cross-legged beside Charlotte. "Have you mentioned the riddle?" he asked quietly. Charlotte shook her head. "I've figured out part of it," Jason said. "Seven steps times seven..." He stared at Charlotte, feeling a bit smug.

"Go on."

"There are forty-nine steps up to the tower."

"There are?"

"When we climbed up there, remember, we counted."

"Now I do," Charlotte added. "Because the steps were so narrow, we had to walk sideways. Seven times seven."

"It's a start," Jason said, "and..." he took a deep breath,

"Friedrich has asked me to go up on the castle wall. I'm to signal troops with the bugle." He did a thumbs-up sign. "It's perfect."

"Lucky you," Charlotte said, looking a bit envious. "Maybe I could come with you again."

"This time, you'd have to ask Friedrich yourself."

"Well, that's as good as saying I can't come."

"Sorry. Anyway, what would we do about Squid?"

"I know," Charlotte said, "but it doesn't seem fair."

They all heard the thump, a heavy thud reverberating in the distance.

"It's started," Bettina whispered, staring at them. She grasped the cross and hung on to it.

"It must be dawn, then," Jason said. "Friedrich said it could start at dawn."

"What was that?" Charlotte asked.

"The siege engine," Bettina whispered, rocking back and forth again. "They'll be aiming it at the front tower, trying to break through."

"The tower wall?" Jason thought about its height, its thickness.

Bettina nodded. "It's not as thick as the castle wall."

"It's still thick," Jason replied. "It won't work."

"I hope not," Bettina whispered.

Jason turned to Charlotte. "Find where life and death both nestle," he began. "I don't have a clue what that means."

"Life and death?" Bettina repeated, twisting the cross back and forth. "Hindel says old daggers and birds' nests. They're life and death."

"How do you know that?"Jason asked, jumping up. He remembered the twigs in the opening under the turret. Maybe there were more, further along.

"Early in the spring," Bettina said softly, "I took the children for walks along the wall." She caught her breath. "It was safe then."

"Yes," Jason said, gently, "you took the children for walks up on the wall." He needed to know more.

Bettina nodded. "And one day a few months ago, Hans pulled a baby bird out from one of those openings." She made a face. "All wriggling and ugly. I was in a dither, I can tell you."

"Exactly where did he find this bird?" Could Jason have found the same nest?

"There are seven towers around the castle," Bettina continued, in a flat voice, almost as if reciting lines. "And between each tower, a turret with an alcove beneath."

"Hans found the bird in one of these alcoves?"

Bettina nodded.

"So what did you do?" Charlotte asked.

"I put it back as carefully as I could, the mother bird screaming and swooping around us..." Bettina paused and shivered. "There was something sharp down there, too, an old dagger maybe. I almost cut my finger. What a stupid place to make a nest."

Bettina stared at the cross for a moment. "I told Hindel about it," she went on, "and he said, birds for life and daggers for death. It seemed so melancholy to me..."

"Thanks," Jason cut in excitedly. "Seven places round and hollow. The seven alcoves."

"Did Hans and Friede look in all of them?" Charlotte asked, staring at Bettina. "Because if they did..."

"No," Bettina said firmly. "I wouldn't take the children up there after that."

The thud repeated, louder this time and followed by shouts. Bettina turned back to the wall, grasping the cross with both hands. "There'll be sappers too," she said. "That's what Hindel's doing. Looking for sappers." She sobbed quietly, pressing the cross to her forehead.

"Sappers?" Charlotte asked.

"Men who dig in from underneath," she whispered. "And they'll find the tunnel, and then we're done."

"No, we're not," Jason said firmly. "The walls are too thick, and Friedrich has dozens of good knights and soldiers. Besides...I'm going to find the parchment."

"The parchment?" Bettina looked up at him, surprised in spite of her grief.

Jason knelt down beside her. "Frau Wölfin gave us a riddle," he began, "that tells where a parchment is that says who was first-born, Heinrich or Otto."

"And that will end all this nonsense," Charlotte said firmly. "For once and for all."

"Do you really think so?" Bettina asked, sitting a little straighter.

"We're sure," Charlotte said, clasping Bettina's hand. "And you just helped us solve the riddle."

"I did?"

"We couldn't make any sense of the life and death part," Jason said.

A knock on the door silenced them. Bettina jumped up and ran to the children. "It's okay," Jason said softly. "it'll be for me." He opened the door a crack.

"Master Jayson?"

"I'll be right there."

"Be careful," Charlotte cautioned.

CHAPTER TWENTY-SIX

J ASON CLOSED THE DOOR AND FOLLOWED THE BOY ALONG the passageway and down the stairs. He was younger than Stefan, not much taller than Squid.

The chapel bell struck seven as they entered the Great Hall. Wounded men lay moaning on straw mats with servant girls hurrying up and down carrying cloths and jugs. Jason couldn't pick out either Hildred or Gunthar, but he knew they must both be there. As he and the boy edged out the door, another knight was being carried in, blood streaming from his arm. How could all this happen in just two hours?

The boy grabbed Jason's hand and pulled him into the shadows. The din was terrific – metal clanging on metal, men shouting, skittish horses clattering out of the stable to be mounted. "Go up the back tower," the boy whispered. "The one nearest the tunnel entranceway. Sound the signal there and at the next tower farther east."

"Thanks," Jason said, but the boy was already gone.

Jason sprinted through the early morning to the tower. The courtyard was still damp and in shadow.

A soldier stepped out of the tower doorway. "Who goes there?" he snapped.

"Jason," Jason faltered and then he remembered. "I'm sounding signal for Lord Friedrich."

"Pass," the soldier replied, moving to let him through.

Little of the morning light filtered through the wall slits and Jason was grateful he had climbed these stairs before. Once at the top, he stared for a moment at the fields and forests beyond. Somewhere out there, reinforcement troops were waiting for his signal. Further along, inside the wall, soldiers stood in what had been their quarters, each guarding a window, bows ready to fire. A shiver ran down the back of his spine.

Above him, on top of the tower, a torch light still flickered, barely visible in the morning light. When he looked past the Great Hall building, he saw a faint flicker from the next tower. The castle wall was egg-shaped, with the largest tower at the front, three towers down each side, and the only entrance at the back. Otto didn't stand a chance. The fighting would be fiercest in front of the castle, a good reason for bringing reinforcements in from the back.

"I sound the bugle beside this tower," he said quietly, "and then again, at the one further east."

His heart pounded as he stepped up to the outside wall. What if another sniper was waiting? What if someone jumped him from behind? He lifted the horn and sounded the call. Tah-tah-tah, tah-tah-tah. Tah-tah-tah, tah-tah-tah, tah-tah-

tah. The sound echoed across the dark fields. Nothing moved. No footsteps.

One down, one to go, he whispered to himself.

He ran down the walkway, keeping as close to the inside wall as possible, hoping he was not visible from the ground. Every moment he expected to hear an arrow, a shout, a footfall other than his own.

He stopped at the turret he and Charlotte had checked, making a quick search, just in case. Still nothing but a few twigs. By the time he reached the second tower, he was so out of breath, he had to wait a moment before he could play. He repeated the exercise and waited. This side of the castle was quieter with only occasional shouts and hoof beats from below.

Jason squinted toward the morning sun, wondering if he would catch a glimpse of movement from the hills. He wondered if all would advance at once or if they would be divided up. He knew so little about military tactics, in spite of having played so many computer games. Then, when he shaded his eyes, he saw them, row after row, swords gleaming in the light, horses galloping down the sides of a distant hill. There must be several hundred, he thought, more than he remembered at the bridge.

As Jason sprinted toward the next tower, his confidence welled up. It would be a snap now. All he had to do was find...

"Who goes there?" Two guards blocked his way.

"I'm sounding signal for Lord Friedrich."

"But the signal has been sounded," one of them said. Jason felt an arm on his shoulder.

"Only twice," Jason heard himself say. "And Lord Friedrich wants it sounded once more. At the front of the castle."

The guard let go. "Are you sure?"

"I am Jason," Jason said, slowly backing up, "guest of Lord Friedrich." Sunlight suddenly flooded the walkway, highlighting Jason's blonde hair.

"Holy Mary," one guard said, staring at him.

Jason held up the bugle. "One more signal," he repeated.

"The shepherd knight?" the other faltered.

"At your service," Jason replied, and broke into a run, stopping only when he reached the next turret, trying to catch his breath as he bent down to search.

His fingers touched something. His heart pounded. He grabbed at it and pulled out a larger handful of twigs and grass. The remains of another nest, he thought. He reached in again, feeling every rough edge. There was nothing else.

Life and death, he whispered. There has to be both. He wondered if this was the opening where Hans pulled out the baby bird. Not unless someone had removed the old dagger. He threw the nest to the ground and hurried on.

When he reached the next tower, the battle noise, a dull clamour further back, was now almost deafening. The battle action was definitely concentrated at the front of the castle. A row of helmets bobbed in the distance, bowstrings twanging over and over, men jostling each other for position. Everyone was shouting – commands, questions, comments. Outside, a roar built up each time the siege engine was launched.

If soldiers were positioned around the next turret, there was no way he could get at it. Somehow, this realization made him all the more determined. He had to search the next turret. He just had to. Sweat trickled down the side of his face as he moved closer, and when he realized they were lined up past the next tower, not before it, relief flooded through him. As long as he was quiet and proceeded slowly, he should pass unnoticed.

As he knelt down in front of the turret, an arrow whizzed above him, clattering to the floor a short distance away. He froze in a crouching position, expecting the worst. When he heard no footsteps, no shout, he reached for the opening, still checking in both directions. His hand hit the wall. He looked up. The turret was directly above. Where was the opening? He ran his hand down the wall and felt a large rock sticking out from the rest. Running his hand around its edge, he realized someone had sealed this hole. Move, he thought, pulling on the rock. Maybe this was it.

As he struggled, the rock slipped enough to reveal a small opening, then refused to budge further.

"Hey, you there," a voice barked, "what are you up to?"

Jason turned to see a burly soldier, a quiver slung over his shoulder, an arrow in hand.

"I'm Jason...sounding signal for Friedrich."

"Aye, and you've done two and you're slated for one more."

Jason took a deep breath. News travelled fast. "I've dropped my pouch down here," he said, pointing to the small hole. "And I can't seem to get it out." If this hole was empty like the others, he was in big trouble.

"We're sealing up these holes," the guard said, picking up

the stray arrow. "Pesky birds won't stop making nests in them."

"My bugle music is in the pouch," Jason blurted out. "And a spare mouthpiece." Far-fetched, but he hoped the guard would go along with it.

The man wiped his sweat-stained brow and stared at him, as if trying to understand this strange request. "Don't know why this one would be part-way open," he went on. He gave the stone a couple of fast kicks and it rolled out, barely missing Jason's hand. Jason reached down into the hole, his heart pounding. Another nest. He pulled it out.

"You see?" the guard remarked. "That's why we're going to block the rest of them. Hurry it up, will you, I have to report in at the next bell."

Jason plunged his hand into the opening again. If this guard suspected he had lied, the man could as easily kick him as pull him to his feet. The tips of his fingers touched hard metal. A dagger? He didn't dare pull it out. The man was shuffling his feet, anxious to move on.

He reached to the very back, pressing hard with his fingers and thumb, the knot in his stomach growing. All at once, he felt a snap, as if part of the stone had caved in. He reached down to feel something soft, cloth-like. "I almost have it," he said, straining until his shoulder ground into the stone edge.

"Well, hurry it up, will you, lad," the guard said. "The main action's up ahead, and I don't want to miss it."

The pouch was longer than Jason expected, and luckily for him, made of cloth. It definitely contained something light and papery. Jason inhaled sharply and jumped to his feet. "Thanks," he said, trying to look nonchalant. His hand shook as he tied the pouch to his belt, hoping the guard would leave.

"I'd better escort you," the man replied, watching him. "Make sure you get safely to that front tower."

Having no other choice, Jason nodded and followed. The noise was deafening: men shouting, bows banging against stone, pages running back and forth refilling quivers. At both front turrets, Jason saw men passing buckets in and out, the smell of hot tar rank in the air. They were pouring hot tar down the castle wall. Jason shivered.

The attack on the castle was in high gear now. It was impossible to tell how anything was going, whether Friedrich was winning or not. A knot twisted in the pit of Jason's stomach. This was the real thing, and it was terrifying and exciting at the same time.

When they reached the central tower, Jason's guide tapped a knight on the arm. It was Lothar. He slapped Jason's shoulder. "Well done!" he boomed. "Our soldiers are advancing round the castle from both sides. If they can get the siege engine down, it should be over by midday."

The clamour on the ground increased, followed by a thud that shook the stones under Jason's feet. A cheer went up, outside. Moments later, a page came running from behind. "Crack in the front tower," he shouted and when no one answered him, he shouted again, "crack in the front tower." Someone whisked him aside then, asking more questions. Lothar barked out a series of commands.

Jason didn't wait to hear more. He pushed his way through

soldiers rushing forward and slipped into the tower stairway. He squinted until his eyes adjusted to the darker interior. It was identical to the one he had climbed on the other side of the wall. Further down, he saw men with wooden poles rushing up the stairs to reinforce the battered wall from the inside. There must be a way to the very top, he thought. Someone had to light the torches. He looked up and spotted a dangling rope and, several metres higher, an opening with sunlight pouring in.

Jason grabbed the rope and, with difficulty, shinnied himself up. Once inside the narrow opening, he pushed with his feet, grasping the rope hand over hand until he grabbed the edge and pulled himself over. For a few minutes, he lay, exhausted, listening to increasing roar from the outside, watching for any arrows that might fly over the top.

The sun was almost overhead now, its rays warm on his back and arms. The siege engine fired again, its impact reverberating up the tower like an earthquake tremor. Jason jumped to his feet and moved to the tower's edge, bugle in hand. He had to do something. Now.

He lifted his head and played toward the sun, its rays flying at him, reflecting off the bugle. He felt a surge of warmth, tremendous energy. This was it, the reason the bugle had brought him here. He felt suspended, almost floating, bugle notes flying out to stop the battle.

A roar rose from the ground, followed by a substantial crash. "Siege engine's down," someone shouted, beneath him. Fierce hand-to-hand fighting broke out around the fallen machine. More soldiers moved in. Soldiers on the wall

continued to fire. The battle noise grew louder as Jason kept playing, note after note soaring to the sun.

Finally someone shouted, "Long live Friedrich." Jason paused as more voices picked it up, chanting the words again and again. The battle was over. Below, the wooden siege machine lay broken with only a few soldiers still in hand-to-hand combat.

Further down the hillside, knights on horseback were shouting at men to drop their swords. Jason felt a pang of disappointment. He'd thought he might be in the thick of it, riding out like the shepherd knight, arrows and swords miraculously missing him. Maybe it wasn't that way for the shepherd knight. Maybe he was just lucky and smart. After all, in the end, he did get killed.

A cheer rose up, both on the wall directly below and on the ground. One or two arrows may have flown toward him and missed. He wasn't sure. It didn't matter. The battle was over and he held the parchment. Friedrich's future was secure.

CHAPTER TWENTY-SEVEN

J ASON STOOD IMPATIENTLY OUTSIDE LORD FRIEDRICH'S quarters, waiting. First the Lord had given a speech to the knights and soldiers who had come to help, and now he was talking to the wounded in the Great Hall below. Jason heard cheers and more cheers. The parchment seemed almost unnecessary now. Otto's men had retreated, the castle was safe.

Jason slumped to a sitting position, his hand on the cloth pouch. He had pulled it out and looked at it, enough to confirm that it was some kind of official document with a red wax seal, but the strangely formed letters were impossible to read.

His whole body ached, partly from staying up all night and partly from his harrowing climb to the tower top and back down. He wasn't sure why he had climbed up there. Had he accomplished anything playing the bugle into the morning sun? His eyes closed momentarily...

"Master Jayson?" Jason scrambled to his feet as a tired Lord Friedrich appeared at the top of the stairs. "Come in, come in."

The man sat heavily and bent down to pull off his boots. "You played magnificently," he said. "The last cowardly bunch retreated when they heard you."

"They did?" Jason was surprised. He didn't remember this. He barely remembered climbing back down out of the tower.

Jason pulled the parchment from its pouch and laid it on the table in front of Friedrich.

"What is this?" Friedrich said, looking it over.

"The parchment."

Friedrich held it to the light, reading first to himself and then aloud:

In the year of our Lord
one thousand four hundred and sixty-two,
born in the Veste Coburg and
attended to by Marta and her daughter Ursula
Twin sons
Heinrich the first-born and Otto the second.
Praise be to God and the esteemed Lord
of the Veste Coburg
AMEN

Friedrich said nothing for a few moments and when he looked up, Jason saw tears in his eyes. "Where did you find this?" he asked.

"Under one of the turrets on the east side," Jason said. "In one of those openings underneath."

"Where those pesky birds were making nests?"

Jason nodded. "This particular one was already sealed up,

but I managed to get the stone loose."

"And it was right there? In plain sight?"

"No, sir. I was pressing against the back wall of it and a piece broke away."

"A hidden compartment?"

"I guess you could call it that."

"All these years!" Friedrich exclaimed, putting the document down and then picking it up again. "And it was right here in the castle. What can I ever do to repay you?"

Jason was too tired to think. "I need some sleep," he said, "and then...maybe a celebration of some kind?"

"I will proclaim a Festival Day," Friedrich said, pounding the table with his fist. "We will have performers and speeches and fireworks." He stood up, pacing back and forth. Jason marvelled at the man's energy. Only a few minutes ago, he'd seemed exhausted, and now he was wired for sound, as his dad would say.

"However," Friedrich said, sitting again, "the first matter of business is a new mayor."

"But Otto..." Jason began.

"The old boar has already fled." Friedrich slapped his knees and laughed. "To a monastery, no less." He picked up the parchment. "And when he hears about this," he added, waving the document back and forth, "he'll be taking a vow of silence."

"What about Gunthar?" Jason asked, impulsively. "For mayor, I mean."

"Who?"

"Gunthar, the apothecary. He is a good man," Jason went on. "Honest, and he cares for the people."

"Gunthar the apothecary," Friedrich mused. "I have

known him since I was a child." Friedrich smiled. "I must say, I hadn't thought of him. There are several in my court, but then again..." He looked at Jason. "I must give this some thought," he said. "But thank you, Master Jayson, I value your opinion."

Jason nodded. He was sure he was falling asleep on his feet.

"You need sleep, my boy," Friedrich said, rising and steering Jason to the door. "Go. We will rouse you when the festivities begin."

Jason wandered back to his quarters in a daze. Inside the room, arrows lay scattered on the floor and window ledge. Someone had been lying on his bed. Jason fell onto it, too exhausted to care.

It seemed only a few minutes later that Liesa was calling him to get up. Jason heard the chapel bell strike three. "Charlotte and Octavius are already waiting by the carriage," she said, pouring fresh water into the washing bowl.

Jason splashed cold water on his face and tried to wake up. The Festival. Fireworks. Maybe Gunthar for mayor. His red velvet tunic and black stockings were waiting, and a hat, also black velvet, with a broad brim. He dressed quickly and picked up the bugle. It shone, but there were several dents in it. He didn't remember being hit when he was up on the tower. Could he have been? He rubbed the bugle with his sleeve and tied it to his belt.

JASON STOOD IN FRONT OF THE GREAT HALL watching the flurry in the courtyard. Everyone in the castle, it seemed, was going to the Festival. Two spectacular looking wagons Jason had never seen before stood nearby. Each was surrounded by servants, ox carts with wine kegs and cooking pots, and piles of baskets, some laden with food, some piled high with cloaks and other clothing. The wagons themselves had tapestry-covered canopies, each brocaded with the Veste Coburg insignia.

Everyone in the courtyard scurried back and forth, lifting items into the wagons, often arguing, returning some, adding others. The stable crew was out currying Friedrich's favourite horses, polishing saddles, equipping a cart with water and hay.

Jason spotted Charlotte and Squid in front of the chapel, again dressed in their court clothes. Squid was running back and forth with a barrel hoop, trying to keep it upright.

"How long is this Festival going to be?" Jason called as he hurried over.

"Only for the day," Charlotte answered, "but Bettina says it's always like this. Cool hat," she added. "Aren't you quite the dandy."

Jason wasn't sure if this was a compliment or not. Squid crashed into him, the hoop falling at their feet.

"Can you make this thing go? Can you, Jason?" he asked.

"Don't you get all dirty now," Charlotte warned. She pulled a fan from her sleeve and began fanning her face. "Hot out here," she said.

"Where'd you get that?" Jason asked, picking up the hoop. Squid ran around the two of them, banging the hoop stick on the ground.

"Lady Katherin gave it to me for helping Bettina," Charlotte replied.

"Is Hindel okay?" Jason had forgotten all about him.

"A few scratches and bruises, but he's fine."

"Are you going to play with me?" Squid asked, pulling on Jason's tunic.

"Not now," Charlotte said. "Besides, look. The wagons are ready."

Bettina rushed out through the Great Hall doors with Hans and Friede. She waved when she saw them and hurried the children toward the second wagon.

"The first wagon is for Lady Katherin," Charlotte whispered, taking Squid's hand as they walked. "She gave Bettina a new dress."

"Master Jayson?" Lothar galloped toward them, his horse snorting and pulling at the bit. He grinned. "Your horse is waiting."

"Lucky you," Charlotte said, lifting Squid into the wagon.

"Where's Squid's drum?" Jason asked. "And your flute?"

"Already in the wagon," Charlotte said, smiling. "See you when we get there."

A page held Jason's horse, and this time he felt more confident mounting the creature. He followed Lothar toward the tunnel entrance, passing the wagons and five or six carts laden and ready.

"Master Jayson," Friedrich said, as they rode up beside him, "You are more awake now, I see." Chancellor Reinhard nodded from his steed.

Jason grinned and looked behind. Several dozen knights in full dress guided their horses into position directly behind.

Wow, he thought, if his dad could see him now. A wave of homesickness hit him but disappeared immediately as a shouted order from behind signalled the procession to move forward.

As they trotted down the stone-arched tunnel into the sunlight, a second group of knights fell into place ahead of them. Sentries waved from the wall above as they proceeded around the stone wall to the front of the castle. Jason waved back and looked up to the high front tower. He could almost see himself up there playing.

Wagons and ox carts behind them creaked, the oxen clop-clopping a steady pace. Knights' horses snorted and pranced and peasants, already lined up, cheered as they passed. Jason's body moved with the gait of his horse, an almost dream-like movement, all of them winding down the hill toward Coburg.

As they approached, Jason marvelled at the stone wall surrounding the little town. Turrets with tiled roofs and look-outs not unlike those at the castle stood at regular intervals along the high stone barrier – sentry lookouts, a necessity in this basically lawless land.

He thought of Otto and smiled. He couldn't imagine the man in a monk's habit, spending the rest of his life in a cold stone church.

Inside the town wall, the late afternoon sun reflected off red-tiled roofs and an imposing church spire. Outside, more houses, many simple thatched dwellings, huddled together for safety. And if there was an attack? These people would be forced to leave everything they owned and flee inside the walls for protection. It seemed an uncertain way to live.

As they came closer, Jason saw groups of people already gathered with wagons and oxen, the air charged with dust and excitement. He faintly heard music and dogs barking, and in the middle of all of this, near the bottom of the hill, he glimpsed an empty wooden platform. Thankfully, someone had removed the gallows scaffold.

Moments later, they pulled their horses to a stop and Jason watched the girls and children tumble from the second wagon, chattering and munching on the kitchen's famous sweet iced buns. They were a distance from the assembling crowd, who had moved in to watch two young men wrestling on the platform.

As Jason dismounted, a line of foot soldiers marched in two wide arcs to surround the wagons. They may have won the skirmish, but Friedrich wasn't taking any chances. The Coburg Lord ran a tight ship, as Jason's dad would say.

Jason wondered what happened to those who didn't toe the line, those who didn't perform up to standard. Friedrich seemed just and fair, but he would still have to pass judgement. Find some guilty. What about the prisoners who were just captured? He glanced toward the wooden platform and shuddered. He probably didn't want to know.

Squid ran up to him. Jason's horse startled and a page was quick to catch the reins and calm it. "You a knight now?" Squid asked. "You going to slay a dragon?"

Charlotte was right behind with Bettina and the children. "No fair," Charlotte whispered, moving beside him. "Girls don't get to ride."

"You'll have to take riding lessons," he whispered back, "when we get home." Charlotte quickly squeezed his hand and let go. He was sure she felt the same way he did about leaving. "What was that other riddle?" he asked.

Charlotte closed her eyes. *"When the hillside fills with singing,"* she began, *"When the night sky seems like day..."*

"When the fog leaps from the fire," Squid piped up, his eyes wider than usual. "How can fog leap from fire, Jason?"

"That's the surprise," Jason said, putting his hand on the boy's shoulder. "That's going to be the big surprise."

Stools and benches appeared and Bettina sat with the children on one of them, playing a string game and singing to them. Lady Katherin sat under a canopy, sipping from a drinking goblet, in animated conversation with Chancellor Reinhard. Lord Friedrich was striding about, talking to knights and inspecting the building of their firepit.

Down the hillside in front of them, other groups of men were busy piling wood, digging similar pits, and lashing crossbeams onto tripod uprights to go over them. "They'll hang whole pig carcasses from those," Charlotte said. "It's to be a gala affair."

"Do you think we'll be asked to play?"

"I would imagine so," Charlotte replied, smiling. "You're the star here, you know."

"Do you mind?" he asked.

"It would have been amazing to be there when you found the parchment," she said.

"It was tense," Jason replied. "This burly guard standing over me, probably ready to kick me if I didn't find anything."

"But you did," Charlotte said, more quietly. "I was worried." She paused. "Bettina was freaking out about Hindel and then the children woke up and Friede started crying. It was a bit of a zoo."

"Sounds like I had the easier time of it."

Several young men approached carrying wide planks and a colourfully painted wooden chest. When they came to the ring of soldiers nearest to them, Jason watched as the men bargained and gestured, obviously wanting to enter the royal circle. One of the soldiers hurried over to Lord Friedrich and, after bowing low, whispered in his ear.

"*Ja, ja,*" Friedrich exclaimed. He was in a jovial mood, the stress of the past few days finally resolved.

The men announced themselves as the *Sommerzeit* Players and had, among other talents, a Punch and Judy Show to charm Lord Friedrich's children.

"Summertime Players," Jason whispered to Charlotte. "Guess they're glad the fighting is over." Charlotte nodded and followed Bettina, who sat to watch with the children on the trodden-down grass. Jason stood behind them, getting a view not only of this performance but also of the general activity farther down the hill.

Once the stage was assembled, the puppeteers disappeared behind a curtain, two other actors in Jester costumes, in front, telling the tale as it was performed. Hans and Friede, who obviously knew the story already, squealed and clapped as soon as it started. Lady Katherin and her ladies, as well as a number of the sundry servants, gathered around to watch the puppets' antics.

Before the puppet show was over, a large group of Mummers climbed noisily onto the main platform further down the hill and began a boisterous song and mime performance, acting out their songs as they sang. They divided into four groups, each group taking one side of the stage so that they were playing all four sides of the platform at the same time. The Mummers' masks were similar to the ones they had worn and Jason recognized a donkey, several birds, a goat, and an ox. The crowd roared and clapped; it was like a rock concert. No matter what, Jason said to himself, he was not going to perform on *that* stage.

The afternoon passed quickly with acrobats and jesters, even a fire-eater, who absolutely mesmerized Squid. Soon the smell of roasting pork drifted up and down the hillside. Minstrels wandered from group to group, singing songs of fearless knights and beautiful ladies. *Wasserale* and wine flowed in abundance and everyone was growing mellow.

Jason stood apart from the others, reciting the riddle to himself again. "*When the fog leaps from the fire...*" What could that possibly mean? When someone tapped him on the shoulder, he turned to find Petra and Wolfgang smiling at him. Elsa and Karl were close behind. "This is great," Jason said, reaching out to shake Wolfgang's hand. Petra embraced him and then pulled back, smiling.

"Does Bettina know you're here?" Jason asked. He looked for her and for Charlotte, but neither were in sight.

"We have talked to her," Wolfgang replied smiling. "She is happy."

"We wanted to wish you well," Petra said softly.

"You'll be going home?" Wolfgang added.

"Yes...after the feast, I think." Jason didn't know what else to say.

"Master Jayson?"

Jason looked up to see Chancellor Reinhard striding toward him.

"Auf Wiedersehen," Wolfgang said, turning to leave.

"Godspeed," Petra added. The four of them waved and disappeared into the crowd.

"When will you and your friends honour us with a concert?" Reinhard asked. "Everyone is asking."

Jason took a moment to answer. He wished Wolfgang had waited. He wanted to tell them...

"Master Jayson?"

"A concert," Jason repeated, focussing on Reinhard again. "Would it be appropriate after we eat?"

"I'm sure his Lordship would agree to that," Reinhard replied. He smiled and turned to leave.

"And Chancellor," Jason added quickly, "instead of being on that stage at the bottom of the hill, could we play up here?"

Chancellor Reinhard looked down to the stage and back to Jason. "Do I understand," he asked, "that you might feel uncomfortable down there?"

Jason nodded.

"I'll speak to his Lordship." Reinhard strode off, leaving Jason feeling unsure. Was it an unreasonable request?

A few minutes later, Friedrich appeared. "I think it best if you begin playing up here," he announced, as if he had come up with the idea. "We will assemble a small platform. Yes, play up here, and then, if you wouldn't mind, wind your way down the hill. My people are so anxious to hear you and I feel it is safe now." He laughed and slapped Jason the back. "Besides, you don't have to worry, with that horn of yours."

Friedrich strode off, shouting orders as he went, planks and tools appearing while Jason watched.

"Are you all right?" Charlotte asked. He hadn't noticed her arrive.

"Friedrich wants us to perform here," he said slowly, "and then weave our way down the hill, still playing."

"Are you all right with that?"

"I...I don't know."

"When?" Charlotte asked.

"I suggested after we eat." Jason scanned the hillside. There were so many people, hundreds, he was sure.

"At least everyone will be relaxed by then," Charlotte said.

Reinhard returned, smiling as he came. "Lord Friedrich suggests that we announce you right before the fireworks," he said. "Come. Look at this platform."

Jason and Charlotte followed him to the newly-con-structed platform and listened while Friedrich insisted it be levelled one more time. Situated directly in front of the royal canopy, the platform afforded a clear view down the hillside where roasted pigs were browning over the glowing firepits. Jason stepped onto its floor and looked out over the crowds.

The chancellor tapped Jason's shoulder and nodded for him and Charlotte to sit under the canopy, where a long table had miraculously appeared, complete with a white cloth and silver serving plates. The sun was low in the sky now and torches were being lit up and down the hillside. Jason knew from experience that the sun set quickly – faint light one minute, and darkness the next.

Even though the food was delicious, Jason found it difficult to eat. It was as if he was waiting for something to happen, only he had no idea what, or even if it would.

Frau Wölfin said they would go home, he thought, forcing himself to chew another mouthful. She looked into her cat's eye and said we would go home. *When fog comes out of the fire.* It seemed impossible.

He looked over at Charlotte. She was chatting to Sir Lothar and Chancellor Reinhard, laughing and being witty. She looked amazing, older than she was. Bettina, too, at the other end of the table with the children, her dress making her look more like a Lady than a servant girl.

After a mountain of sweet buns and tarts had been passed up and down the table twice, Friedrich and Reinhard rose and strode to the platform. "Good friends and noble knights," Reinhard boomed. "We have tasted sweet food after sweet victory." Everyone cheered and fists thumped on the table.

"Lord Friedrich has an announcement of great importance to make," Reinhard shouted. Voices at the various firepits quieted; faces turned up toward the two men standing on the platform. Jason noticed four soldiers escorting someone up the hill – two, no three people. The fading light made it difficult to see.

"We need a fanfare," Friedrich called suddenly. "Master Jayson, will you oblige?"

Jason jumped to his feet and ran toward the platform. A fanfare? Why hadn't Friedrich mentioned this? His hand shook as he stepped onto the stage. He looked up to see Gunthar, looking somewhat out of place and a little dazed. Hildred and Hindel were standing off the stage, Hildred nervously smoothing down her skirt. Gunthar moved from one foot to the other, adjusting the sleeves of a long brown velvet robe.

Jason grinned and lifted the horn, sounding the notes he had used on the castle wall. A cheer went up from the crowd below.

"I am pleased to announce," Friedrich shouted, "that from this day forth, Gunthar will be known to the citizens of Coburg as...Bürgermeister Gunthar." Chancellor Reinhard stepped forward and placed an elaborate gold chain clanking with keys over Gunthar's head. "The keys to the town of Coburg," he called. Jason remembered that chain, clanking on the table in front of him. The keys belonged to Gunthar now, and he would use them wisely. Two soldiers hoisted Gunthar onto their shoulders and Friedrich shouted again, "Welcome Bürgermeister Gunthar."

Cheering rose again from the hillside. Gunthar waved and looked pleased if not a little amazed. All this had happened so quickly, Jason thought. The man would have had no time to get used to it. A bench appeared on stage and Friedrich led Gunthar to sit on it beside the chancellor.

"I have one more announcement," Friedrich shouted, nodding to Jason. "Before the fireworks, Master Jayson and his friends have kindly offered to play for you."

A cheer went up and someone started chanting. "Jayson, Jayson," and it spread down the hillside, voices calling, interspersed by hoots and whistles.

"Wait," Friedrich said. "They will silence. Give them a moment or two." He was right. By the time, Charlotte and Squid joined him on the platform, a hush had fallen, so that only the crackling fire embers and the odd whistle could be heard.

"Here we go," Jason said, his heart pounding. They played "The Bugle Call" through twice, the second time marching around the platform, Squid in his glory pounding for all he was worth, Jason bringing up the rear. He closed his eyes and played as he had never played before, the notes pouring from somewhere inside himself that he hadn't realized existed. When they stopped, an even louder cheer rose up from the hillside. People pounded on barrels and clapped and whistled. Jason and Charlotte and Squid bowed again and again.

"They're not going to stop," Charlotte called over the noise, "until we play more."

"What can we play?" Jason called back.

Charlotte put the recorder to her lips and played the first line of *"Die Gedanken sind frei."* The crowd hushed, straining to hear.

"But I don't know it," Jason whispered. "I've never played it, not the tune."

"You can do it," Charlotte replied. "Think the tune inside your head and it will come out. Trust me." She moved slightly forward. "I'll begin," she said, softly. "Think shepherd knight. Think home."

Charlotte played again, her clear notes filtering down the hillside. Jason joined in on the second line, hesitantly at first, feeling for the notes. They were there. He was playing it. Squid marched to the edge of the platform and jumped off, rat-a-tat-tatting as he went. Charlotte followed and then Jason, the notes taking over, the bugle almost playing by itself. They marched past the firepit and down onto the hillside.

The second time through, several voices sang out: *"Die Gedanken sind frei,* my thoughts freely flower..." More voices joined in. *"Die Gedanken sind frei,* my thoughts give me power..." By the time they were halfway down the hill, everyone was singing, "no scholar can map them, no hunter can trap them. No man can deny, *die Gedanken sind frei."*

The sun dropped below the horizon and, without warning, fireworks burst from the castle wall, cascading down toward the hillside. The sky lit up and, simultaneously, fires were doused, causing clouds of steam to pour from the firepits.

Jason and Charlotte and Squid marched through the steam. It was as thick as fog. Figures close to them appeared and disappeared. *When fog leaps from the fire,* Jason thought. This is it. The singing slowly subsided as everyone turned toward the castle, watching burst after burst of fireworks explode into the night air.

Billows of steam pouring down the hillside pushed into cool stream water, sending a fog rolling back up the hill. Jason turned into this fog, playing *"Die Gedanken,"* then "The Bugle Call," then a combination of both. He had no time to think, only to play notes and march on, one foot after the other, a ring of water droplets slowly forming on the rim of his bugle.

A moment later, the fog rolled back and he thought he glimpsed a sign of some kind, but it slipped in and out of sight so quickly he couldn't be sure. When a car horn sounded, Jason slammed into Squid, sending him flying onto the dirt path.

"A car," Squid exclaimed, and they watched the red tail lights dissolve into the fog.

"Sorry, little guy," Jason said, pulling Squid up and dusting off his jeans. Jason glanced at his own legs. His jeans, his sneakers. Everything in place.

Charlotte was just behind them, staring at her shiny silver flute, tears running down her cheeks.

"We're home," Squid said. "We're home, Lottie."

"What day is it?" she asked. "What time is it?"

Jason automatically looked for his watch. And it was there, on his wrist. "It's...it's 4:30 by my watch." He felt dizzy, displaced, as if he'd fallen out of something and landed on the path.

"If it's the same day," Charlotte whispered, "we've only been gone thirty-five minutes."

"Can we go back to Gran's now?" Squid asked, pulling on Charlotte's arm. "I'm thirsty."

"It's still foggy," Jason said, looking about.

As they stood there, the fog melted back, late afternoon sunlight filling in the empty spaces. On the black, ploughed field south of them, long fingers of fog drifted like tattered curtains just above the soil, moving back and back as if the lake was pulling them into its waters.

Jason shook the droplets of water from his horn. It was dull again, dull and dented. An old WWI bugle. He looked up to see Charlotte fingering the valves on her flute; Squid was staring at the yellow cord on his tin drum.

"I guess we did it," Jason said, breaking into a grin. "Do you think anyone will believe us?"

"Die Gedanken sind frei," Charlotte replied. "My thoughts freely flower," she sang. Then Jason joined in, "My thoughts give me power, no scholar can map them, no hunter can trap them, no man can deny..." And with Squid, *"Die Gedanken sind frei."*

"We haven't forgotten," Charlotte said, laughing.

"Could we do it again tomorrow, Lottie?" Squid asked. "Could we?"

"Aren't you tired?" Charlotte asked, tousling his hair. "I don't even want to think about tomorrow."

Squid pulled at Charlotte's arm. "Gran's, Lottie," he kept saying, "let's go to Gran's."

"Come over tomorrow?" Charlotte asked, giving in to Squid's tugging.

Jason nodded. *"Auf Wiedersehen,"* he called.

"Auf Wiedersehen," they echoed back to him.

Jason watched Squid take off down the path, his short legs almost a blur, Charlotte right behind.

When Jason turned, he realized he was past his own place – they had landed between the two houses. The road was perfectly clear now, as if they had simply walked into town, turned around and walked back. The bugle was all dented and in need of polish, almost worse, he thought, than when he'd found it in the attic.

Halfway up his own driveway, he stopped and put the horn to his lips. He played the first line, not well, but he could still play. He felt suddenly lead-legged and wondered if he would make it through the gate and into the house.

His dad was in the kitchen, drinking coffee. He smelled pizza in the oven.

"Good practice today?" his dad asked, grinning. "I thought maybe you kids had hit the road, joined a circus or something."

"No," Jason said quickly, slipping past his dad. "I'll go and wash. I'm starving." He tore up the stairs.

The realness of everything leapt out at him – the carpet seemed luxurious and his room enormous. He shoved the bugle under his pillow and fell back on the coverlet, breathing in the room's familiarity. Home. He was home. Charlotte would be too. And Squid? Would he blab it all to Gran? Spin off what would seem to her just another of Squid's *little stories* as she called them?

Jason stared at the electric light fixture in the centre of his ceiling. Electricity, he thought. TV, computers, microwaves...

"Jason? Hey buddy, I thought you were starving." His dad was standing in the doorway, the overhead light glaring in Jason's eyes.

"Yeah, Dad," he said, jumping up, "I'll be right there."

"Your mom called," his dad said as Jason followed him down. "I told her you were playing up a storm on that trumpet."

"It's a bugle, Dad."

"A bugle, right," his dad continued. "Well, she sounded pleased you were working so hard at it and she wants to know all about Charlotte's grandmother."

"She's cool," Jason said, jamming his mouth full of pizza. It tasted awesome, even better than awesome.

"Hey, slow down," his dad said, laughing and putting another slice on Jason's plate. "You'd think I hadn't fed you properly since your mother left."

Jason felt a stab of panic. How long *had* he been gone? "I thought...I thought mom was away for two weeks."

"Not enough students signed up. They've postponed the course. She'll be home in a couple of hours."

Jason felt his body relax. He folded his arms on the table. How many days had they been in Germany? Six or seven, for sure. And they'd been gone from here only thirty-five minutes. When he tried to think about each day there and what had happened, he couldn't. His mind kept going numb. He'd sort it out tomorrow...with Charlotte.

"Hey, buddy," his dad said, shaking his shoulder, "you're falling asleep at the table. It's okay. You don't have to eat the whole pizza tonight. Save some for breakfast."

"Thanks, Dad," Jason mumbled, getting up from the table. He made a heroic attempt to saunter to the stairs and once out of sight, dragged himself the rest of the way up into his room. Tomorrow he'd go over to Charlotte's. Tomorrow they could sort it all out.

Auf Wiedersehen. Danke. Wolfgang and his family. Otto and the dungeon. Lord Friedrich and the castle. Bettina and Hindel. Gunthar and the town of Coburg. Frau Wölfin and her furballs. The battle. The fireworks. Everything blurred, ran together like colours spattered with raindrops, like bugle notes drifting into the fog.

ACKNOWLEDGEMENTS

FOR THEIR ADVICE, EXPERTISE, AND SUPPORT, SPECIAL thanks to Sheila Dalton, Kathryn Cole, Bonnie Symons, Marguerite Andersen, Diana Storen, Helen Pereira, Judy McCrosky, Janet Read, Ruth Hircock, the Saskatchewan Writers' Guild Winter Colony, and Barbara Sapergia, my editor. In Germany, to Hubert Limpert, Gunthar Buchgreber, Elke Walthes, Walter Knapp, and Dr. Manfred Stammberger.

PHOTO: CINDY TALOR PHOTOGRAPHY

ABOUT THE AUTHOR

Linda Hutsell-Manning has written fiction, poetry, non-fiction, and theatre and television scripts. Her work has been produced on television and the stage, and published in anthologies and periodicals of many kinds. Her juvenile fiction books include *Dinosaur Days* (1993), *Animal Hours* (1991), *Cooling Off* and *Wondrous Tales of Wicked Winston*. *Dinosaur Days* was a Reader's Choice award winner, and she has received honours for poetry and playscripts as well.

Born in Winnipeg, Linda Hutsell-Manning trained as a teacher and has lived in many Canadian communities, from Kamloops, British Columbia, to Cobourg, Ontario, where she now makes her home.

IN THE SAME BOAT
CELEBRATING CANADIAN DIVERSITY

THE WATER *of* POSSIBILITY
by Hiromi Goto

Twelve-year-old Sayuri may be the only one who can save Living Earth from a terrible fate.

ISBN: 1-55050-183 6$9.95CN/$8.95US

LITTLE VOICE
by Ruby Slipperjack

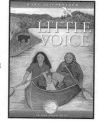

An Ojibwa girl comes of age during a summer spent in the bush with her grand-mother.

ISBN: 1-55050-182-8 $9.95CN/$8.95US

LOST *in* SIERRA
by Diana Vazquez

A young Canadian girl unravels a family mystery while visiting Spain.

ISBN: 1-55050-184-4 $8.95CN/$7.95US

ESCAPE PLANS
by Sherie Posesorski

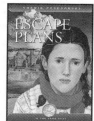

Thirteen-year-old Becky confronts her fears at the height of the Cold War.

ISBN: 1-55050-177-1 $9.95CN/$8.95US

I HAVE BEEN *in* DANGER
by Cheryl Foggo

Two young sisters grow closer together as one struggles to save the other.

ISBN: 1-55050-185-2 $8.95CN/$7.95US

ANDREI *and the* SNOW WALKER
by Larry Warwaruk

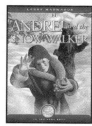

Old and new worlds collide as Andrei moves from Ukraine to Canada in 1900.

ISBN: 1-55050-213-1 $9.95CN/$8.95US